Praise for Beth V *ıty*

4 Red Hearts "THE E ill have the reader gasping for more with each page turned. Ms. Williamson delivers a wild ride from start to finish and will capture the reader's imagination... With each page, Ms. Williamson delivers a story that had this reader smiling, sighing and rooting for Nicky and Tyler to admit their feelings as well as find out who is pulling their strings. Run to grab this wonderful first book in the series and be transported to another place and time. THE BOUNTY is a great read to read on a sunny afternoon and a wonderful way to be introduced to the Malloy family." ~ *Dawn, Love Romance*

Blue Ribbon Rating: 4.5 "...THE BOUNTY is the first book in the Malloy family series and is destined to become a big hit. I read this book from beginning to end in one sitting and was ready to read it again. This is Beth Williamson's first book and she is definitely an author to be looking out for in the future. Mrs. Williamson's next book is THE PRIZE which is the second book in the Malloy family series and this reviewer will be eagerly waiting for its release." ~ *Dina Smith, Romance Junkies*

"...I really enjoyed how Beth Williamson used Nicky's toughness as a cover for her tender feelings for Tyler. Speaking of Tyler, I was getting a bit worried at his stubbornness and refusal to see reason, but he came through and was the better man for it. The Bounty is the first book of Ms. Williamson's Malloy Family series and I can't wait to read more from this wonderful family! I am officially hooked! I very much enjoyed The Bounty by Beth Williamson because I love nothing better than a kick-butt western with masculine heroes and their loving mates. Yeehaw!" ~ *Talia Ricci, Joyfully Reviewed*

5 Angels and a Fallen Angels Review Recommended Read! "The Bounty reaffirmed my love for the historical genre! With the backdrop of a land where men were strong and loyal, Ms. Williamson takes us back into time and place where we lived off the land and were one with nature. Ms. Williamson created a fascinating couple that provides entertaining communication, leaving me laughing one minute and emotionally spent the next. ...The Bounty was an exceptional story that made me smile and shed a couple of tears, and earned itself a top spot on my list of books to revisit over and over and over again" ~ *Rachelle, Fallen Angel Reviews*

The Bounty

By Beth Williamson

A Samhain Publishing, Ltd. publication.

Samhain Publishing, Ltd.
2932 Ross Clark Circle, #384
Dothan, AL 36301

The Bounty

Cover by Scott Carpenter
Print ISBN: 1-59998-209-9
Digital ISBN: 1-59998-047-9
www.samhainpublishing.com

First Samhain Publishing, Ltd. electronic publication: April 2006
First Samhain Publishing, Ltd. print publication: July 2006
This book has been previously published.

The Bounty

By Beth Williamson

Dedication

To my readers and friends on the CowboyLovers group. Y'all are always an inspiration. Thanks for everything.

Prologue

April 1880, Cheshire, Wyoming Territory

It was, without a doubt, the absolute worst day of Nicky Malloy's life. And every terrifying, miserable minute was her own damn fault. Her nose was clogged, her eyes felt like she had a cup of dirt in them, and her throat was raw. She could barely swallow her own dry spit.

She and her brother Logan were standing behind the main barn on the Hoffman ranch, out of sight of anyone approaching. Twilight was setting in and shadows were beginning to creep in around them.

"My God, Logan. I still can't believe it."

He grimaced. "Neither can I."

"I should never have made you come here with me. Of all the stupid, asinine—"

"Stop it, Nicky. I would have come with you no matter what you said."

She wiped her clammy palms on her jeans. "What are we going to do when Owen gets here? I know you can hear them coming. They're somewhere near Buffalo Pass."

"Yeah, I can hear them. But *we* aren't going to do anything about Owen. *I* am." He turned his face toward her. "You are going back up that rise, put those two women on Shadow, put the boy on the saddle in front of you, and ride hell-bent for leather toward town and the sheriff."

She felt as if he'd punched her in the gut. For a moment, she couldn't even speak.

"You're crazy," she shouted. "You think I'm going to leave you here, alone, to face him? After what we just found in his root cellar? Not a chance."

"No, Sissie," he said, looking down at his feet for a moment. "I am responsible for you, even if I'm only two minutes older. I will not, *will not*, allow you to be here when those riders get here. It's not just a matter of pride, or just being a man."

When he glanced back up at her, she saw in his eyes that somewhere in the last fifteen minutes her brother had become a man. He looked so much like Papa that tears burned her eyes. *Why now?*

"I have to do this. Do you understand? It's who I am."

She covered her mouth with one hand and held back the sob that threatened to erupt. God help her, he was telling the truth. She had to leave him to face a pack of at least half-a-dozen armed riders that were sure to be furious when they found out what she and Logan had done. He pulled his knife from his boot and held it out to her.

"Take my knife and go."

She looked down at the leather sheath she had made for him last Christmas. How frivolous life had been then, she realized. She listened to the approaching riders, only minutes away now.

"It's time, Sissie. You need to go."

"I can't," she said, looking at him with hot tears blurring her vision.

"Yes, you can. You're strong, hell, stronger than me. You can do this. You will do this. Don't worry about me. Owen can't hurt me without Papa coming down on him like a thunderstorm."

Oh, but she knew better. Owen would hurt him, just as he had hurt her. She knew the devil that hid behind his watery blue eyes.

"I don't have time to argue with you. Just go."

He shoved the knife into her boot and pushed her toward the rise that marked the border between their ranch and Owen Hoffman's.

"Goddammit, Nicole Malloy. Get your ass in gear and get out of here. Run!"

She took one last look at his face and nodded. Then she ran for the rise, certain to come back after she had put the two women and the boy on Shadow, and pointed them toward town. She knew she should take them herself, but they were strangers, and Logan was her brother. She would help them, but she would return to help Logan. And damn the consequences.

Chapter One

May 1883

Tyler Calhoun pretended not to notice that most people sidestepped him when he passed through a town. It was, after all, instinct on their part. He was big, formidable even, over six feet tall, two hundred twenty pounds plus. Two Colt pistols were strapped to his thighs, there was a ten-inch knife on his back, and a Winchester repeating rifle hung from his saddle in a fringed scabbard. He was all in black: black hair, black mustache, black clothes, black saddle, black horse, hell, even black boots. And he had a twisted enough sense of humor to name his black horse Sable. No one else, it seemed, got that joke.

But what put most people off was what they saw when they looked into his eyes. An ordinary blue, but he knew there was emptiness in them. What was left of his soul was as black as his heart. Too many years had passed since Tyler had felt anything. Life had become predictable and nearly distasteful.

If someone had asked him why he'd accepted this particular bounty, he couldn't have answered. It was a hell of a long ride from Texas to Wyoming, and, in late spring, the weather was fickle. The lure could have been the three thousand dollars; it was finally enough to hang up his bounty hunter hat for a long while, if not for good. It could be the fact that the man he was after hadn't been caught in over three years, and Tyler loved a challenge. Or it could be neither of those reasons. Something had compelled him to make the long trip.

Owen Hoffman had written to him a month ago about his problem—a problem with Nicky Malloy, an outlaw who had killed Hoffman's brother and stolen a small fortune of the man's money. No one had been able to spot Malloy, or even catch the scent of his trail, but now it was Tyler's turn. He could find a single grain of sand in the desert if it had a price on its head. He had no doubt he'd find Malloy even if the trail was as cold as a whore's heart.

Reining Sable in as he reached his destination, it was all he could do not to snort in disgust. Cheshire, Wyoming wasn't even a town. It was eight buildings and a barn huddled together pretending to be a town. It didn't seem like there would be anybody handing out three dollars, much less three thousand, for a bounty within a hundred miles of this little piece of nowhere.

No help for it, he'd just have to ride into town—he mentally winced at the word—and ask if anybody knew how to find Owen Hoffman. Tyler kneed his horse forward and before he knew it, he was in front of the general store marked Goodson's. He dismounted, then rubbed his horse's nose for a moment before he secured the reins to the hitching post.

His boots thunked on the plank sidewalk as he approached the door. A pretty blonde was on the other side, fixing to turn the sign to Closed when she saw him. Her pink lips made the shape of an O as she halted in her task. Smiling, she opened the door for him. A small bell tinkled overhead as the smell of cinnamon and the heady scent of a woman rushed over him.

"Good evening, sir. Can I help you?" she said as she gestured for him to come inside.

Tyler stepped into the store and took a quick survey of the interior. There didn't seem to be anyone else around. He touched his right index finger to the brim of his hat as he moved into position with a shelf of canned goods behind his back.

"I'm looking for Owen Hoffman. Can you tell me if he lives hereabouts?"

She opened her mouth to answer him, but was cut short by someone else.

"Who in the hell are you? And what are you doing alone with Regina?"

A trio of men stood in the doorway, staring at Tyler. They were good-sized men, all with similar features marking them as kin to each other. Only one was wearing pistols and he was behind the leader, a little younger and a little hotter under the collar by the look of him. They had no idea that he could kill all three of them within the time it took them to take a breath. Like shooting fish in a barrel.

"Raymond," the blonde rebuked softly. "Where have your manners gone to? This nice gentleman," the gun-toting young one snickered loudly, "was only looking for information."

"I'll bet that's what he was doing," said the leader. Tyler assumed he was Raymond. "Did he push his way in here, Reggie?"

"Of course not," she answered. "The store was still open when he came in."

Sort of a half-truth, but Tyler didn't correct her. His eyes were trained on Hothead's hands and his pistols.

"I've asked you repeatedly not to call me that," she said with a sniff.

"Fine, Regina," he drawled her name, perhaps to irk her further. "Mister, you didn't answer my questions. Who in the hell are you and what are you doing alone with my intended?"

Ah, so that was the way of it.

"Name's Calhoun. As I was telling your intended," he paused, "I'm looking for Owen Hoffman."

He thought Raymond had seemed annoyed before, now he appeared absolutely livid. His green eyes practically spit fury. That, of course, did not bode well for getting the information he needed. Sometimes it was too hard to be patient with regular people.

"You won't find that information here. Get out."

Regina looked quickly from one man to the other. She pursed her lips and sashayed over to Tyler.

"About five miles due west of here, Mr. Calhoun. You can't miss it." She turned and leveled an expression of triumph at her fiancé. "Step aside, all three of you. And get your hands away from those pistols, Jack."

"Jesus Christ, Regina. I can tell by looking at this 'gentleman' that he's just a goddamned bounty hunter. And you're telling him where to find the bastard that set men like him on Nicky's tail." Raymond was forcing the words through clenched teeth.

"There's no need to get so upset, Raymond. He could get the information from anyone in town. I was only being neighborly," she said.

Tyler could see there was a hell of a lot more going on here than a simple lover's spat. He didn't want to know about it and he sure didn't want to be part of it. Time to go. He stepped toward the door, ready in a moment to do battle, strangely hoping he wouldn't have to. He had respect for men who protected their own. Nonetheless, he'd kill them if necessary.

"You don't want to dance with me," he spoke softly, but clearly. No one moved. No one even flinched from their position.

"Raymond, Jack, and Trevor," the little blonde interjected, "I will never forgive any of you if harm comes to this stranger because of the three of you. Now, move out of the way and let him pass."

Dead silence met her order.

"Raymond Malloy. You move this instant, or I will let the whole town in on our little secret this Sunday in church."

The men blocking the door looked shocked. They all stopped like deer in a hunter's sights.

Tyler took advantage of the moment and headed out the door. As he passed, the men stepped inside as if in a slumber. They weren't paying much attention to him any more. Apparently the little blonde's threat was enough to numb them like a mountain stream. Definitely time to go.

"Much obliged, ma'am." He glanced at Regina as he passed. He forced himself not to react when she winked at him.

Holy shit.

Whatever her secret was, it was a powerful one—powerful enough to keep a man, and his brothers, whipped into submission.

"Watch your back, Calhoun," hissed Raymond. "Nicky has a lot of brothers."

Tyler didn't bother to answer. He moved into the deepening darkness outside and untied his horse. None of the men followed him out, but he felt at least one pair of eyes glued to his back. He was waiting for a bullet from the Hothead to slam into him. But nothing happened.

Was that disappointment or relief?

Mounting Sable, he turned west and headed out to find Owen Hoffman's ranch and accept the bounty on one Nicky Malloy. This could get really interesting. He loved it when there was more to a story than a simple robbery and murder. Hostile brothers added a little spice to his life.

⁂ ⁂ ⁂

Following the little blonde's directions, Tyler reached the Hoffman ranch just after nightfall. As he headed up toward the buildings in the distance, he noticed a few men hanging around the corral watching him. By the look of them, Tyler would bet that at least half of them were either escaped convicts or wanted men. He'd captured or killed enough of them to know these fit that bill. Apparently Owen Hoffman liked to hire some unusual ranch hands.

Ranch hands, my ass, more like mercenaries. They were there to kill who needed killing.

Owen Hoffman was obviously not the upstanding rancher he painted himself to be in his letters. Yet a little bit more flavor for the mix.

When he arrived at the big red barn, a skinny kid was waiting outside. He had filthy brown hair, no shoes, and his pants resembled a bizarre clump of patches rather than an entire piece of clothing. He looked to be about fifteen, undernourished, and as clean as a pig in a wallow. Reminded him a bit of himself about fifteen years ago.

"You Calhoun?"

Tyler nodded.

"Mr. Hoffman expects ya at the main house," the boy mumbled.

Hoffman clearly wanted to get to business immediately. Tyler was the same way. He didn't accept, or deliver, any shit. "Make sure he gets oats," Tyler said as he handed the reins over to the boy. "And a good rub down."

"Yessir." The boy gulped as he studied the dirt under his feet.

Grabbing his saddlebags and the scabbard containing his Winchester, Tyler headed toward the sprawling homestead. He wasn't going to leave anything of value for any of those sons of bitches to grab. He didn't want to have to kill them for it. It was too late in the day for that.

"Calhoun?" asked a nasally voice as Tyler approached the ranch house.

Tyler saw a portly man standing in the door, the light illuminating his balding head. He nodded in response to the question even as his hand tightened on his rifle. Every one of his well-honed instincts was at attention. Regardless of his appearance, this was a dangerous man.

"Come on in."

Tyler followed the man into the house, surprised to see him turn his back on his guest. Tyler turned his back on no one, especially someone armed as well as he was.

The house was enormous by ranch standards. It was also furnished to the hilt with chairs, tables, a piano, what he thought was a harp, gee-gaws, and all kinds of shiny-looking objects filling every corner and cranny. A huge stone fireplace dominated the room. No expense was spared to create this household. Turning to speak, Hoffman indicated to a rather ugly chair.

"Sit," he ordered.

Tyler made no move to sit. Hoffman eyed him as thoroughly as he himself was being scrutinized. Hoffman's eyes had a rheumy cast; his nose was red and mottled. A sheen of perspiration covered his forehead and wisps of gray and blond hairs stuck up, forming a frizzy halo. He huffed out a long breath.

"You *are* Tyler Calhoun?" he asked.

Tyler nodded. "I am."

"Then sit and let's get down to business." Hoffman went over to the table by the far wall and poured himself three fingers of whiskey into a thick crystal glass. He didn't offer any to Tyler. And Tyler did not sit down.

"I expected you last week. Don't know why you took your sweet time about getting here, but I'm glad you finally arrived. As I wrote, I need you to track and find Nicky Malloy. Been gone more than three years now. I tried six bounty hunters without any luck. There's a file right there next to you on the table, reports and such. Read it. You can read, can't you?" Without waiting for an answer, he continued. "You're supposed to be the best. Find Nicky so I can have the pleasure of hearing that skinny neck crack at the end of a hangman's noose for the murder of my brother."

Tyler nodded again. This man made the hackles on the back of his neck rise, and his gut instinct told him not to trust him. But no one ever said you had to like the person offering a bounty, just the money he paid. He picked up the leather file and tucked it under his arm.

"What about the money Malloy stole?"

Calhoun harrumphed. "Doubt there's anything left of that. After three years, I'm sure it's all spent. I just want revenge, boy, sweet revenge."

No one had called Tyler "boy" in twenty years. He didn't like it then, and he sure as hell didn't like it from this puffed-up peacock of a man.

"The name's Calhoun, not boy."

That seemed to catch Hoffman's attention. The man's brows slammed together as he looked at Tyler over the top of his whiskey glass. Damn, he should have stopped at that shit-ass saloon in that pretend town for a drink of bad whiskey. Watching this fool drink what was sure to be prime whiskey was pure torture.

"Okay, Calhoun. There's a guestroom, head of the stairs. Bunk there tonight. Read up and we'll talk in the morning." Hoffman downed the last of the amber liquid in his glass and smacked his lips noisily as the glass hit the table with a thump.

He's dismissing me like a young'n underfoot.

"Do you have a description or a wanted poster?"

"There's an old tintype in the folder and some wanted posters. As if they did any good."

Tyler was silent. He reminded himself again that he didn't have to like Hoffman to work for him. Money is money, dirty or clean. "The reward."

"What about it?"

"It's three thousand total then."

"Yes, yes, of course. I told you that in my letter," he said with a wave of his hand.

"I want to see it."

"What the hell are you talking about?" Hoffman's face flushed.

"I said I want to see it. My rules for my services."

"Listen, boy, I have five hundred times that alone in the bank, not to mention this ranch, the cattle, and other investments," he said, puffing out his chest. "You do your job right and you'll get your reward. I'll tell you what, if you bring Nicky back alive, I'll double it." His facsimile of a smile almost made Tyler step back a pace.

"Double sounds reasonable to me. I still want to see it." He paused, then repeated, "My rules for my services. And I'm only going to tell you one more time, the name is Calhoun, not boy."

Tyler's eyes never moved, never blinked, never faltered. Hoffman looked away with a snort.

"Oh, fine, then," Hoffman said, flapping his hand in the air again. "I'll show you in the morning before you leave. Is that acceptable to you?"

"Morning is fine. And I want two hundred up front."

"Pushy bastard, aren't you?" Hoffman practically sneered. "Fine, I'll give you that in the morning, too."

Tyler nodded. "Agreed."

"My housekeeper left a plate on the table for me. You might as well eat it." Hoffman reached for the whiskey as he pointed in the direction of the doorway that apparently led to the kitchen.

Tyler gritted his teeth. This man was definitely trying his patience. "Thanks for the hospitality, Hoffman."

Hoffman chuckled under his breath. "Just find Nicky."

"I'll find him, and bring him back alive." Tyler would be an idiot to turn down a double reward. Hopefully Malloy wouldn't do something stupid to get himself killed along the way. "There isn't a man that can't be found if I'm the one doing the looking."

"Calhoun?" Hoffman said, that frightening smile appearing on the older man's lips again. "I thought you knew. Nicky is short for Nicole. She's a woman."

Tyler heard a few clocks ticking in the silence. He cleared his throat and took a deep breath before he spoke. "A *woman*? You've been hunting a *woman* for *three* years and can't find her? Who the hell did you hire, a bunch of schoolmarms?"

Hoffman's eyes narrowed. "She's a goddamn *murderer* and a *thief*. She took what was mine, and I intend to see her pay for it."

"Look, Hoffman, I'm not bragging, mind you, but people usually call on me to find a true hard case, not a girl. I don't think I would have ridden this far for a woman's bounty, but I'm here anyway. Are you sure you're not wasting your money?"

Jesus, a woman.

"She's a hard case, believe me. Is you or ain't you going to take on this bounty?"

Tyler opened his mouth to say no, but his inner voice pulled back from that negative response. Six thousand dollars to bring in a woman alive? He was hoping for more of a challenge, but money was money, clean or dirty.

"I'll take it, Hoffman. I won't argue with you about it, but you'd better hand over the six thousand when I bring her back alive. Or you and I will have a problem."

"I always settle my debts." Hoffman rubbed his hands together as he grinned. He looked like an image from a funhouse mirror rather than a real man, and most definitely unsettling.

Tyler wondered if he had just made a deal with the devil.

* * *

A woman.

Tyler felt himself grin. He had read the reports written on Nicky Malloy. She had avoided some of the best, that was for sure. But how? Tyler picked up the faded tintype of Nicky that was in the folder. She looked to be about sixteen or seventeen in the print. She certainly didn't look like a dangerous outlaw, but he had studied the warrant sworn out against her. A thief and murderer at the ripe old age of nineteen. She did have the most extraordinary eyes though, almond-shaped and kind of cat-like.

Tyler shook himself. What was he doing? This was an old tintype. The wanted poster had aged her a little, but not much. She still looked fresh and innocent. He snorted. She was twenty-two now, and life on the run was hard for a man; for a woman, it would have been twice as bad. She certainly wasn't innocent anymore. Tyler had no doubt he'd find her.

Setting the folder on the floor next to him, he lay down on the guest bed in Hoffman's house, completely clothed except for his boots. Although it was a cool night, Tyler did not turn down the blankets. His rifle lay on the bed next to him, and a pistol rested just beneath the pillow. He started to drift off to sleep when he smiled again.

A woman.

It didn't seem like much of a challenge. And for six thousand he was sure to bring her back alive.

Chapter Two

August 1883

Three months later, Tyler grudgingly accepted the fact that hunting a woman was not as easy as he first thought. Not quite on his knees, he was hanging by his bloodied wrists, strapped to two solid wooden poles, in the middle of nowhere. The relentless heat of the summer sun beat down on his back, criss-crossed with shallow knife marks. The blood had long since caked and baked on his skin. The pain had turned to numbness for the moment. He couldn't feel his arms, shoulders, hands, or fingers. Hell, he didn't think he could even stand up anymore.

"So, *gringo*," came the rough voice from behind him. "You are ready to tell me, no?"

Using a well of strength he didn't know he had, Tyler lurched to his feet, rising to his full height. Ignoring the screaming agony of his shoulders as the weight was lifted off them, he looked out at the horizon.

"Told you no before, *amigo*, but I guess since you're so stupid, I need to repeat myself," Tyler rasped, hoarse from three days without water. Turning his head, he looked at the man behind him. "No. You want me to say it in Spanish? *No*."

The bandito, known as Hermano to everyone, smiled at Tyler. "You dig your own grave, *señor*. I just want to know why you're asking questions about a woman, and who sent you. Not hard questions to answer, I think. You are not a bandito, or an outlaw, so me, I think you hunt for bounty, no?"

Pulling his knife from its scabbard, he caressed it as if it were a pet. The dirty chaps he wore over his pants bore a multitude of old bloodstains, and other things that Tyler didn't want to think about. The bandito's gray shirt was open at the throat, which was tied with a bandanna of an unidentified color that resembled dirt. Tyler's fingers itched to grab hold of that filthy bandanna and teach Hermano a lesson in hospitality.

Pushing back his sombrero, a hank of black hair fell over his forehead as he surveyed Tyler. "You will not last past tomorrow."

"Too bad, isn't it?" Tyler wasn't about to give this piece of shit the satisfaction of seeing him break.

Shrugging his broad shoulders, the bandito sheathed his knife and walked around Tyler. "Your choice, *gringo.* Tell me what I want to know and you can go free." He spread his arms wide with another smile that never reached his black eyes. Tyler knew he'd never go free, no matter what he confessed to. To an outlaw, a bounty hunter was as much an enemy as a lawman. To a bandito, he wasn't worth the space he took up on this earth. Better off dead and buried beneath it.

Tyler remained silent. Hermano's lips curled back to bare his teeth as his fist smashed into his prisoner's stomach, stealing the breath from Tyler's body. With a muttered curse, the bandito strode away toward the cluster of crude dwellings the outlaws lived in as they passed through the valley.

His brief well of strength depleted, Tyler saw stars as he desperately tried to suck air into his lungs, then all was black.

⁂ ⁂ ⁂

It was dark when Tyler woke. Someone was crouched beside him, silently watching. Without moving, he opened his eyes to narrow slits to see the stranger. It could have been a child, a woman, or a man for all he saw. A cloud had spread its wings over the moon.

"I know you're awake. I've done my share of playing possum, mister, so don't keep it up on my account." The soft whisper floated across the night air.

It sounded like a young boy, an *American* boy in a bandito hideout in Texas.

"What do you want, kid?" he ground out through parched lips.

"I'll set you free, mister, but you've gotta tell me something first."

Tyler was instantly, completely awake. He struggled to his feet and willed away the spots dancing in front of his eyes and the agonizing shafts of pain blossoming in his arms and shoulders. "What?"

"I need to know if you're looking for somebody in particular." The boy stood and lifted a skin of water to Tyler's mouth.

After lapping greedily at the cool liquid, Tyler felt like a baby denied his mother's breast when the stranger took it away almost immediately. It was near agony.

"All right, who?" he snarled, desperate for the water.

"Are you looking for a woman?"

At the boy's question, Tyler forgot his thirst completely. Who was this boy? And why would he ask a question like that?

"I don't need to get laid, kid, so peddle your sister's skirts somewhere else."

With an impatient huff, the dark form stood. His head reached past Tyler's shoulder, so he wasn't short, but he didn't look like there was much to him from what Tyler could see.

"Don't play games with me, mister," he hissed. "You know what I meant. Are you looking for Nicky Malloy?"

Nicky was good, but Tyler Calhoun was better. He'd tracked her to Hermano's hideout and then had stupidly gotten himself strung up like a Christmas goose.

"What's it to you? Is this Hermano's latest trick?"

The dark figure shook its head. "Hermano doesn't know I'm here. Let's just say that Nicky and I look out for each other. I need to know if Owen Hoffman is still sending bounty hunters after her. You sure look like a bounty hunter to me, and Hermano is convinced that's who you are. So, I'm asking you again, are you looking for Nicky?"

Tyler weighed his options. If he said yes, would the kid let him go? Or would he let the banditos finish him off in the morning?

"Yeah, kid, I'm looking for Nicole Malloy. For nearly three months now."

The boy let out a sigh that sounded desperately sad. "That's what I thought."

"You gonna let me go?"

"You've got to tell Hoffman that you couldn't find her. Promise me that you'll do that and I'll cut you free," came the boy's ragged whisper.

Was he kidding? Did this boy actually believe a bounty hunter would follow through with a promise made in the middle of the night to a faceless, nameless stranger? And how in the hell did he know who had hired him?

"I can't promise you that, kid."

The boy turned and took a few steps away. For a moment, Tyler thought he was going to keep walking.

"Your horse is over by the trees, saddled and ready. There's some food, and you can have this water." He dropped the skin to the dusty ground by Tyler's feet.

The moonlight burst through the cloud as the boy stepped next to him. Tyler was completely captured by the young, agonized face illuminated by the moon. He would recognize it anywhere. The faded tintype he'd studied for the past three months didn't do her justice. She was dressed as a man, with dirty cheeks and shapeless clothes, but it couldn't hide her. It was Nicky. He leaned toward her to make sure he wasn't hallucinating, but she stepped back quickly. The moonlight glinted off the knife, a well-used looking instrument, which sat comfortably in her hand. It had a beautiful pearl handle with intricate detailing. He wondered where she'd stolen it from.

"Nicole."

Her eyes widened. "Don't come looking for me."

"You know I will."

"You won't find me, bounty hunter."

"Yeah, that's what they all say."

His breath caught in his throat as the knife glided toward him. She turned to cut the leather strap binding Tyler's right wrist. "You'll have to free the other hand yourself."

"Why are you letting me go?" He was completely flummoxed by her act of kindness.

"Human beings should never be bound, mister, pure and simple. I don't want to see you die like a dog, even if you are a mangy bounty hunter."

Before he realized what she was doing, she cupped the back of his neck and kissed him hard. He tried to grab her, but all he caught was air. She moved silently, like a shadow in darkness. She touched her fingers to her lips, then turned and disappeared into the night.

The woman outlaw he'd chased for three months had just kissed him and saved his life. She knew he was going to continue to chase her until he caught her, yet she let him live.

What the hell?

Tyler stared after her for several minutes, before he shook himself mentally. He had to get his wrist untied and get his ass out of there as quickly as he could.

⁂ ⁂ ⁂

Nicky threw herself on her horse and took off into the inky night. She had let the bounty hunter free. And he'd be after her again. Even beaten, bloody, and dirty, he'd been magnificent. His hair was as black as soot, matching the stubble that graced his strong jaw. Earlier, even from a distance, she saw that his eyes were a bright blue, and up close, they were devastating. He was dark, forbidding, and mysterious. She couldn't stop herself from kissing him. It was as if her body had taken over her mind for a moment.

She was a woman with no future, obsessing about a bounty hunter who wanted to drag her back to Wyoming to hang.

Damning herself for having a soft heart, she rode on through the night as silent as the moon that lit her path. Hermano had been right all along. The bounty hunter was after her and he'd infiltrated the outlaws' valley hideout, endangering all of them. But she couldn't stomach the thought of the man's death on her conscience. She already had enough to deal with on that count, thank you very much.

She supposed Hermano had been the closest thing to a friend, and a brother, she'd had since her life had become an unending nightmare...since Owen Hoffman's bullet and her own rash impulsiveness had gotten her twin brother killed. A brief hiccup of memory tried to surface, but she quelled it with iron will. Now was not the time to start acting like a woman. It was time to start acting like a ghost.

Chapter Three

September 1883

It was raining as Tyler rode into Willowbend, Oklahoma. The raindrops were barely more than a mist, but after three hours of riding in them a man could get soaked, which did nothing for his already dark mood. There was a sucking noise each time his horse's hooves pulled out of the mud in the street, mud that seemed determined to hang onto the gelding.

It had been six weeks since he'd escaped from Hermano's hideout. Six long weeks. Nicky's visage had haunted his thoughts—especially that kiss. Hell, he had even had a few dreams about her. Not that he'd admit it to anyone, but her act of kindness had touched something in him that he thought was dead and buried. He didn't want to see her hang, but money was money, clean or dirty.

He'd checked every whorehouse for hundreds of miles and come up with nothing except a nose full of cheap perfume and more than a few propositions. He had also carefully checked the known outlaw hangouts but, of course, no one had remembered seeing her, much less heard of her. He'd checked housekeepers, shopgirls, hell, even schoolmarms. And he had only found one small piece of information about the elusive lady outlaw. Only one measly lead—someone sort of meeting her description, with a pearl-handled knife sort of like hers, may have been seen in Willowbend at the saloon some time in the last month. The idiot cowboy who provided the information probably needed help finding the outhouse.

I need a drink.

Tyler stopped his horse at the Dogleg Saloon and dismounted with a creak of leather and a splat of mud on his boots, then secured his horse to the hitching post. As he stepped onto the planked sidewalk, Sable whinnied in protest and shook his rain-soaked mane, spraying Tyler with even more water. He glared at his horse.

"Damn horse," he muttered, trying to shake the rain off himself. "A little rain, and you turn into a woman, Sable."

The horse nickered in response to Tyler's voice.

"Apology accepted," Tyler said quietly as he rubbed Sable's wet nose. "I'll get you out of the rain soon, boy."

With one last scratch for his horse, he turned and strode into the building.

* * *

Nicky saw him enter the saloon from the card table in the back, and promptly forgot to breathe.

Oh, sweet Jesus, it's him.

She'd recognize him anywhere. In fact, she had dreamed of him nearly every night for six weeks, sometimes frightening, always erotic dreams. She pressed one hand to her palpitating heart as her eyes followed the big man around the room. He approached the bar with the grace of a big cat. A big, dangerous cat.

The barkeep this time of day was Joey, a red-haired kid covered with freckles. He stopped wiping glasses and looked like a rabbit facing a big bad wolf with eyes as wide as saucers.

"Whiskey." The stranger slapped down a coin on the bar.

"Yes, sir." Joey squeaked and jumped as though the bounty hunter had bitten him. The kid grabbed a bottle from behind the bar and poured a shot glass full of the amber liquid, spilling a good amount in the process. He set the bottle down for the stranger to use up his fifty cents' worth of whiskey.

"Are you cheating, Jesse?" Willard said very loudly, much louder than he should have. "What in tarnation is wrong with you? You're as white as milk."

The bounty hunter's steps faltered for a split second as he walked toward a table with his bottle and glass.

"I'm fine. As if I need to cheat with the way you play poker," Nicky hissed.

The bounty hunter laid his wet coat on a chair to dry, then sat down with a sigh.

"Got any grub here?" he asked Joey. "I'm mighty hungry."

"Yessir, got some stew and cornbread in the back if'n you want some. It's still h-hot," Joey answered, his voice breaking on the last word.

"Much obliged, kid. You can take the cost of the meal out of my half dollar, and then keep the rest. You'd best take the bottle back. I don't need to come home drunk on an empty stomach. The missus would have my hide."

Nicky tried not to snort out loud at that one. Missus? Ha! The man probably was born from a nest of rattlesnakes. He surely didn't have any family, much less anyone like a wife to worry about him.

The man held the bottle out to the boy. Joey hesitantly approached him and made a swipe to grab it. Then he turned and went through a door in the back to get the meal as the big man stretched out his legs to wait.

"Feels mighty good to sit down," he said to no one in particular.

In the back of the saloon, Nicky expelled the breath she had been holding. Her hands started to shake so she pressed them down into the table to stop the trembling. From beneath her hat brim, she glared at the man who had called attention to her—he was a gray-haired, older man with a weather-beaten face who at the moment, looked like he wanted to be anyplace else but there. He had the decency to look chagrined. “Sorry, Jesse. Too much whiskey, I guess.”

“I’ve got to get out of here,” she whispered. She felt as if an army of ants had landed on her and were busily crawling up and down her skin. Why did Willard have to get loud and half-drunk when that bounty hunter was here in the saloon? Damn, he was good. Too goddamned good. He tracked her to Hermano’s and now here, two hundred miles away. Her cards were suddenly a blur in her hand, so she folded, then clenched her hands together under the table. She glanced up at the other two card players, Nate and Rusty, who were eyeing her suspiciously. She knew they hadn’t heard her whispered conversation with Willard, but she didn’t trust them for a minute.

She turned her gaze to the bounty hunter again. He seemed to be napping while he waited for Joey to bring him some dinner. Perhaps Lady Luck would smile on her today. Rising quickly, she scooped up her winnings and shoved them into her pocket.

“That’s it for me today. I’m gonna head on over to Rosie’s for some dinner. I’ll see you fellas back at the ranch.”

“Mind if I join you?” a deep voice asked from behind her. Nicky had to bite her lip to stifle the shriek that tried to escape her throat. How the hell had he gotten back here so fast? Like a stealthy black panther.

“Sure thing, mister,” said Willard. “Long as you got the money, we’re willing to let ya give it away.”

Willard let loose a low whistle as he took a good look at Tyler’s large frame. “Whooee! You’re a big boy. You ever work the range?”

"Time and again."

"Damn, I'll bet ya can lift a full grown steer by yourself." Willard chuckled. "Name's Willard. This here is Nate, Rusty, and Jesse."

The stranger didn't offer his name.

Nicky yanked her hat down farther on her head. Time to go.

"You from around here?" Willard asked the stranger.

"No."

"In town fer pleasure?"

"No."

"Talkative, ain't ya? Makes no never mind. Ante up, fellas."

Nicky tried to get around Willard without raising her head into the light.

"Wait, Jesse, you'd better get on over to the store to pick up that new fancy cookpot Missus Benson asked you to get. Old man Perkins will be closing up soon for his afternoon siesta."

"Dammit!" She could have kicked him for reminding her. "You're right, Willard. I'd best be getting along then."

She grabbed her coat and walked with as much dignity, but as quickly, as she could. Hopefully no one noticed she was running for her life.

As Nicky exited the saloon, a huge sigh of relief exploded from her chest. Turning in the direction of the general store, she ran across the muddy street. She skittered into the store, earning a disapproving glance from Mr. Perkins.

"Boy, I tol' you before, don't be runnin' in my store."

"Sorry, Mr. Perkins." She truly made an effort to be polite, and it was an effort. Jesus, the bounty hunter could be after her already. "I came to get the cookpot for Mrs. Benson at the Rocking R."

"Well, then, just so we're clear on that runnin' thang. Already got a gob of mud on my floor, and lookit the water." His gaze roamed over the planked floor. "Missus Perkins is going to have my hide."

"Sorry, Mr. Perkins," she repeated. "The cookpot?"

With one final scowl at her, he picked up his order book from behind the counter.

"Let's take a lookee." He began to turn the pages slowly. Excruciatingly slowly, blindingly slowly, maddeningly slowly. Nicky thought she might just have to knock him upside the head and steal the cookpot.

"Here we are," Mr. Perkins announced with a flourish. "It didn't come in."

He peered at Nicky over the top of his glasses.

She swallowed the angry words that rose to her lips. He didn't slow her down on purpose. How was he to know she was running from some stranger in a saloon who was hunting her outlaw hide?

"Do you expect it soon?" she asked as politely as she could.

"I reckon so." His brows came together. "Mud has slowed everyone up this week."

"Okay, then." She started back through the store to make her escape. "Willard will likely come by next week to see if it's come in."

"Young man, wait just a minute," Mr. Perkins started to say. Nicky closed the door behind her with a thud.

⁂ ⁂ ⁂

Tyler stood waiting beside the general store, moving a coin between his fingers. He listened to the conversation in the store. He heard the door close and the footsteps heading straight toward him. Stepping from the shadows, he waited for her.

"Fool errand. Didn't even have the damn thing and now I've wasted my..."

As she raised her arm to put on her coat, she turned and ran right into Tyler's chest. A muffled "Oh!" preceded her raising her face to look at what she'd run into. The coin made a loud ting as it hit the boards beneath them.

It was her. He couldn't believe his luck. That voice in the saloon had been so achingly familiar, he was hard-pressed not to grab her then and there in front of her friends and kiss her. No, not kiss her, *capture her.*

"Hello, Nicky."

Those green eyes widened and then she was gone, running like the wind across the road, the coat dropped at Tyler's mud-encrusted feet. Tyler was after her like a shot. The rain had turned the street into a slippery, muddy mess. The two of them must have looked like circus performers as they careened down alleys, between buildings and through a corral, trying not to fall.

Tyler could see holstered guns thumping against her thighs and was glad she hadn't pulled one on him. He wanted to get that extra three thousand for bringing Nicky back alive. And she would be dead if she tried to draw on Tyler. No doubt about it. If he concentrated on hitting an arm or a leg, not generally his preferred target of course, he could just bring her down if he had to. But damn, that woman was fast. She had legs that ate up the ground like a goat in a cabbage patch.

Breathing hard and out of patience completely, Tyler's long legs finally gained the advantage. On an open stretch behind a hotel, he caught up to Nicky and tackled her.

They landed with an *oomph* on the muddy ground and slid a good ten feet before they stopped. Immediately she put up a fight, punching and twisting and kicking. The kicking was the worst. He hated to be kicked, and his back still wasn't completely healed from that bandito's carving job. He had to stop her before he actually cried out in pain.

"Get off me, you son of a bitch!" She punched him in the balls. That did it. Before he knew it, he'd stopped her with a sharp uppercut to the jaw. After he'd done it, he simply stared down at her. He'd hit a woman. His stomach was rolling with nausea from her well-aimed punch and his balls ached like they were on fire.

"Let go of me! Son of a bitch! Get off! Get off! *Get off of me*!"

Jesus, his mother was rolling in her grave. He had hit a woman for God's sake and now he was sitting on her. Tyler immediately unbuckled her gun belt and took her knife from its sheath in her boot. He quickly rose, then yanked her to her feet. Still breathing heavily, he pulled off her muddy hat. A mass of chestnut-colored curls sprang up like a jack-in-the-box. Her hair was shorn like a man's, but *no* man had hair like that—it looked like pure silk. She rubbed her jaw where he'd punched her.

Damn, now he was sure both his mother *and* his grandmother were rolling in their graves. How the hell did he lose control like that? Tyler took a good look at the woman he'd finally captured. She was dressed in jeans, a blue shirt, and men's boots, but Tyler noticed, couldn't *help* but notice, the womanly curves beneath the disguise now that the mud had plastered her clothes to her body.

"Are you going to gawk at me all day?" She bracketed a hip with her free arm. "Lonely, bounty hunter? Haven't been with a woman in a while? Did you miss me?"

He shook her arm. "You'd best keep your mouth shut, Malloy," he growled, all too aware her remark hit a nerve. It had been quite a long time since he had scratched that particular itch, but it was none of her damn business. He fixed her with his hardest expression. She didn't flinch, didn't blink, but instead looked back at him with fearless determination.

"I'll never go back to Wyoming with you," she said in a voice laced with bitterness and challenge.

"Yes, you will." He all but slammed Nicky's hat back on her head and pulled her forward. "Sorry I had to knock you around a bit, girl, but when you punch a man in the balls, you're aiming for some payback."

"Was that an apology?"

"Of a sort," he said through gritted teeth. The strain of not limping along and cradling his nether regions was enough to make him break out in a sweat, even in the cold rain. Damn, that woman had a hard fist.

They walked back to the saloon with their feet making godawful noises through the muddy street. Tyler kept a firm grip on his prisoner's arm. The second time she slipped in the mud, he stopped and glared at her.

"Do you need to be carried?" he snapped.

"No. This goddamn mud is slippery. And it doesn't help that you're dragging me along like a farm plow."

"I think you'd prefer this to bouncing along on my back when I throw your little ass over my shoulder."

"Just try it, bounty hunter." She stuck her chin up at him. "I'll be happy to go another round with you."

"The bounty is dead or alive, Malloy. You'd do best to remember that."

"As if I could forget," she snorted as he yanked her forward again. "How did you find me anyway?"

Tyler didn't answer. He was still surprised the idiot cowboy had been right.

She scooped up her discarded coat from the sidewalk as they passed the general store. She tried to get some of the mud off it, but it was too wet and she ended up smearing the mud like yesterday's dessert. "Can we at least wash the mud off?"

At that moment, the mist of a rain became a steady downpour. The mud started to run down their faces like dirty tears.

"Does that answer your question? Looks like Mother Nature is doing the washing for us."

Nicky stuck her tongue out at him as he turned away from her. He promptly ignored the jolt that went through him at the sight of her pink tongue. A tongue he was sure had featured itself in at least one of his dreams. *Damn her for kissing him.*

When they reached the saloon, Tyler asked, "Which horse is yours?"

"The dun mare."

Conveniently, his horse was directly next to Nicky's. Funny how things like that happen. Tyler was nearly dragging her now.

"You feel like a boat anchor, woman. Would you mind walking for yourself?"

She dug her heels even further into the mud. "I'll do anything I can to make this as hard for you as possible."

As they neared the horses, Tyler got a clear look at the mare. He couldn't help but be impressed with the fine horseflesh—Nicky's mare was a beautiful animal. She looked well taken care of, and Nicky's saddle and tack were well oiled and in great shape. He didn't want to remember that he normally respected people who respected their horses so much. Outlaws had never fallen into that category, until Nicky Malloy, anyway. Shaking the unwanted thoughts from his head, Tyler grunted as he dragged her the last five feet to the horses.

With one hand, he rifled through her saddlebags searching for weapons or anything else he needed to confiscate. Something cold and metallic touched his hand. He pulled it out to discover that it was a man's pocket watch.

"Don't you touch that." She dropped her coat in the mud again and reached for the watch.

"Something you stole?"

"No, you stupid son of a bitch, it was my brother's. Give it back to me," she said, voice full of fury as she tried to wrestle the watch out of his hand.

"Fine. Here, take it." He handed it to her.

As she made a grab for the watch, it almost slipped out of her wet palm. Releasing a shaky sigh, she kissed the watch and tucked it into her pants pocket.

Brother, my horse's behind.

"Brother? Hermano's watch, more like it. Reckon he took care of you right nice."

Her gaze narrowed. "Not that it's any of your business, *bounty hunter*, but it did belong to my brother, a brother who gave his life for mine. He was more of a man than your sorry ass will ever be."

Tyler quirked a dark, disbelieving eyebrow at her passionate defense, but said no more on the subject.

"Put your coat on, woman. You're not going to do yourself any favors by getting any wetter than you already are."

Nicky glared at him as he helped her not-so-gently slip the coat on without ever letting go of one of her arms. After hooking her gun belt over the horn of his saddle, he tucked her knife into the saddlebags and pulled out his custom-made shackles. They allowed him to shackle a prisoner to his saddle and still ride a comfortable distance on another horse. As he turned to her, shackles in hand, her eyes widened.

"Are you planning on riding out *now*?" she protested. "It's pouring."

Tyler was silent. He had no intention on letting her in on his plans, not that he'd made any specific plans yet other than to head north. He secured her hands with the shackles and ran the length to his own saddle. She wasn't going anywhere without him. He lifted her up onto her horse, strangely aroused by the feeling of her soft flesh in a man's clothes. His cock was beginning to recover from the fist, and lurching to life.

"These aren't very comfortable, you know," Nicky continued, her voice high and tight. "Can we at least eat something first? I was, uh...heading to the restaurant before you decided to tackle me. I can't eat Joey's stew no matter how hungry I am."

Her husky voice was beginning to grate on Tyler's nerves. What happened to the quiet stranger in Texas who had saved his life? Swinging up into the saddle, he held both pairs of reins as they started out of town.

Through the saloon's dirty window, Tyler noted that the old man, Willard, had watched as Nicky was secured to her horse. He hadn't taken his eyes off the woman for a moment.

Tyler and Nicky rode in silence for a while as the town grew smaller and smaller behind them. He was reciting hymns in his head to calm the lust that seemed to want to join the party. Finally his blood stopped rushing and he felt more in control of himself.

The rain tapered off within a short time, and then the silence between them grew larger and larger. He knew Nicky wasn't going to keep quiet much longer. Her anger was almost physical, radiating in waves, and it was aimed at Tyler. It at least distracted him from the dull throbbing in his balls as his body recovered slowly from his first run-in with a she-cat.

"Don't talk much, bounty hunter?" she finally said.

"I don't talk to murderers and thieves."

Nicky's eyes widened. "What? Is that what Owen said?" she asked, her voice breaking. "That I'm a *thief* and a *murderer*? Incredible. What did I steal?"

Tyler noticed that she didn't deny the killing. "Ten thousand dollars."

Tyler had learned not to trust outlaws, but this woman looked sincerely surprised. "*Ten thousand dollars*? Holy shit! I didn't steal any money from that snake. And protecting yourself isn't murder. Did you know Owen Hoffman is a cold-blooded murderer?" Her voice grew cold with fury. "That he killed my brother? Shot him in the head while he was bound and on his knees?"

"Was he thieving too?" Tyler knew he'd made a mistake as soon as the words left his mouth. Nicky's face clouded with rage and she let loose a war cry that would curdle milk. She lunged for him, muddy fists raised and shackles clanging. The horses bumped into each other, startling them into a gallop. Tyler tried to slow the horses down with one hand while fending off blows from Nicky with the other.

"Enough." He grabbed both of her wrists with one powerful hand and yanked her hands over and pinned them to his thigh.

"Whoa, boy, whoa." Tyler crooned to his horse. He pulled hard on the reins, slowing the horses to a trot and then stopping them. Nicky looked up at her captor with disgust. Tyler returned the look.

"Look, Malloy, we've got a lot of miles to cover. It's gonna be even longer if you keep fighting me," Tyler said through clenched teeth.

"Then it's gonna be longer because I'll never bend to your will, mister. What is your name anyway? I want to be sure they spell it right on your tombstone."

"Calhoun. Tyler Calhoun."

"Okay, got it, *Calhoun*," she sneered. "I'm warning you now, bounty hunter, don't ever, *ever* speak about my brother like that again, or I'll kill you myself."

Tyler brushed away her threat like a horse flicking away a pesky fly. "You'd better learn to control that mouth, *Nicole*, or I'll gag it shut."

They stared at each other with controlled rage. Tyler had never met a woman with such fire. She had even landed a couple of good punches to his jaw, which was throbbing in tune with his crotch. She was breathing hard, and her eyes were shining like green fire. Tyler's sleeping lust woke up with a snarl. He wanted to yank her off that horse, go to the nearest tree, and bury himself inside her until neither one of them could think straight. Tyler could almost see her legs wrapped around his waist as he pumped into her. Shaking his head, he tried to dislodge the image. Did she guess at his erotic thoughts? Disgusted with himself, he leaned forward and stared directly into her eyes.

"Don't push me too far." His voice was low and dangerous. "I guarantee you won't like it."

"I grew up with six brothers. Your scare tactics don't mean spit," she said as he slowly let her hands go. She straightened up in the saddle.

He snorted and spurred the horses forward. There was no way Nicky Malloy was getting under his skin. She was, after all, just a woman, just an outlaw.

Chapter Four

Three hours later, they stopped for the night. Nicky was relieved they were finally stopping, affording her an opportunity to attempt escape from the bounty hunter. Tyler dismounted in a grassy meadow near a small patch of cottonwood trees. He secured the horses to one of the trees and set off to find some kindling to start a fire. In the dark, it wasn't going to be easy.

"Calhoun? Are you just going to leave me here?" Nicky yelled.

Tyler ignored her. Nicky was so angry she could have killed him if given a weapon. She was also terrified, absolutely quaking-in-her-boots terrified. After three and a half years, she'd been caught and she was headed back to Wyoming where she was sure that she'd swing from the nearest tree. She shuddered at the memories that were creeping up on her in the dark. She had repressed her feelings for so long—she had only allowed her survival instincts to function. And now they were coming back at her like a runaway locomotive. The shackles were a vivid, cold reminder of what had happened. It was something that had replayed itself hundreds of times in her nightmares.

She wasn't surprised Owen had made up stories about her. *Thief?* Never. *Murderer?* No. She had done what she had to do in self-defense. Hoffman's brother was going to rape her and would have killed her without a second thought afterwards. Her eyes suddenly filled with tears as a tide of emotions threatened. *Don't do this now,* she told herself, *hold on.* The shackles clanged noisily as she wiped the tears from her eyes before that bounty hunter saw them.

"You can't escape from those, Nicole." Tyler's deep voice was suddenly next to her. "They're not made of leather like Hermano's. That's cold steel and even your sharp little teeth can't bite through it."

She glared down into his unreadable and cold blue eyes. She tried to wrestle her foot from the stirrup to kick him, but he caught hold of the back of her thigh. The touch of his large hand on her leg sent goose bumps clear up to her ears, and she felt a dampness between her legs. What was it about this man?

"I'm going to start a fire, so sit tight and I'll get you down in a minute," he said as he turned away from her.

As soon as he was out of earshot, she slid down from her horse as quietly as she could and crept toward the tree where the reins were secured. As she reached up, the shackles clanged, and she froze in mid-motion. Tyler was instantly behind her.

"You don't listen good, Malloy," he growled, grabbing her and pulling her by the collar of her shirt back to the horses, the heels of her boots dragging along the ground.

"Let me go, you stupid bastard."

"Malloy, I think you know more cuss words than I do. What a mouth you've got."

After plopping her back on her horse, he twisted the shackles on her saddle in a way that she couldn't move more than six inches. She tried to kick him again, but he easily sidestepped her long leg.

"Tsk, tsk. Don't waste your energy," he warned as he went back to gathering firewood.

True to his word, he started a small fire and then came back to get Nicky. He unlocked the shackle from his saddle and secured it to one wrist. She gaped at him as he lifted her out of the saddle, her bound breasts brushing his chest lightly. A shiver of goose bumps danced up her spine again as his long fingers almost touched at the center of her back.

"I'm going to be chained to you now?" she cried, aware her body had betrayed her.

He simply stared down at her, a novel experience for her. Generally speaking, she either looked at or down at most men. Tyler Calhoun topped her by more than six inches. She couldn't read what was in the depths of those icy blue eyes, but she thrust her chin up in her typical defiance, refusing to be cowed by this man.

"Are you at least going to let me relieve myself or shall I pee in my pants?"

"You can go behind a tree," he muttered, his voice thick as he dragged her toward the nearest one.

"What?" She was caught off guard by his command. "Where am I gonna go? I demand that you unchain me."

His lips curled into a smirk. "I don't trust you, Nicole."

"It's Nicky. My mama is the only one who calls me Nicole, and you certainly don't deserve the privilege."

Tyler's expression remained as flexible as a rock.

Nicky turned abruptly, heading to the trees with her head held high. She wasn't about to let Tyler see the effect he had on her. Unfortunately for her, she forgot how short the chain was that bound her to Calhoun. She was jerked backwards and straight into Tyler's arms. Nicky felt those goose bumps turn into a hot flash of something else entirely as she found herself pressed up against this man's hard, muscular chest. Tyler reached down and pulled off Nicky's hat. For a crazy, heart-stopping moment, she thought he was going to kiss her. And oh, God, she wanted him to. She didn't dare take a breath.

"You'd better remember how short your leash is," he said softly.

Damn the man! Nicky was flushing as she extricated herself from his arms. She couldn't think of a single retort to his remark, so she hauled off and punched him in the stomach, which was as hard as granite. Her fist was now aching painfully and his unperturbed expression made her angrier.

"Calhoun, are you made of stone everywhere?"

He seemed to find her anger amusing as he half-smiled at her. "Not all the time."

Her body still hummed from the contact. She was excited by him. Excited by the very man that wanted to bring her back for money, like a whore. She didn't want to think about how hard his body could actually get...and where.

Turning her back on him, she clenched her jaw in frustration at her own stupidity. "I'd like to relieve myself now."

What she thought was a rather rusty chuckle erupted from behind her. "Right this way," he said, pointing to the small copse of trees.

Nicky walked carefully to the trees, keeping as far away from Tyler as possible. She turned to glare at him.

"I'm not who you think I am. Owen Hoffman made up a thief and murderer for the law and bounty hunters to chase. But I am *not* that person."

She worked hard to maintain her dignity under the bounty hunter's piercing gaze. She couldn't help but appreciate the raw, untamed power that was evident in his eyes, his stance, and his hard body. No doubt about it, this was a cold man with iron in his spine. It was going to take some serious planning to escape. But she would escape, of that she had no doubt. She chose to ignore the little voice in her head whispering, *he found you twice, what makes you think he wouldn't catch you again?*

"I'm getting paid to bring you back to Wyoming. How I feel doesn't matter one way or the other."

Now what the hell did that mean? Do bounty hunters actually feel? She opened her mouth to ask him what he meant but one strong finger landed on her lips to stop her. She resisted the urge to lick it.

"Take a piss right now or you can sit in wet pants all night. Your choice."

Embarrassingly, Nicky felt her nipples stir under her bindings. The touch of his callused digit was arousing too.

She chose the coward's way out and headed behind the tree to pee. She wondered if he was going to look at her while she did it. Then wanted to rip the thought from her head when the idea excited her.

* * *

Tyler breathed a sigh of relief when Nicky opted not to fight with him over taking a piss. When she'd slammed into him, he hardened like a stone. He had to physically restrain himself from looking at her when she pulled her drawers down in the darkness to do her business.

Why the hell did he have to want her so much?

He led her over to the fire then sat her down with a grumbled curse. She watched him through shuttered eyes by the light of the campfire. As he quickly made the batter for johnnycakes in his skillet, he felt her eyes on him. Tyler was also quietly studying his prisoner. She thought she was being so smart in her sneaky perusal, but he wasn't the best bounty hunter for no reason. He had needed the reminder of just who and what she was.

"You can just hurl your escape plans right into this fire." He had trained his voice to be without a drop of emotion. "You are not getting away from me."

He turned his head to release the full force of his penetrating gaze on the outlaw. Many men had lost all hope because of that gaze. Others had literally shaken in their boots. Nicky, however, just quirked up one eyebrow and pursed her lips in a slight smirk. The firelight danced across her hair, making it glisten with its own fire.

"Scary. Does that nasty look usually work?"

A muscle twitched in his cheek as he ground his teeth together in frustration. He'd been saddled with a witch. Oh, perhaps she didn't dance under the full moon and sacrifice chickens, but he didn't doubt she was a witch through and through.

"Maybe you can try harder." She shrugged.

He was startled to notice a bruise on her chin where he'd punched her back in Willowbend. He forced his conscience to take a nap on that one. She obviously knew the rules of the game, too, since she hadn't made a peep about it. Of course, all the reasoning in the world didn't change the fact that he'd hit a woman, something he'd never, ever done before. He sure as hell wasn't proud of it either.

At the sound of approaching hoofbeats, Tyler rose in a split second, pistol cocked. Before Nicky had time to stand, two riders came into the circle of firelight on lathered cow ponies.

Tyler's gaze surveyed the newcomers, their abilities, and their weapons. He remembered them from Nicky's afternoon card game. Two-bit cowboys without a brain between them. Nobody treated a horse with such disregard when it was your only link to survival out on the prairie or the range. They were dressed in dirt-encrusted chaps, even dirtier shirts—couldn't tell what color they were—and had ragtag, poorly made saddles.

He waited with a pistol at the ready, his rifle hanging from his left hand.

"Hey there, mister, Willard tol' us you took Jesse from town today," drawled the bigger one. "We come to take him offa your hands." He had crooked teeth, looked like he hadn't bathed in a month or two, and his greasy brown hair hung down to his shoulders. His partner had corkscrew red hair and dull, empty eyes.

"Go away, Nate," Nicky said in her "manly" voice.

"Well, Jesse, from where I'm sittin', I got the drop on yore bounty hunter here." He leered as his gaze fastened on her chest.

"I said, go away. I don't need or want your help," she growled as she rose to her feet.

"Too goddamn bad," said the one she'd called Nate. "I been waitin' too long fer ya to drop yore drawers for me. Now I aim to finally get ya with a reward to boot."

"What the hell are you talkin' about, Nate? You want a man to drop his drawers fer ya?"

"No, no. Jesse's really a woman, ya ijit. I saw her taking a bath one day in the crick. Mi-tee-fine titties." He licked his lips, leaving a trace of spittle from one side to the other like a dog waiting for a meal.

"Jesse's a woman? I cain't believe it."

"Believe it. And, she's mine now."

"The only way you're getting in my drawers is to wear them, you stupid bastard," Nicky shouted.

Tyler wasn't about to give up six thousand dollars for two mangy cowboys with stiff peckers. "You heard the lady." His voice sliced through the heated conversation. "Be on your way."

"Ya think ya can take both of us?" sneered Nate. He leaned forward on his saddle and caressed the butt of his pistol.

"No question." Tyler brought his rifle up to point directly at Nate's heart.

Nate's eyes grew a bit wider and darted back and forth between Nicky and Tyler. One grimy hand yanked at his crotch. He snorted noisily then spat a huge amount of some disgusting looking spit on the ground in front of them.

"Let's go, Rusty. Don't think you're scaring us away, mister," Nate called as he turned to go. "Ya gotta sleep sometime, then that bitch will be mine."

After one last venom-filled look at Nicky, the two idiots spurred their horses around and headed back into the darkness. Nate's laughter faded into the distance as they rode away. Tyler turned to Nicky as he replaced the pistol in his holster.

"Smart fella. It's always good to let on what you're going to do to ambush somebody before you do it. Old beau of yours?"

She snorted and rolled her eyes skyward. "A rat wouldn't keep company with a lowdown skunk like that."

Tyler shrugged with a casualness he didn't really feel. First there was a constant battle with his lust. Now this. He wasn't at all certain as to why he felt protective toward this woman. It was an odd and unsettling emotion he couldn't ever remember feeling, except perhaps for his mother. That was another lifetime ago. And Jesus Christ on crutches, he didn't want to drag that up now.

Nicky shook her head back and forth. "Why did God create man?" she muttered. "If they can't kill something, they want to fu—"

Tyler cut her off with a jerk on her arm. "Watch it, Malloy."

"Too close to the truth, bounty hunter?"

He stared at her long and hard. "If you're wanting company, I can ask the two of them to come back."

Nicky blanched. It was the first time he'd seen a reaction other than anger from this little spitfire. Then her cheeks turned into a blaze of red heat and she clenched her hands into fists.

"No one, *no one* will ever force me to do that with a man. I'll cut off his prick before he touches me."

This woman really did have an amazing vocabulary. "With what? You're not even armed," he scoffed.

She smiled at him with no warmth in her eyes. "Can't wait to find out?"

God Almighty, she was tough.

"Won't have to. Never had to force a woman. Don't intend on starting, especially with you."

Nicky visibly flinched and averted her eyes to the fire. "Your supper is burning."

"Dammit!"

As Tyler tried in vain to salvage the johnnycakes, Nicky dropped to the ground with a thump.

"We'll be moving camp after we eat."

"I figured that one out all by myself."

While they ate a dinner of chewy jerky and water, Nicky complained about the cold meal, the hard ground, and everything else on God's green earth that was bothering her. Tyler was more than ready to gag her as he had threatened earlier.

As he cleaned up the simple fare, he glared at her until her chattering stopped and she was finally silent.

"Listen, magpie, I need you to just shut the hell up for a minute. We've got to be smart about moving our camp tonight. Those two idiots are still out there, waiting. You can either help, or your friend Nate can get his chance with you."

Nicky took a deep breath and closed her eyes. "What do you want me to do?" she finally said.

"Put everything back in the saddlebags. Follow me, and stay low to the ground until we're far enough away to get a fix on them. We're going to walk the horses for a spell in a few circles. I don't suspect they have good tracking skills between them. Keep those pink lips quiet, and *obey* me. Do you understand the word *quiet*?"

She nodded.

"How about the word obey?"

Her jaw clenched tightly, but she nodded again.

"Good. Keep both of those words in mind and we'll lose those bastards."

As Tyler doused the fire, she gathered their belongings and began putting them into the saddlebags. She hesitantly rooted around in his.

"No weapons in there, Malloy. Move that sweet behind before I have to spank it."

Oh, hell, why did he have to say that? Another fantasy danced across his overactive mind.

Nicky harrumphed at his remark, but completed her task without any further ado. They crept to their horses and slung the saddlebags up. After making sure the shackles were secure, he grabbed the reins of her horse, and pulled her forward along with the horses.

"Let's go."

For hours, Tyler pushed Nicky in the darkness to keep walking. He kept bringing up Nate, hoping it would inspire her to keep going. He was tired, so he figured she must be completely exhausted.

"You're a demon from hell, aren't you?" she said with more than a hint of weariness.

He grinned into the darkness. "No, but you're not the first person to ask me that."

"No doubt. Too bad I don't have some holy water to heave at you just to be sure. Or perhaps lay my hands on you and yell 'begone demon'."

Tyler had to swallow a snort of laughter. "Believe it or not, a traveling preacher tried that outside of Amarillo once. He ended up on his ass in the dirt after his righteous spittle hit me on the nose."

"A spitting preacher tried to get rid of your demons?"

"Something like that."

He thought he heard a chuckle, but the darkness absorbed the sound too quickly.

"I had a preacher once tried to convince my mama that I was a demon."

Tyler's eyebrows shot toward his hair. He had to bite his tongue not to laugh. "And your crimes against the church?"

"You'll laugh."

"No, I won't."

Silence met his assurance. "Really, I won't laugh."

"If you do laugh, I have permission to punch you in your spittle-covered nose."

"Agreed."

"I wasn't wearing a corset or a dress—always wore britches—so he was convinced I was a demon in disguise. He said demons can't wear lace. It chafes their scales."

Tyler laughed, then swerved just in time to avoid a small white fist sailing at him. He grabbed her arms and halted her attack.

"What the hell are you doing?"

"You said I could punch you in the nose if you laughed."

"Well that was before you said demons can't wear lace because it chafes their scales."

"Lace does chafe. Damn sissy stuff. I hated it and I refused to wear it. Still don't, goddammit!"

He bit his tongue and tasted blood, but he didn't laugh again.

"So does that mean you're a demon after all?"

"Very funny. You must keep your prisoners in stitches all the time."

"Yup, but they're not laughing with them. They're bleeding from them."

Tyler immediately regretted his words. He had been enjoying their banter. Too much. She didn't speak another word.

Tyler decided it was time to stop after putting sufficient distance behind them, and far too many tracks for those fools to follow. He spotted another clump of trees on the horizon.

"Mount up, Malloy. Almost bedtime."

Nicky hauled herself up in the saddle with a grunt. She didn't stay on the horse for long. Tyler saw her start to slide out of the saddle and caught her about the waist.

"Won't be that easy to escape."

He pulled her limp form onto his saddle. When she nestled in front of him with a sigh, he realized the monumental error he had just made. It was like having a little piece of heaven sitting in his lap. Now why was he not surprised her sweet behind was so goddamn soft? Good thing it was only for a few minutes, or she was sure to feel more than his pistol poking her in the back.

He held the reins with one hand, while the other settled on her waist. Seemingly without thought, he rocked against her and shuddered at the sensation as his cock decided to rise to the occasion. Dammit! He had to stop himself. Now. He wasn't about to fuck an unconscious woman. Even an outlaw.

When they reached the trees, he dismounted quickly, then pulled her down with a plop. She was like a life-sized rag doll.

He didn't want to put his hands on her any more than necessary.

"Come on, Malloy, stand up," he growled.

Nicky stood, albeit shakily, biting her lip as she watched Tyler open her bedroll. He grabbed her arm and led her to it like a small child.

"Sleep."

As he watched, she dropped like a sack of potatoes. Her hat popped off and rolled a few feet away. She was asleep in the blink of an eye. Tyler had to tear his gaze away from her finely rounded bottom, to forget how it felt to be pressed up against it so intimately. To forget how badly he wanted to pull down those jeans and plunge into her.

As he tried to will away the terrific hard-on in his pants, he briefly scouted the area, but neither heard nor saw any pursuit. Hopefully they had confused the hell out of those two idiots, and had seen the last of them.

Now if only he could stop wanting to get into his prisoner's pants.

⁂ ⁂ ⁂

Nicky couldn't get back to sleep. She woke up as suddenly as she had fallen asleep, and now her mind was racing. Although she had washed the mud off her face and hands, her clothes were stiff with it. And she was chained to this bounty hunter, had to sleep next to him. It didn't matter that she was on her own bedroll; he was so close she could hear his even breathing, and if she turned her head, they would be nose to nose. Close enough to kiss. She sighed, gazing up at the moon. It was almost full and bright as a new coin.

She couldn't believe all the effort she'd made to cover her tracks was wasted. This man had found her, and a nice fat reward waited for him, she was certain of that. She had disguised herself so well for years, survived on her own, learned to shoot like a damn gunslinger, and here she was chained to a bounty hunter. A man that made her remember what it was to be a woman, to want, to desire, to lust. A disturbingly handsome bounty hunter with hair as black as soot, and eyes the color of a Wyoming winter sky.

Wyoming.

Unbidden images of Logan's final moments came into her mind. *Oh no, here it comes.* Her throat closed with emotion. She missed him, she missed her parents, her other brothers, and even missed Wyoming. Now she found out they thought she was a thief and a murderer. She choked on the feelings, hidden for so long as she had struggled to hide, to survive. Rage, fear, hopelessness, and most of all, grief. Now her family would see her swing from a tree. And Logan's death would never be avenged.

Silent tears coursed down her cheeks.

Oh Logan, I'm sorry I couldn't save you. It should have been me who died.

This was definitely not the time to become a crybaby. She stifled a hiccup as the tears slowed. She needed to think about how to escape from this bounty hunter, not weep about how she would die if she didn't.

Chapter Five

The sun peeked over the horizon the next morning, painting the sky a soft shade of pink. Tyler was awake with the dawn. As his eyes focused on the sky, he was disconcerted to find it was the same shade of pink as his prisoner's lips. He was even further disconcerted to find that Nicky was snuggled up against him, with one leg slung over his. In sleep, those pink lips were slightly parted, her long lashes closed in repose, and her face was smudged with dirt. In something akin to horror, he realized that another part of his anatomy was waking with a vengeance. Hard, long, and hungry.

Nicky's hair was splayed out beneath her head. *How did she ever control those locks?* It really did look like it was made of silk, and was probably softer. She truly was a beautiful woman. He refused to torture himself and think of what she would look like wearing a dress. She was enough to look at in jeans and a baggy shirt. He squashed the urge to smile. It was replaced by the stronger urge to kiss those sunrise-pink lips, and run his hands through her curls. He berated himself for desiring this strange woman...this outlaw. Disgusted at his body's weakness, he pushed at Nicky's shoulder to wake her up. She slept on.

Tyler leaned over her face and took a deep breath.

"Wake up, woman!" he shouted with a certain perverse satisfaction.

Nicky awoke with a start and sat up so quickly she knocked her head soundly into Tyler's jaw.

"Ouch!" She rubbed her forehead.

Tyler hid his pain by rising to his knees, pushing her leg off his. "You sleep like the dead."

Nicky regarded her captor with an icy stare. "I'll soon be dead if you take me to Wyoming."

Tyler ignored her comment. As he stood, he pulled her up with him, the shackles clanging noisily. She looked sleep rumpled and still goddamned desirable. He groaned inwardly at this continuing lust. No more wasting time, he'd push her as hard as he could to get to Wyoming.

* * *

Tyler knew, he just damned well knew, he should have followed his instincts and told her no. But she pestered, and pestered, and pestered until he thought he'd lose his mind. He briefly wondered how magpies tasted after they were roasted over a spit. She wanted to take a bath and change her clothes.

"The mud is itchy. I really have to get clean," she whined.

So he relented, and took her to the creek on the other side of the trees.

"You aren't going to keep me chained now, are you? You're going to have my clothes...where can I go?"

Tyler finally gave in to her demands, and unlocked the shackles only after she'd taken off her jeans, and her shirt hung by one sleeve. He averted his eyes from her half-dressed body. The fact that she was wearing men's long underwear did nothing to detract from her innate sensuality. God, how he wanted this woman.

As she washed up in the creek, she asked him if she could wash the mud off her clothes, too. Without thinking, no, perhaps he was thinking of nothing but her taking a bath, he tossed her muddy clothes to her. As he stared off into the distance, he realized the splashing had stopped. And Miss Nicole Malloy was hightailing it across the prairie wearing a wet pair of men's long underwear. And dammit to hell, she ran like the wind.

Tyler cursed heartily as he ran to the horses to give pursuit to his wayward prisoner. He untied the reins from the tree, then hauled himself up into the saddle. Leaving her mare behind, he took off after Nicky.

* * *

I did it. Best bounty hunter, my ass.

The rocks that were hidden in the tall grass were starting to cut the bottoms of her feet, but she kept going. She was running flat out and putting quite a distance between herself and the bounty hunter. Now if only she could find a farmhouse with some nice people that would believe her story of being kidnapped.

The sound of rapid hoofbeats threw her into a panic. She began running haphazardly, trying to keep out of his direct line of fire. Her foot slipped into a gopher hole and she tried to use her arms to regain her balance and stop her downward fall. She ended up sprawled face first in the dirt. Her nose took the brunt of the fall.

* * *

Tyler wanted to laugh when he saw her fall. *Some escape.* As he dismounted by her prone body, he grew concerned that she was truly hurt. He gently rolled her over. Nicky stared up at the sky with her eyebrows slammed together and blood running from her nose.

"Son of a bitch. Why can't I ever be graceful enough to be a woman?"

"Maybe when you start acting like one," Tyler said, realizing her pride was more hurt than her body. Damn, the woman had grit. He pulled a bandanna from his back pocket, and pressed it to her nose. "Here, hold this."

He scooped her up into his arms, then flung her stomach first over his horse. After he mounted, he turned the horse around and headed back toward the creek.

"You know, you're not supposed to treat an injured woman like this," came her muffled, somewhat nasal shout.

"You're not a woman to me, you're an outlaw. You're lucky you only hurt your little freckled nose. In a second, my Winchester was going to stop you."

Tyler tried not to look at her behind, but his eyes seemed to have a mind of their own. The wet material hugged her derriere, outlining the sweet curves. *God Almighty, it is perfect.* His musings were cut short when he saw the soles of her feet—they looked to be painted crimson.

"Dammit, woman, why can't you just do what I tell you to do?"

"What did I do now?"

As they arrived back at the makeshift camp, Tyler dismounted and pulled her shivering body from the horse. Dropping her on her bedroll, he threw his blanket around her shoulders, then grabbed his nearby saddlebag and started rummaging around for salve.

"What are you doing?" she asked around the bandanna.

"Looking for something to clean up your feet." He washed the blood off her feet with water from his canteen, then put salve on the cuts. Taking one of his shirts from the saddlebag, he cut strips of bandages for her feet, and bound them after the bleeding had slowed to a trickle.

When he glanced up, she was staring at him with a confused look in her eyes. Her nose had stopped bleeding, and dried blood had crusted on her cheeks. He took the bandanna from her and rinsed it out, then bathed her face, mindful of her sore nose.

"You're probably gonna have a helluva shiner," he said as he finished his ministrations.

"Why did you do that?"

"I didn't want to have to haul a corpse four hundred miles when those cuts turn gangrene. You're enough trouble alive."

If she'd had the courage to question him on why he offered that particular lie, he couldn't have answered. He just didn't know.

Chapter Six

Over the next several days, Nicky took it upon herself to study Tyler Calhoun, to gather all the information she could about the tight-lipped bounty hunter. Something she could use to escape, a weakness, anything. Trying to keep her plans unknown, she studied him when she thought he wasn't looking. As they rode side by side across the plains each day, he never seemed to be interested in her at all, which gave her the opportunity to complete her surreptitious study.

She decided that he truly was as extremely handsome as she had originally thought. He had a broad chest and shoulders, narrow waist and hips, and thick black hair which all fit together in one nice package. His jaw was set in a hard line, his chin was covered with light stubble only hours after he shaved, his nose was straight and fine, his thick mustache rode a pair of lips that were just the right size for kissing.

She had to stop thinking about kissing him. It was a one time occurrence—never to repeat itself. If she kept telling herself that, she might believe it.

It was his eyes that truly haunted her. She'd never seen eyes quite that shade of blue before. They suddenly flicked over to hers. He had caught her looking at him. Chagrined by her actions as well as her pitiful, susceptible heart, she pasted on an innocent expression.

"You've been staring at me for two days. Something you need, Nicole?"

She didn't trust that soft tone for anything.

"Yes." She scrambled for a reason. "Since this is going to be a long journey, I thought we could at least talk. The silence is making me jumpy."

He shook his head, then turned his gaze forward again. Nicky squeezed her lips together in determination. Now he'd pissed her off by dismissing her. She would make him talk.

"How long have you been a bounty hunter?"

The silence was only broken by the sound of the horses' hooves clopping on the hard-packed dirt and the jangle of the chain that bound them together.

"Have you caught many men?"

Still nothing. He obviously underestimated a woman that grew up with six older brothers. She could be a pest's pest when she wanted to. Time to get dirty.

"Was Hermano the first time you'd been captured? How embarrassing."

Clip-clop went the horses' hooves.

"Where are you from? Texas? Sounds like it. You went all the way from Texas to Wyoming for this job? Owen must have waved a lot of money under your nose."

His hands tightened on the reins, and she smiled at his growing impatience.

"Wife? Children? Friends? Enemies? Favorite things to do?"

Tyler finally turned his head toward her. His eyes glittered like chips of blue ice, cold and hard.

"You're worth six thousand dollars to me...alive, anyway. That's all you need to know. What makes you ask all these questions about me?" His tone certainly did not match the look on his face.

Her heart dropped along with her stomach. They were dragging behind the horse now.

Six thousand dollars. That's a damned fortune. Who in their right mind would turn that down to capture an outlaw?

"Ah, well, ah...y-you seem to know, um, to know everything there is to know about me..." she stammered.

His gaze raked up and down her body. Those ice blue eyes found hers. His expression hadn't changed. "No, not everything," he said as he turned away from her again.

"You know more than most men," she retorted.

His gaze snapped back to hers. The coldness had intensified in his eyes. Thankfully, the sun burst through the clouds at that moment and the brim of his hat shaded most of his face.

"Have you known many men? Like Nate maybe? I couldn't find you in any whorehouse, but maybe that means you had your own business going. You're a nice piece of calico—it could happen."

Nice piece of calico?

Now she was getting angry. She was no whore, dammit. And one kiss didn't change that fact. She yanked on the chain that bound her to his saddle. Tyler grabbed the chain tightly with one hand.

"What I have or have not done with men is none of your damned business, Calhoun. Why are you being so all-fired nasty to me?"

"I could ask you the same question."

"All I wanted to do was pass the time. You wouldn't talk so...I made you talk. I win."

He snorted. "Bull, Malloy. Now shut up and keep riding."

His voice was firm as he kneed his horse to a faster pace.

"I still win. Can we stop for dinner?"

He didn't answer her.

"I will throw myself from my horse and drag you down with me," she said sweetly but with a touch of ice. "If you don't stop and let me rest."

Calhoun turned to look at her. She saw a flash of something—irritation?—cross his features, then he was his cool self again.

"As long as you'll stop your blathering, magpie," he said through his clenched teeth.

So, too much talking bothered him? She wasn't normally a chatterbox, but being talkative could be an easy weapon to wield against her captor. Oh, joy! She mentally rubbed her hands together at the newfound information.

"Thank you, Calhoun," she cooed with a bright smile.

Tyler snorted at her thanks. He stopped the horses at a small pond, and dismounted in one fluid motion. After unlocking the shackles from the saddle horn, he reached up to lift her down.

Nicky's arm bumped the brim of her hat, knocking it off and letting her curls loose in a small explosion of hair. They tumbled down, brushing Tyler's face.

Nicky caught her breath at the desire she saw flame in Tyler's eyes. His hands felt like branding irons on her sides. Ever so slowly, her feet touched the ground. Her breathing quickened as they stood between the horses, his hands still on her waist.

Kiss me.

It seemed like a moment frozen in time, as if they existed outside here and now. Nicky licked her lips as she searched Tyler's eyes. For what, she didn't know. His scent exuded from him like a beckoning knell. She breathed deeply, inhaling Tyler into her body, then raised her hand to his face. When her fingertips made contact with his cheek, he didn't jerk away. He closed his eyes. Nicky would swear she felt him shudder.

She didn't dare take a breath. The moment was as fragile as a butterfly's wing.

Kiss me.

In answer to her silent plea, Tyler's eyes opened and he pulled her to him hard as his mouth descended on her parted lips. His body was long and muscled but curved into hers like a key in a lock. Nicky expected his lips to be as hard as the rest of him, but they were soft and demanding. His mustache tickled her cheeks, sending delightful shivers down her back. His tongue was tracing the outline of her lips.

So sweet, so sensual. God, it was like heaven.

Her heart was hammering against her ribcage so loudly she was sure Tyler must hear it. Uttering a small moan, she opened her mouth to his slick tongue and pressed herself against him fully, her hands probing his muscled chest. This is what she wanted, what she craved, what she *needed.*

Tyler released a primitive, animal-like noise deep in his throat as his hands roamed up and down her back. One hand settled on her behind, squeezing gently. The other anchored itself in her hair. His tongue delved into the dark recesses of her mouth where no man had ever been.

Nicky's head was spinning as she kissed him with every fiber of her being. Every nerve ending jangled, every inch of skin sang. Her breasts felt constrained in her bindings. Her jeans felt too tight as an incredible ache between her legs intensified with the kiss. The rawness of her reaction was frightening.

Nicky clung to Tyler for dear life as a near maelstrom swirled inside her. Never, *never* had she felt anything like this for a man.

And oh, sweet Jesus, she wanted more. Her hands clutched at his shirt pulling him closer. The ridge of his arousal pressed into her mons and she clenched deep inside. She let her body take over and just feel.

"Free my hands, Calhoun," she said against his lips.

He dragged his lips from hers and stepped back, getting as far from her as possible. The chain from the shackles bound them together as the two regarded each other. Both were breathing raggedly. Nicky's cheeks were hot, and her lips felt puffy.

Tyler wiped the moisture from his lips with the back of his hand. Nicky's heart hiccupped at his obvious disgust.

"You should keep your hands to yourself, Malloy. Don't try escaping by using that tempting body of yours," he said, his voice raw.

She spat on the ground as well as any man.

"How dare you? How dare you kiss me and then put the blame on me? I'm chained to you. I don't have the key or the freedom. As for using my body..."

Her eyes narrowed as she approached him with a stiff spine. She poked one finger at his broad chest.

"I have never, ever used it with anybody, for anything. I am untouched, and plan on remaining that way until I get married." She cursed the extra huskiness in her voice. It was a lie and she choked on it. "And if you ever try to kiss me again, I'll kick you so hard your grandchildren will still be feeling it."

His expression remained unchanged, but a muscle jumped in his cheek. No, he sure as hell didn't believe her. She was just about to climb into the grass and invite him to join her. Her goddamn body betrayed her. Her head told her no, but she couldn't seem to control the rest of her.

Angry at her own weakness, she turned quickly to her mare and reached into the saddlebag. He was on her in a flash, wrestling her hands out of the saddlebag. Nicky let out a yelp of pain as her wrists twisted in Tyler's hands. When she let go, her book fell to the grass. Tyler stared at the book as if he'd never seen one before in his life.

"Calhoun, what are you doing? Trying to break my arms?" He was so frigging fast and so strong, he could have broken her arms easily. She had no idea he had that kind of speed, along with his obvious brute strength. Her heart was still racing from the kiss, and this pushed her pulse up even faster. She needed time to catch her breath before Calhoun realized the effect he had on her. She could never allow him to see the power he unconsciously, or consciously, wielded against her.

"What is this?" Tyler bent to pick up the book.

"It's a book. It's got letters and words in it, in case you haven't heard of them. Sonnets written by a man named Shakespeare. Ever hear of him?"

Tyler thrust her book at her as he clenched and unclenched his jaw.

"'All men are bad, and in their badness, reign'," Tyler said so quietly, Nicky almost didn't hear him.

But she did, and it about knocked her on her ass. It was part of a sonnet, a Shakespearean sonnet. "*You've* read Shakespeare?"

He scowled at her. "What makes you think I'm an idiot?"

"I never said you were an idiot, Calhoun. I'm just surprised you've read Shakespeare, even more so that you can quote from a sonnet."

"Same here."

"Oh, so now I'm an idiot?"

"I never said you were an idiot, Malloy." He mirrored her words with a bite to his voice that stung.

Nicky opened her mouth to speak again, but then closed it and turned away from Tyler. Willing herself to ignore the man, and her hungry body, she patted her mare affectionately as the horse drank from the small pond, then sat herself down on the soft grass. Opening the book, she glanced up at Tyler.

"Are we going to eat?" She shaded her eyes from the sun with her free hand. "Where's my hat gone to?"

* * *

Tyler could barely keep from strangling Nicky. Scooping up her hat from the ground, he threw it to her. She was acting as if nothing had just happened, as if he hadn't just come close to fucking her in the middle of nowhere, then quoted Shakespeare to her. *Son of a bitch!*

He'd never met a woman who vexed him like this one. Usually they were all fluttery and demure, or scared shitless of him, but not Nicky. Tyler shook his head to dispel his wayward thoughts. Six thousand dollars was a hell of a lot of money and no lay, no matter how good, was worth that. Not even the luscious Nicky Malloy was going to deter him from getting that money.

After listening to Nicky chatter on the rest of the day about everything from buttons to boot heels, Tyler was at the end of his patience. When they stopped for the night, he threatened to gag her if she didn't shut up. She shrugged and kept herself reasonably quiet, and went to sleep without a sound.

He awoke that night, startled by a noise. He sat up quickly, surveying their makeshift camp. An owl hooted somewhere, and the drone of crickets was steady, but he heard nothing unusual in the night. Then he heard the noise again and realized it was Nicky whimpering.

He looked down at her sleeping face, bathed in the moonlight. It was twisted in the most painful grimace Tyler had ever seen as tears ran down her cheeks from her closed eyes. He was perplexed that she was crying in her sleep. He'd never heard of such a thing, but then he'd never met anybody like her before. She was obviously cunning, resourceful, and...okay, intelligent. She always had a fresh barb ready for him, never giving an inch of her pride. And, Jesus, the woman could talk from sunup to sundown.

"Oh, Logan," she whispered. "I'm so sorry."

Tyler frowned. She was whispering another man's name in her sleep. So what? It didn't, shouldn't, *couldn't* matter to him.

She whimpered again, then shivered. Tyler leaned down and pulled her blanket up, tucking it around her body. He felt his face flush with the intimacy of his gesture. Why should he care if she was cold or crying? He didn't know why, but he knew he did. He had come to respect Nicole Malloy and was bone-deep scared that it might become more than respect if he didn't keep his distance from his prisoner. A prisoner who was whispering another man's name in her dreams. That was something that shouldn't bother Tyler in the least. And, of course, neither should that kiss.

Chapter Seven

The next day began gray and dreary, mirroring Nicky's mood. Her plan to annoy Tyler with her chattering worked all too well. When he threatened to gag her yesterday, she had been frightened that he meant it. She could hardly bear to be shackled, much less gagged. As a result, familiar nightmares had plagued her sleep last night, and she was exhausted.

They broke camp quickly and efficiently by unspoken agreement, against an ominous sky. She felt as if she hadn't slept in years, and Tyler was his usual tight-lipped self. And it looked like it was going to rain—hard. All in all, it was a depressing day. Tyler surprised her by settling his horse closer to hers as they headed north.

"Tell me what you've been doing for the past three and a half years," he said.

"*You* want to talk to *me*?"

"Believe it or not, magpie," was his only response.

Nicky sat up straighter in the saddle, suddenly feeling more hopeful. Perhaps if she could convince him she was innocent, he wouldn't bring her back to Cheshire. *Fat chance.* She scoffed at her own optimism.

"Start whenever you want. Yesterday or three years ago."

"Three years ago?"

Before she could call upon her rigid self-control, Nicky was awash with painful memories. That first afternoon when she woke, she was horrified to find dried blood all over her hands and face. She nearly scrubbed her skin raw with the sand from the creek she used to wash. It couldn't, and didn't, wash away the guilt. She remembered the painful days alone when she slept during the day and traveled at night. And then when she saw the boy again, what he did, she very nearly—

Using an incredible reserve of strength, she regained her self-control and forcibly pushed aside the pain. Instead, she concentrated on convincing the bounty hunter of her innocence.

"After I left Wyoming, I went to Nebraska for a short time. Then I drifted around for a few months, taking short jobs at local ranches. Since I grew up on a ranch, it was the only thing I knew how to do. That's how I met Hermano. I was in Texas, heading out from the ranch I'd just quit. He was surrounded by three men who had beaten him and tied him."

"What did you do?"

She shrugged. "I evened the odds. I don't like to see anybody outnumbered or tied up like an animal."

"So then what?"

"Hermano became like a surrogate brother to me. He brought me back to his valley hideout for a week or so. I found another job and moved on."

"And that was a few years ago? Then why were you back there in August?"

She sighed. "When I was between jobs, Hermano's was a safe place to be for a bit. At least, until you found me there."

"Just doing my job, Nicole."

"I know, but I can never go back there again."

Nicky had been at Hermano's a few times over the last two years. After she'd freed Calhoun, she left for the last time. The sentries had let her pass—they all knew the bounty hunter was there for her, but they wouldn't give her up. No one dared risk Hermano's wrath. And he treated his little *Roja*, his red-haired *gringa*, as he would his own blood. To harm her would be certain death for anyone.

"Why not?"

"I put them all in danger. Even with Hermano, they would kill me if I went back."

"Right. So, what brought you to Oklahoma?"

"I ran into Willard. He and I knew each other from a few years back at another ranch in Kansas. He got me the job as a wrangler at the Rocking R."

"Did they know you were a woman?"

She shook her head. "No, just Willard. When we'd first met, he got suspicious as to why I didn't bathe in the creek with the rest of the men, or visit the whorehouse on payday. I confessed to him about how I was trying to avenge my brother's death and not get my neck stretched in the process."

"Didn't this Willard want to turn you in for the bounty?"

"No. I don't think he ever really believed I was a wanted woman, but by then he was like an uncle to me and would never betray me."

"I can believe you're a wanted woman."

Nicky glanced at Tyler. His face was a hard, emotionless mask. She wasn't sure how to interpret his remark, so she let it pass, but damn she couldn't help the flip that her heart decided to do.

"Did you keep up with the rest of the men as a hired hand?"

"Of course. I was always one of the top hands, but my specialty was cutting calves from the herd," she stated proudly, noting the flicker of surprise in his eyes. "Didn't know I was a real rancher's daughter, huh?"

"It doesn't say much about you as a person in my file. Just what you did, and how many men have tried to catch you, without luck of course," he answered, with the smallest smile in the corner of his mouth.

"I'd like to find out how you caught me."

"I'm the best there is. I found your trail, even though it was cold and near impossible to see." He shook his head slowly. "I have to tell you, when I first found out the bounty was for a woman, I figured it would be a week, two weeks at most to find you." He laughed without any real humor. "That particular mistake I don't plan to make again. I've learned that a woman can be harder to find than a man."

"Thanks, I think."

His glance slid over and back. "I guess you can consider that a compliment. The reason I found you in Oklahoma was because some drunken cowboy had spotted your knife. It's pretty unique, you know. Probably shouldn't have shown it to me."

Nicky grimaced. "Damn! I didn't even remember that I had."

He glanced down. "It was the night you saved my life. I don't know why you did or what would have happened if you didn't, but all the same, you have my thanks."

That must have been a pretty hard thing to say. Especially to an outlaw like her. But he had.

"You're welcome. I think I'm pretty much regretting it now," she said as her lips twisted. "Especially now that I know you spotted my knife and that's how you tracked me again. Damn softhearted woman."

As if in answer to her sagging spirits, the first fat raindrops began to fall on them.

"This is just wonderful," she muttered at the gray sky.

Within moments, the rain was a steady downpour, running in rivulets off the brim of her Stetson and down the collar of her coat. It was as if God was punishing her for what she had done, or didn't do.

"I think I see a barn in the distance. Let's see if your mare can keep up with Sable." He urged his horse into a gallop.

Nicky automatically kept up with Tyler, the chain that bound them together clanking noisily in the rain as they flew across the prairie. She could hardly see where she was going and hoped there were no trees to hit or any fences to crash into. After ten minutes of hard riding, the rain was almost painful on her face. She could barely discern the outline of a barn as they rode up hard and fast.

As they came closer, Nicky laughed. It was a pitiful excuse for a barn if she ever saw one. The entire structure was leaning to one side, with various boards missing like gaping tooth holes, and the grass grown up around the outside of it. At that moment, the sky truly opened up, and a torrent of rain pounded them.

Tyler pulled his horse to a stop and dismounted simultaneously. He quickly removed the shackles and yanked Nicky down from her horse. Holding onto her arm with his right hand, and the horses' reins with his left, he was left with no other choice but to use his foot to open the curiously crooked barn door. With a mighty kick, it moved a few inches. Nicky chuckled.

Frowning, Tyler gave an even mightier kick, and the door opened a few more inches. Nicky guffawed.

Tyler gave one last try with a manly grunt and the door swung all the way open. Nicky was still chortling as they entered the barn, the horses in tow.

"I don't see anything funny about drowning out there," he growled at her. "Tend to your horse." He removed her shackles and dropped them to the dusty floor.

"Her name is Juliet."

"Shakespeare, again." He snorted. "Figures."

She smiled as she turned to wipe Juliet down with some straw, and an ear-popping crack of thunder split the sky, followed immediately by a blinding flash of light. Tyler was watching her. A wicked grin spread across his handsome face.

"You're not scared are you, Nicole?" he drawled as he wiped down Sable.

"Don't be an idiot." She kept her back to him.

The next crack of thunder was even louder, making the hard-packed dirt beneath their feet rumble. When the next bolt of lightning lit up the sky, Nicky yelped.

"You're *scared* of a thunder and lightning storm, magpie? You? Fearless ranch hand and outlaw?"

That, as they say, was the straw that broke the camel's back. Fury bubbled up inside her like a fire burning out of control. Nicky turned and with a scream hurled her body at him. They landed on the ground heavily.

"Jesus Christ, woman!"

"No more, no more, no more!" She pummeled his chest with her hard fists.

"Nicole," he bellowed, grabbing hold of her wrists in a punishing grip. "Stop it."

She halted in mid-swing, surprised by the depth of her rage. Wondering why it was all directed at this man. She stared at him with regret and confusion. Releasing her wrists, he sat up and wrapped his arms around her, snuggling her like a small child. She was shivering with fear, cold, and countless unnamed demons. Holding her closely, Tyler stroked her back.

Nicky opened her mouth and words just started tumbling out.

"Logan was always there for me when a storm came. We'd usually play a game or read. Poems were my favorite. He used to tease me that I was a cat afraid of a little water," she whispered against his chest. "But he didn't know the real reason. He never knew because I begged my parents not to tell him. I grew up on the ranch next to Owen Hoffman's. Our families were usually friendly-like, and we all knew each other. When I was five, Owen locked me in an abandoned root cellar during a violent thunderstorm—his idea of a practical joke. It was a very leaky root cellar, which is why it was abandoned. I huddled in a corner listening to the storm scream around me like a banshee searching for a fresh meal of little girl. My brother Ray finally found me."

"How long were you locked in?"

"Three hours." She paused. "By then, the water was up to my neck, and my throat was hoarse from screaming for help."

"God Almighty," he whispered.

"Owen got caught, but never got into much trouble, because his Pa was so rich. He was a mean young man, and it just got worse. My parents couldn't see the evil that was part of his soul, but I could. I could always see it." She squeezed her eyes shut and willed the tears back. "I never shook the fear of a storm...even when I was old enough to realize that what Owen had done was for his own twisted games. Now when there is a storm, I know that Logan will never, *ever* be here to comfort me. And it's *my fault.* He's dead and it's all my fault."

"Shhh," he crooned as he held her close.

"If I hadn't been so nosy, so curious, so damn sure of myself, we never would have gone over there." She snuffled loudly. "Have you ever lost anyone you loved?"

Tyler's body stiffened at her question. "Yes."

"Then you know what it's like to have your heart ripped out, to feel as if your soul was empty. I felt it, still feel it, and know it was my own doing. I gambled with his life and lost."

"You were very close."

"He was my twin brother, the other half of me." Her throat felt raw. "I haven't been a whole person in a very long time."

He was silent for a moment. "How did he die?"

"I already told you. Owen Hoffman and his outlaw ranch hands murdered him. They beat him senseless, tied him up, then shot him in the head." Her voice was loud with fury. "And I'll never have the chance to avenge his death, will I?"

As the thunderstorm raged like a demon outside the musty barn, Tyler held Nicky close, giving comfort when there was none to be had. She seemed to be turning her back on everything that was familiar to her.

She grappled for him, her lips seeking his. It was more than a kiss, it was a battle. She tried to take control, but he was stronger. His lips gentled and she sighed, giving control over to him. Her kissing experience was limited, but obviously his wasn't. His lips moved over hers, brushing his mustache against the sensitive skin above her lips.

She was drowning in the sensation of being beneath him, of having his body lay on top of hers. He was hard, yet supple, like his lips. He licked the seam of her lips until she surrendered and opened her mouth. His tongue swept in and Nicky was lost.

The darkness seemed to intensify in the barn as the hairs on the back of Nicky's neck rose to attention like little sentries. Something was wrong. It sounded like a locomotive, but she knew what it was before it even hit the barn. Tyler tore his lips from hers and their eyes met. She could see his mind rush to the same conclusion as hers.

A twister.

A deafening, whirling noise preceded the roof of the barn being ripped clean off the sorry building.

Tyler immediately shielded Nicky's body with his own as the wind howled above their heads. Nicky thought she had been scared before, but this was mortal danger, and Tyler was protecting her. *How did that happen?* She felt his grunt as something slammed into his back. The wind spun around her, crazily kicking up dust and hay. She could barely see or hear anything except the shrieking wind. The warmth from Tyler's hard body felt like a protective blanket. Nicky could definitely get used to that feeling.

It seemed like hours, but was probably more like two minutes, until it was over. As suddenly as it came, the twister was gone, and a light rain was falling on them through the ruined roof of the barn.

Tyler groaned in her ear as he tried to straighten.

"Are you okay?" Nicky asked.

He nodded. She was surprised to find them both relatively unhurt. The horses had bolted from the barn when the twister hit, but she didn't think they'd be far. The rain began to slack off to an occasional drip.

She looked at him, still stunned. "You protected me."

He stared at her unblinking for a moment.

"You're worth twice as much to me alive. Let's go find the horses."

Nicky tried to swallow the lump of pain that blossomed in her throat at his callous words. As if he hadn't been wrapped in her arms with his tongue in her mouth five minutes earlier. Her bounty hunter was proving himself to be a cold bastard. Too bad her body craved his heat.

Chapter Eight

Two days after the brush with the twister, they stopped for the night in a small town called Clayton. They were about two hundred fifty miles or so from Cheshire but, to Tyler, that two hundred fifty miles yawned like an empty cavern in front of them. He was so wound up, he felt like a pistol with a hair trigger and too much powder, ready to go off at any second. He seemed to have a constant semi-erection and had to stop himself from pulling his prisoner into his arms. He could still taste her lips and feel her supple body against his. It was enough to drive him insane with want.

Tyler immediately steered the horses to the local hotel and dismounted, snapping the end of the shackles to his wrist. After tethering the horses, he let Nicky down from her horse, careful to remove his hands quickly. Keeping his distance from her was impossible, and the strain was almost unbearable.

He walked across the road with long, dirt-eating strides, Nicky in tow. She didn't say a word or ask where they were going. When he stopped in front of a small building on the corner of the main street, dawning realization sprang in her eyes. It was the sheriff's office. He meant to imprison her there.

"You can't," she said simply.

"The hell I can't. I can and I will."

He held her firmly by the upper arm and opened the door of the sheriff's office, stepping into the cool, dark interior. He felt her hesitation, but he ignored it and yanked her forward. It was too important to be away from her. Even for just a night.

"Nothing you do or say is going to change my mind, magpie, so make it easy on yourself," he whispered.

She looked back at him as though slightly dazed. She was, however, blessedly silent. He turned his attention to the jail and as his eyes adjusted he saw a middle-aged, sandy-haired man seated behind the desk. The silver star gleaming on his chest marked him as the man in charge.

He tipped his hat. "Sheriff, name's Calhoun. This here's my prisoner Nicky Malloy. She's wanted up in Wyoming and I'm bringing her back. I was wondering if I could use your jail for the night."

The sheriff's right eyebrow raised in a questioning arc as Tyler spoke. He stood and walked over to the two of them. He was the same height as Nicky with a large belly that spoke volumes about someone's cooking. He laced his fingers across his belly and rocked back and forth on his heels.

"Bradley. Emmett Bradley," he said by way of introduction. "You a bounty hunter or a marshal?"

"Bounty hunter."

Bradley nodded, assessing with his sharp eyes. "She's wanted back in Wyoming, eh? I don't suppose you got yourself a wanted poster or any type of paper to prove it?" he asked politely.

Tyler pulled the warrant and the wanted poster from his back pocket and handed them to the man. The sheriff unfolded the papers, read them both thoroughly, and then handed them back to him.

"Okay, but we only got but one cell. If'n we have to put somebody else in there, it's likely to be a man."

"Nicky can handle herself against any man, believe me." She was certainly tying *him* into knots.

The sheriff nodded. "Okay then, why don't you take off those fancy shackles and we'll get her locked up."

Tyler would not look in her eyes, but he sensed that she was frightened. He told himself he didn't care at this point. He needed to be free from her for a night, to shake her out of his system, especially after the confusion of the last few days. He found himself unable to sleep next to her, knowing how soft and yielding her body was. He busied himself unlocking the shackles.

Nicky rubbed her wrists. Tyler ignored the reddened skin with some effort. Hell, the skin wasn't broken, it was hardly even chafed. His hand closed on her upper arm. She started a bit at that, but didn't try to pull away.

"Lead the way, sheriff," Tyler said.

The sheriff took a ring of keys from his desk drawer and led them through a thick wooden door at the back of the building. It was a small room, not more than eight feet by eight feet. A cell was taking up much of the space. In it was a cot with a straw mattress encrusted with various varieties of dirt, along with a rather frightening looking chamber pot in the corner. A window the size of a loaf of bread was on one wall, weak light filtering through it.

"Believe it or not, we don't get too many visitors in here." The sheriff seemed a bit ashamed of the accommodations.

Tyler grunted in response as the sheriff opened the door to the cell. The key scraped in the tumblers with a small shriek, then the door swung open.

"In you go, miss." He gestured inside.

Nicky made no move to enter the cell. Tyler tightened his grasp on her arm and forcibly walked her into the cell. When he let go of her, she swayed toward him. He backed off before he did something stupid like change his mind. Nicky hugged herself and glared at Tyler.

Tyler stepped out of the cell and the sheriff closed the door, twisting the key to lock it again. Inside, he breathed a sigh of relief.

"Bessie brings me dinner from home. I'll send her word to bring an extra plate for you," he said to Nicky.

She nodded in response.

Tyler finally looked her in the eye. The fear he saw there hit him like lightning. Outlaw that she was, she'd apparently never spent the night in a jail cell before. He felt himself waver and clamped down on his lust-driven soft heart. A night's peace was more important to him right now. He had to have at least a few hours without her company to continue this journey. The reasons why were secondary.

"I'll be back for you first thing." *Magpie.*

He stopped himself from voicing the little nickname he had given her. He never felt guilt when he locked up the male outlaws he'd brought to justice. He shouldn't feel any for locking up this one. At least that's what he told himself. His inner voice was howling in protest as the object of his obsession was behind bars, unreachable.

She stared at him mutely. Her lips were pressed together so tightly, they were nearly white. And her hold on herself was as tight as the damn shackles.

"Much obliged, Bradley," Tyler said to the shorter man.

The two men walked out of the room, shutting the door behind them with a solid thump. With forcible effort, Tyler didn't jump at the sound.

⁂ ⁂ ⁂

After an amiable conversation with the sheriff, who was a little astounded, and a bit uncomfortable, that his prisoner was a woman, Tyler went back to check into the only hotel in town. It wasn't fancy, but it looked clean enough. He retrieved his saddlebags and automatically took hers too. He didn't know if anyone would steal anything, but felt obliged to look after her things.

He went into the hotel room, dropped their gear, and headed for the saloon. As soon as he walked in, one of the soiled doves made a beeline for him. She had honey brown hair, blue eyes, and an ample bosom. Each more than a handful. Just the way he liked it.

He ordered a whiskey and sat at an empty table with his glass. The woman followed him to the table, wiggling her hips as she walked. She smiled at him while she licked her lips and waited for an invitation to join him.

Now this is exactly what I need to flush that little magpie out of my system.

"Care to join me?"

"I thought you'd never ask, honey." She practically oozed onto the chair next to him, affording him a full view of her large breasts, which looked nearly ready to pop right out of the green dress she was wearing. It was almost the same shade of green as Nicky's eyes.

Don't think about her.

"Buy me a drink, cowboy?"

"Sure thing."

"Cal, give me a whiskey, would ya?" the woman called to the bartender. "My handsome cowboy is paying."

Tyler flipped her a coin as she retrieved her drink.

She ran her fingertip up and down his arm as she spoke. "What's your name, sugar?"

"Tyler."

"Tyler, darling, if you're game, I can give you a half-hour of the best loving you've ever had."

"Is that so?" He was fairly certain it wouldn't be the best loving he'd ever had, but hell, right now all he needed was to get laid. Not loved.

She leaned forward and pressed her soft breasts into his arm. "Sure thing," she whispered into his ear as she gently bit his earlobe. She smelled of cigarettes and whiskey and, up close, her pancake makeup looked clownish.

"What's your name?"

"Whatever you want it to be," she breathed, her response tickling his ear as her hand meandered toward his belt buckle.

"Okay, then, I'll call you Nicole."

Jesus Christ. Now why the hell had he said that?

"Then I'm Nicole. Dollar for a half-hour, sugar. I can promise ya that you'll hardly be able to walk when I'm done. And from the looks of you," she eyed him up and down with a hungry look, "I may not be able to walk, either."

Tyler hesitated as he looked at the obviously well-trained whore working her wiles on him. Nicky had no claim on him; no woman did. And he damn sure needed to work that magpie out of his system.

Why not?

"Okay, Nicole, you've got a deal."

She turned his face to hers and landed a warm, soft kiss on his lips. His cock twitched to life. Perhaps this was a good idea after all. If he released his sexual tension, maybe he wouldn't be lusting after Nicky like a randy hound. Deep down, he wasn't sure it would change anything, but he wanted to try anyway. He had to do something to break the spell his prisoner had cast over him. It was as if there was an invisible thread between them that had wound them closer and closer together. Unfortunately, she was on the wrong side of the law, he was on the right side. Sooner than he wanted, they were going to collide. He was helpless to stop it. That was a feeling he didn't like in the least. Tyler always wanted to be in control. He drained his whiskey in one satisfying gulp. Time to gain control of his body and perhaps his heart would follow suit.

The saloon girl gave him a hand up, then squeezed his ass and led him to the staircase. Following her swaying hips up the stairs, Tyler had to avert his eyes from the green fabric that swished in front of him. He wasn't going to think of the green-eyed woman sitting in the filthy jail cell.

"Here we are, sugar," she announced as she opened the door to her room.

Tyler entered the whore's bedroom and took a deep breath. It was as he expected. Covered with red satin and filled with cheap furniture. And it stank of unwashed bodies and old sex. Instantly, any thoughts of bedding this Nicole vanished like a puff of smoke, along with his partial erection.

He turned to face her as she began to disrobe. He stayed her hands.

"Hold on. I changed my mind. I, uh, can't," he offered lamely.

She looked a little annoyed, but didn't voice a complaint. Instead she studied his face for a moment.

"Okay, cowboy, I understand."

He pulled a rumpled dollar out of his pocket and pressed it into her hand.

"Take a half-hour off."

She took the money and tucked it into her cleavage. She apparently wasn't proud enough to turn down a dollar for doing nothing.

"What's your real name?"

She hesitated a moment. "Martha." It was probably something she didn't advertise. Most men didn't want to sleep with a whore named after the first president's wife. Better business sense to let the man choose who he wanted you to be.

"Thank you, Martha." He kissed her cheek.

"Sugar, I hope Nicole is worth it."

Tyler opened his mouth to refute her statement, then closed it without making a sound.

⁂ ⁂ ⁂

After a few more shots of whiskey, he found himself back at the hotel, sprawled on the bed, bleary-eyed and lonely. He didn't allow himself to think about her locked in that tiny, dirty cell while he lay on this somewhat comfortable mattress.

Damn Nicky. How could he get so attached to her in such a short period of time? How could he possibly miss her or feel so all-fired guilty about locking up an outlaw?

As he wrestled with his conscience, he passed out and entered a sea of dreams about a woman with green eyes and chestnut curls dancing in the sunshine with two beautiful little girls, sporting the same curls, following along behind her.

My girls.

⁂ ⁂ ⁂

Growing up in the Wyoming territory, Nicky had endured quite a few hardships. She certainly wouldn't call herself prissy or weak, but the cell she found herself locked in was beyond the scope of anything she had ever experienced. She listened to the rats and felt them brush by her every so often. She felt the bugs infesting the mattress crawling all over her as she scratched and tried in vain to ignore them. She smelled rather than heard the drunk passed out on the floor of the cell. He was some inebriated fool the sheriff had brought in as Nicky lay in the dark, trying to force herself to sleep. It was cold in the cell, too, colder than it had been sleeping under the stars next to Tyler.

She closed her eyes, unwilling to think of *him*. *He* had put her here. *He* was sleeping in a soft, clean bed. *He* didn't care. Why should she? As the pink rays of the sunrise began to peek through the little window, Nicky drifted off into a light slumber cursing the name Tyler Calhoun.

⁂ ⁂ ⁂

As Tyler walked across the road to the sheriff's office, he berated himself again for drinking the whiskey. His reward was a Texas-sized hangover that thrummed in his head to its own excruciating beat. He'd fallen asleep in his clothes, slept well past his normal wake-up time, and now he was rumpled and grumpy. He hoped Nicky wasn't going to rankle him today, because in this mood, he was like a wounded bear. To top it off, he hadn't screwed that pretty whore last night so his dick was scratching to be let out like a tomcat.

Goddammit all to hell!

The sheriff was already behind the desk although it was just past dawn. He looked up from his cup of coffee as Tyler entered.

"Calhoun. Good to see you. I was hoping you'd collect your prisoner before mine woke up."

Tyler's brow furrowed as his frown deepened. "Your prisoner?"

"A local. Drunk as a skunk. I had to throw him in there last night after he passed out in the middle of the street."

Tyler took a deep breath. He hadn't honestly expected anybody else to be put in the cell with her. He nodded curtly to the sheriff. *Son of a bitch.*

"Let's get her then."

As the sheriff was opening the door, a woman's cry assaulted their ears. A fierce, cold fury swept through Tyler as he pushed past the sheriff. The local drunk had his hands on

Nicky's body, pushing her down on the bed. She was kicking and clawing with all her might. Tyler's blood thundered through his head as he saw Nicky struggling. All his common sense and training flew out the window on a breeze. All that mattered was helping her.

"The keys!" Tyler bellowed as he grabbed them out of the sheriff's hands. He twisted the key in the lock and rushed in, yanking the man off Nicky with the force of two men.

He held the man by the collar, shaking him like a rag doll. "Didn't your mama ever teach you not to touch a lady without her say-so?" he snarled.

The unshaven, slobbering fool actually burst out crying, begging Tyler to let him go. He hadn't meant any harm—thought she was one of the saloon girls or something so what's the big deal? She was wearing britches, for Pete's sake.

"Tyler?" came Nicky's voice. His Christian name sounded strange coming from her lips.

Tyler's gaze snapped to hers as she spoke his name for the first time. Not "Calhoun" or "bounty hunter"—no sneer, no sarcasm, no anger, and no censure. Like a magic wand, her voice broke the spell of fury that had taken hold of Tyler. He dropped the man unceremoniously on the floor as he turned to her, easing his features. She was sitting on the bed, dirty, disheveled, and obviously badly scared.

"Are you okay?" Her green eyes almost looked worried.

He wanted to laugh at her question. Was he okay? Sure, he was fine. How could she ask if he was okay when it was she who had nearly been raped? Now his inner voice was laughing like a lunatic. Tyler was not only worried about his prisoner, but he felt *guilty* for what happened to her. Holy hell.

He held out his hand to her. She ignored it and rose from the stinking mattress with as much dignity as she could muster. He followed her out of the cell, clenching and unclenching his hands. The sheriff shut the door behind them, swiftly turning the key in the lock. He looked at Nicky with embarrassment.

"I'm sorry he done that, miss. If I knew he was awake, I could've taken you out of there before he...well, before he attacked you." His apology was strained.

Nicky didn't speak.

"Thanks for your hospitality, sheriff," said Tyler in clipped tones.

He steered Nicky out of the building into the new morning sunlight. She squinted, then pulled her elbow out of Tyler's grasp.

"Where are we going?" she asked tightly.

"The hotel. I thought you might want to clean up and change." As he spoke, he kept his eyes facing forward, not daring to look at her. He was having a hard time not going back in there to beat the shit out of the bastard that dared to touch her.

"I would have preferred to sleep in a bed that didn't crawl with bugs and smell of a hundred drunken men."

Tyler did not comment—he knew she was right. She twitched her nose then leaned toward him and sniffed.

Tyler realized he should've changed his clothes. Too late now.

Oh shit.

"Why do you smell like a whore?" she asked through clenched teeth.

He decided to try distraction. "And how do you know what a whore smells like?"

She stiffened her spine even more as she eyed him with murder in her eyes. "I've spent enough time in saloons over the last three years to know what a whore smells like, Calhoun.

Cheap perfume and unwashed sluts are pretty distinctive. So, I'm going to ask you again, why do you smell like a whore?"

"Why do you care?"

"I don't, bounty hunter. But I think it would about make me mindless with rage if I found out you were poking some whore while I sat in that putrid jail cell last night," she ground out, her face flushed with anger.

Before he could tell her it was none of her business, he opened his mouth and told her the truth.

"Even though it's none of your business, I didn't poke anybody last night, Malloy. Nice language by the way. That's not to say it wasn't offered to me. Not every woman thinks I'm hell's spawn."

She stared into his eyes for a full minute before she apparently decided he was telling the truth. "Pity for those women then. They don't know what they're lusting after. I'm surprised you don't have a forked tongue and a tail."

His mouth turned into a sardonic grin. "You know what my tongue feels like, don't you? It's not forked at all. And I'd be happy to show you my tail."

Nicky flushed. "Bastard. Why don't you go back and find that whore and leave me alone?"

She turned and stomped to the hotel with Tyler right on her heels. She didn't notice the men in town staring at her as she walked past them. Tyler did. Even dirty and rumpled, she was a sight to see in her jeans. He sent fierce, quelling looks at them. Like a jealous dog guarding his bitch. He had to stop himself from punching two of them.

⁂ ⁂ ⁂

Nicky had a lukewarm sponge bath and put on fresh clothes. The hotel room had a nice, tall screen to give her privacy. What she really wanted was a real bath, but there wasn't time according to Calhoun. At least he was letting her have this small luxury.

She reached into her saddlebags, finding her brush. She combed her hair briskly. *Stupid hair.* It was already growing. It grew like garden weeds, and she had to cut it once every two weeks. She had been due for a cut before Tyler caught her, and now it was getting close to touching her shoulders. She didn't have anything to secure it, so she gathered it up into her hat instead.

When she stepped out from behind the screen, she felt like a different person. Tyler stood with his back to her. He watched out the window, silhouetted against the bright morning light streaming in. A lump formed in her throat for the way Tyler had pulled that lecherous drunk off her. He had been so angry at that drunken fool, she could almost believe he cared. In his eyes, she swore she saw concern and regret.

Nonsense. All he cared about was the reward money. Being shackled must have rattled her brain. She reminded herself that he'd at least spent some time with a whore last night while she was sleeping with bugs and filth.

Rat bastard.

"Ready," she announced.

Tyler still would not meet her eyes as he turned, swinging his saddlebags up on his wide shoulder.

"Calhoun?"

"What?"

"Look at me."

He raised his eyes to hers and she saw a flash of guilt in their depths. Good, she hoped he was feeling it, too. "I hope that when I get to Wyoming they string me up right away because I'll take my own life if I have to spend another night in jail."

He didn't respond, but Nicky was satisfied to see him twitch as though she had poked him with something. She was telling him the truth about jail, and fully intended to escape before he could put her in another one of those nasty little rooms. That was a promise she intended to keep.

⁂ ⁂ ⁂

Tyler should have expected it, but he didn't. They had stopped for the night in an abandoned farmhouse. He had just brought in wood to feed the fire in the old cookstove so they could have a hot meal. That's when it happened.

He heard the wind whistle sharply and knew something was coming at his head. He dropped the wood and feinted left into a crouch, and his shoulder took the brunt of the hit. He sprang to his feet and there she was. Like a goddess of old. Her hair was in a flaming halo around her head, the block of wood in her hand like a sword. Nicky was ready to battle him. Tyler respected that.

She swung again, but he was ready this time. He stopped her in mid-swing and ripped the wood from her hands. She squeaked in protest when he yanked her against him so her behind was flush against his groin.

Immediately his body reacted and rose like the good soldier it was. Her indrawn breath was the only indication she felt his arousal, as if she couldn't feel the iron bar in his britches.

"That wasn't very nice, Nicole," he breathed into her ear.

"Fuck you."

"Tut, tut, you've got a mouth like a muleskinner."

She grunted and tried to break free, and that just pressed her more firmly against him. He hissed as the cleft of her ass cradled his rock-hard cock.

"Let me go."

"Not yet. We need to get a few more ground rules here."

She pulled against him again. "Let me go."

His hand snaked around her waist and slid downward toward her core.

"What are you doing?"

"Making sure you're not a man. I could swear there's a pair of balls down here somewhere."

As his fingers crept down inside her pants, she continued to struggle, but not with any real effort. She sucked in a breath when he finally settled on her pussy. She was hot. Not only hot, but damp.

Hell, he had all he could do not to rip off the jeans and feel that heat firsthand. She moved against him, rubbing, feeling. He heard her moan low and deep in her throat. She was so damn wet and so damn hot.

Tyler started moving himself up and down against her even as his hand rubbed her. She picked up his rhythm and together they built up a pace designed to bring them both pleasure.

"Oh God, what are you doing to me?" she asked brokenly.

"Fly with it, Nicole. Fly."

She apparently understood well enough. As his balls tightened signaling his release, she jerked against him and moaned again, this one longer and harder. The sound was enough to push him over the edge. He clenched her against him as the waves of orgasm rolled through him.

The quiet was only broken by their breathing. Hers was short and choppy. His sounded like a steam engine.

What the hell had he just done?

Tyler pulled his hand out from inside her pants and stepped back. Before he could stop himself, he tasted her essence from his fingers. His body was screaming at him to throw her down on that dusty old straw mattress in the corner and fuck her until neither one of them could move.

His head was kicking his own ass for touching her. Again. Only this time it was worse. He knew what she felt like, sounded like, hell, even what she tasted like.

He should have screwed that whore back in Clayton. Now all he could think about was getting his prisoner naked. He quickly cuffed her to the chair and backed off like he was facing a grizzly.

Tyler practically ran outside with a bucket swinging from his hand looking for water. The same hand that smelled and tasted like Nicky's passion. He didn't give a shit what she thought of him, as long as she stayed put while he cleared his head.

He listened for water and heard a stream nearby. As he stomped toward it, he told himself he wasn't going to touch her again. No siree. No more touching.

* * *

Nicky was trembling. For the first time in a long time, her body felt alive. Her blood was flowing like a strong river and her head felt clear.

She hadn't expected it. The pleasure, the yearning or the hunger. She was sitting in the chair, trying to slow her heart rate down. Trying to yank her damn head out of the clouds.

Nicky knew he had found his own pleasure. She heard the guttural cry that escaped from his throat and had felt his hard cock up against her ass. Lord, the man was big...and he was as hard as an iron bar. That meant he was not unaffected either. Something she could use to her advantage if she was smart. She could take as many opportunities as possible to rub against him, to touch him. A man itching to get into a bed was a man liable to make mistakes. A mistake could afford her the opportunity to escape.

Now if only she could stop trembling.

Chapter Nine

They fell into a pattern over the next few days, following a routine for everything. They were a regular two-man platoon. It was driving Nicky insane like an itch she couldn't scratch. She couldn't get close enough to him to brush him, even with her fingertips. He kept his distance as if there was two foot of wall between them.

To top it all off, she was bored silly. He didn't talk, didn't have a deck of cards, and he wouldn't let her read either. She had to do more than sit on a horse or on the cold ground watching Tyler perform every task efficiently. She was used to being busy, not sitting on her ass and doing nothing.

They had just stopped to make camp for the night, and Tyler was planning to snare a rabbit for dinner.

"Let me come with you. I'm tired of just sitting around. I can help."

"Yeah, you'll probably help me right out of my pistols and into the ground six feet under," he said, lips twisted.

"I don't need your pistol to catch a rabbit."

"Look, Nicky, just let it go, would you?"

"No, I can't. I'm going crazy doing nothing."

He rolled his eyes and put his hands on his slim hips. Damn the man for looking so good. Her body heated just looking at him.

"Then go crazy. I'm not going to let you roam around on your own. Do you think I'm some kind of idiot?"

"You don't care if I'm crazy or not, I know. Six thousand dollars goes a long way to salve a conscience, doesn't it?"

"Jesus Christ, Malloy. Give it a rest."

He went over to his horse and pulled a rope from his saddlebags. She watched him, frustrated and angry, and although she tried to ignore it, excited by their argument. It was exhilarating. It was something other than sitting on her ass. Well, bullying was definitely not the tactic to use with him. Time to switch back to female mode.

"Please?"

The "please" must have given him pause. He closed his eyes for a moment and sighed. She was hopeful. "You're not going with me, Nicole." Tyler's voice was firm. "So stay here and I'll do it."

Well, she wasn't hopeful anymore. He crouched down to check her shackles again, then he rose and walked away with his usual feline grace.

"Calhoun," Nicky called to his retreating back as he ambled into the trees in the twilight. "Thanks so much for your consideration." Her sarcasm wasn't satisfying as Tyler calmly ignored her.

"What is it with men?" she wondered aloud. "Is there one on God's green earth that will treat a woman as more than a piece of property? I can snare a rabbit better than he can, any day."

She kicked at the dust with the toe of one boot, disgusted with the situation and her helplessness. He had twisted up the chains again, and wrapped them around her ankles so that she was practically hog-tied, and could hardly even straighten up to walk. Pushing aside her fear of being chained was getting easier each day, although her nightmares continued on a regular basis.

The way Calhoun had shackled her now, even if she could reach her horse, she couldn't ride, which was exactly the reason why he did it. Her pride smarted from the way he treated her as a common criminal. How was she supposed to escape when she couldn't even get up to pee?

"Goddamn bounty hunter," she shouted. As she watched his back disappear from view completely, she sighed long and hard. "Goddamn beautiful bounty hunter."

Since the incident in the farm house, her body had seemed to come alive. To become aware of the world, aware of Tyler. Her nipples hardened and her pussy grew damp when she saw him washing shirtless. Lord God, that man was incredible. And apparently they had some deep connection now. A physical connection that went beyond what her brain and her heart told her to do.

As she struggled against her body's betrayal, a dirty hand clamped over her mouth.

"Gotcha, Jesse," came the warm, fetid breath on her cheek. "Thought I wouldn't catch up to yore fancy bounty hunter, didja? Thought he was so smart leaving all kinda tracks to follow. I found ya anyway, didn't I?"

Son of a bitch! Nate!

Nicky bit down hard on one filthy digit.

"Shitfire!" Nate choked back a yelp. "I'll get ya for that, ya little bitch," he exclaimed in a heated whisper.

As Nicky opened her mouth to yell for Tyler, Nate backhanded her so hard her head whipped around and she saw stars dancing in front of her eyes. The coppery taste of her blood coated her tongue. The next thing she knew a dirty rag was stuffed in her mouth, and another wound around her head.

She still struggled as best she could, like an undulating snake trying to escape Nate's grasp.

"Help me get her back to the horses."

"Let's take hers," Rusty suggested.

"No, he hobbled 'em, it'd take too much time. Just cover me while I carry her. I plan on riding double with her." Nate chuckled thickly.

As the two men made their way back to their mounts with a struggling Nicky, she silently called Tyler with her mind.

Calhoun! Help me! Where the hell are you when I need you?

* * *

The rabbit was almost in the snare when Nicky's voice intruded in his thoughts. Tyler pushed it away, but it kept returning. The hackles on the back of his neck rose, and he whirled with a pistol drawn, but saw nothing. He berated himself for jumping at shadows, and when he turned back the rabbit was gone.

"Damn, even when she's not here, she's ruining my life."

He rubbed the back of his neck.

Calhoun!

There it was again. Nicky's voice was actually in his head. What was that all about? What could she possibly—

Where the hell are you when I need you?

She was in trouble.

A certain dread began to wind its way around Tyler's body like a snake of smoke. There was a new connection between them, one he had tried to deny. Now that connection pulsed through him. As the feeling of dread became overpowering, he found he couldn't ignore it—he was a man who lived by his instincts. He stood and ran back to the clearing where he'd left his prisoner. He knew before he even arrived that she was gone.

As he examined the tracks in the dust, he realized two men had taken her, and that she'd struggled with them. *Nate.* That stupid son of a bitch had found them after more than a week. Now she was Nate's prisoner, and there was no doubt what he'd do with Nicky first. His leer had been as apparent as the sun on a cloudless day. Nicky was a strong woman, but being raped might destroy her spirit. He wasn't about to let that happen.

Help me!

After gathering up the saddlebags, and unhobbling the horses, he vaulted onto Sable, then grabbed the mare's reins and started following the trail. He wouldn't let his conscience remind him that the real reason he was following her was not for the bounty.

⁂ ⁂ ⁂

Nicky felt like she was going to pass out as she bounced, stomach down, across Nate's lap on the cow pony. The saddle horn dug into her side painfully and her nose was bleeding from Nate's blow. The blood was making it hard to breathe. Nate held her down by keeping a firm grip on her jeans. To her horror, his fingers kept dipping lower and lower onto her behind. She was trussed up, gagged, and helpless—fodder for her nightmares. All she could see was the ground and the horse's belly. She could, however, smell Nate. He exuded a sour, rancid odor that was so different from Tyler's scent, it made her wonder if Nate was a man or a pig. Tyler's scent made her want to inhale deeply, and was downright intoxicating. Nate's foul smell made her think of a swamp, teeming with nasty creatures. It was repulsive. She hated to think what he smelled like when her nose wasn't clogged with blood.

"You sure do have a nice ass. Can't wait to see it close up."

She shuddered in revulsion. She was not about to let Nate or Rusty get their hands into her pants. A rock came flying up from the ground when the horse's hoof dislodged it. It knocked Nicky squarely in the forehead, both startling and painful. Tears pricked the backs of her eyelids, from pain and possibly fear—although she wasn't about to admit that, even to herself. She tried to muster her self-control, her inner reserve of strength, to fight back against drowning in self-pity.

She thought of what Tyler would do in this situation, and it wasn't snuffling and crying. That gave her a pulse of courage. She would fight Nate and Rusty with everything she had, but she couldn't stop that little tiny voice that still wished for the bounty hunter to come to her rescue. She tried to imagine Tyler in a knight's suit of armor. He'd probably throw the armor to the ground and wonder why the hell anyone would want to carry that kind of weight around when all you needed was a fast gun.

To her horror, Nate stuck his fingers between her legs. She grunted and tried to wriggle out of his grasp.

Don't you touch me! She screamed with her mind, eyes, and soul. Nate didn't notice, or didn't care. She could feel him rub his dirty hand against his burgeoning erection in his equally filthy pants.

"Oh, yeah, baby girl. You and me are gonna have *fun.*"

He went back to groping her wherever he could. His touch was painful and sickening. Nicky tried her best to stop him, but her efforts were in vain.

Calhoun, where are you?

She'd sooner die than submit to Nate.

※ ※ ※

Tyler was sure he was gaining on them as he squatted to examine the tracks on the ground. These prints were no more than ten minutes old. Just as he thought, one set of prints cut deeper into the scrubby ground. One horse was carrying two people for sure. A small dark spot next to a hoofprint caught his eyes. As he reached out to touch it, he knew what it was. Blood. *Her* blood.

He'd tear those dirty bastards apart with his bare hands.

⁂ ⁂ ⁂

"Think we lost him?" Rusty asked.

"Don't know fer sure. I looked, but I ain't seen nobody followin' us."

Nicky rolled her eyes at their stupidity. Did they think a bounty hunter as skilled as Tyler would announce his arrival with trumpets and a loud "Howdy"?

"I think we can stop fer a rest." Nate's pronouncement was like a bell tolling in the night for the doomed.

Nicky's head felt like it weighed more than the rest of her body combined, and her stomach was spinning like a top. Much as she wanted to stop, she knew if they did Nate wouldn't keep his hands off her. She was more afraid than she'd ever felt with Tyler, even that first night. It was as if she could sense that the real Tyler was different deep down inside. He wasn't the type of man who would rape a woman. Unfortunately, she knew Nate was that type of man, even a woman who was bound and gagged. Nicky's heart was hammering, her mouth felt like cotton, and she could hardly get a breath in.

Jesus, please, help me be strong.

Nate shoved his hands between her legs and groped her mercilessly. A single tear leaked from one eye as she kicked and bucked against the invasion of the filthy hand.

"Ooh, she's ready, Rusty. Let's give this mare a ride she won't forget."

Don't show him you're afraid.

Nate hauled her off the lathered horse with a jerk. Nicky's momentum was great because of her efforts to throw off Nate's grip. She slammed onto the unforgiving ground and the back of her head hit a small rock. All the breath was knocked from her body, and blackness roared through her like a mountain lion's scream.

* * *

Tyler heard the low murmur of voices as he crept catlike across the damp ground. The dew had already coated the prairie grass, making his approach silent and slick. He was nearly upon them when he heard one clear his throat to speak.

"Is she dead?"

A wave of red-hot fury crashed over Tyler when he heard the offhand question. *Dead?* She *couldn't* be dead. He had to restrain himself from rising from the grass with his guns blazing. If they'd killed her, there would be two fresh carcasses for the buzzards to feast on. He needed to keep his wits about him so he forcefully tamped down on his bloodlust. First, he needed to find out where Nicky was, and more importantly, if she was alive.

Get control. You're no good to her if you're dead.

"I don't know. She ain't moving, though. Could be a trick. Damn, and I'm good and ready for her, too."

He peered cautiously toward the voices and saw two figures in the light from the moon. One squatted down and fumbled with another dark shape on the ground.

Nicky.

"Oh, hell, she bled on my bandanna. That was my good one too." He backhanded the dark shape viciously.

Tyler flinched at the sound of flesh on flesh. Only the lowest form of scum would hit an unconscious, *not dead,* woman.

"Well, is she dead?" repeated the other figure as he turned and grabbed his saddlebags.

"I don't think so. Dead people don't bleed. Let's leave her there for a spell. See if she wakes up. I like my women awake when they feel my prick sliding in."

Dead people don't bleed. Her blood still stained Tyler's finger from when he'd found it earlier. He wondered what part of her had been bleeding, was still bleeding even as he sat in the shadows waiting to strike.

The two cowboys walked about ten paces away, found a fallen log to sit against, and pulled out jerky and hardtack from their saddlebags, blissfully unaware of the predator watching them with narrowed eyes, gauging their readiness for battle.

Is she dead? As Tyler circled around behind them, the question kept repeating in his brain. He could see her body lying on the ground by the horses, bathed in the moonlight. Goddamn idiots left her to be stepped on or kicked by the horses. If she wasn't dead, she could be in an instant.

I like my women awake when they feel my prick sliding in.

Tyler didn't know if that meant Nate had already had her once, or he hadn't touched her yet. The fire of his fury was going to scorch those bastards. As he raised his pistols to fire, a moan escaped from the prone form. He froze in place like a part of the landscape. *She was alive.*

"Didja hear that, Rusty?"

"Yeah. Was it her?"

"I think so. Go see if she's awake."

"Now, how'm I supposed to tell that in the dark?"

"If'n you're that stupid, I ain't gonna tell you how."

One of them rose and approached Nicky's inert body.

⁂ ⁂ ⁂

Nicky had come into consciousness slowly, unsuccessfully stifling her moan of pain. She heard Nate and Rusty talking, but couldn't make out the words. When she heard boot heels crunching the dry leaves and twigs, she decided to stay unconscious. Since she was still dressed, they obviously hadn't decided to rape her while she was out. Thank God for that small reprieve. A finger poked her in the shoulder.

"Jesse?" He paused. "I don't think she's awake yet, Nate."

"Give her a wallop. That oughta wake her up. I need to dip my wick in that one."

"Okay."

Nicky braced herself for a fist, but none came. She heard a grunt, then felt a gust of air blow past her. A gentle touch caressed her cheek.

"Hang on, magpie," Tyler's warm voice whispered in her ear.

Her heart leapt into her throat at the sound of his voice as tears once again pricked her lids. *Thank God!* She never thought she'd be glad to see Tyler Calhoun. She opened one eye and saw Rusty lying in front of her. She wasn't sure if he was dead or alive.

"Rusty, what the hell are you doing over there? If'n you're humpin' her, I'll beat you into next week."

As Nate's footsteps came closer, Nicky held her breath.

"No one takes what's mine." Tyler's voice was cold as ice. He stood beside Nicky, legs spread wide, hands resting lightly on his pistols. His eyes blazed, a veritable avenging angel.

Nate's eyes widened at the appearance of the bounty hunter. He went for his gun, but Tyler had already cleared leather and fired in a blur of movement.

"Ya shot my hand, ya son of a bitch." He squealed as he stumbled backward and the gun dropped to the ground. "Goddammit, she ain't that good of a lay, mister."

Tyler calmly shot him in the foot. Nate screamed like a stuck pig as he fell to the ground in a moaning, screeching heap. Tyler scooped up the other man's gun with one swipe of his big hand.

As he stuffed the pistol beneath his belt, Tyler turned back to Nicky. He helped her to sit up, and unlocked the shackles.

"You came for me."

"No one takes what's mine." Before she could react, he grasped her face with his big hands, lowered his head and kissed her breathless. When he pulled away from her lips, she was shaking.

Nicky was not afraid of Tyler's arousal, as she had been of Nate's. She tried to read his eyes in the moonlight, but they looked as dark and mysterious as a deep well. Nicky rose on shaky legs, and approached Nate. She kicked his wounded foot, and then spit on him when he howled in agony.

"That's for me, you bastard."

As she walked back to Tyler, she saw him raise his pistol at her with deadly speed. Speechless, she could only stare with her mouth unhinged. How could he kiss her senseless one minute, then hold a gun on her the next?

It seemed like the world had become as small as a moment. The glint of steel heading toward her was the only warning she had before Tyler jumped in front of her at the last possible second.

She yelped as she hit the ground yet again, this time with Tyler's big body on top of her. When she caught her breath, she started to yell at him. "Tyler, are you trying to get yourself killed?" Then she saw a knife protruding from his arm. "Nate, you bastard!"

Tyler pulled his bandanna out of his pocket, then calmly removed the knife from his arm. As the blood flowed freely from the wound, he tied a tight tourniquet with his right hand and his teeth. He wiped the blood off the knife on the wet grass, then tucked it into his boot. He knocked Nate unconscious with one blow of his fist.

"Shut the hell up, you piece of shit," he growled, then he slapped Nate and Rusty's horses' rumps to get them running into the night.

"Let's go," he said as he returned to her.

"What about them?"

"I don't give a damn about them."

Grasping her elbow, he steered her toward their horses, hidden nearby. Although she tried to hide it, she was feeling very weak and disoriented after riding with those two varmints for hours. At least she wasn't weeping and blubbering, which was a feat in itself.

Wordlessly, he placed her on her horse without shackling her. As they rode off into the darkness, Nicky's mind was a tumult of confusion and pain. Tyler had almost looked and acted like he cared for her, and that kiss. Her toes still tingled from it. And although he held Juliet's reins, he hadn't shackled her—that alone made her want to shout for joy. The man was a complicated puzzle. She couldn't fathom what was going through his mind.

⁂ ⁂ ⁂

Tyler was trying not to show a reaction to her bruised, bloodied face. He was also fighting the nearly ferocious urge to go back and kill the two cowboys for what they had done. All he could think about was how they had mistreated her. And how much that fact bothered him.

After riding for what seemed like forever, but was probably no more than an hour, Tyler found an acceptable place to camp for the night. He didn't want to let her know that his arm was worse than he'd thought. Matter of fact, it was throbbing and hurting like a son of a bitch. He also felt a little lightheaded from the blood loss. He needed doctoring and his little outlaw was the only one available. As he dismounted, he couldn't hold in a grunt of pain.

Nicky's brows knitted together as she looked at him.

"You look terrible," she said flatly. "Let me stitch up that wound."

Although that was exactly what he wanted, he was still pugnacious enough to glare at her. "You don't exactly look like you've been picking flowers, woman. Your face looks like a punching bag."

"It can't be that bad, but fine, I'll wash my face so it doesn't bother you anymore. Do you have anything to stitch your wound with?"

"Yeah." He retrieved a small pouch from his saddlebags, and thrust his medical supplies to her.

"How about some whiskey?"

He quirked up an eyebrow at her. "Thirsty?"

"For the wound, Tyler."

"No, don't have any."

"Well, we'll just have to make do with some hot water then."

After rinsing the blood from her face with water from her canteen, she gathered twigs and wood for a fire. Tyler was startled to realize that she had the opportunity to escape, but she didn't. She could have jumped on her mare and left him behind, weak from his wound, but she didn't. The question was, *why not*?

Seemingly unaware that she was throwing away her opportunity to escape from Tyler, she quickly made a fire as she chattered on about anything but Nate and Rusty. He studied her efficient movements with a touch of admiration. She really was a very competent person. And how she handled herself would make any husband proud.

Husband?

Tyler was momentarily nonplussed by his wayward thoughts. Where the hell had that come from?

"Take off your shirt and I'll mend the tear."

"You can do women's work, too?"

She pursed her lips in aggravation. "Yes, but I can't do needlepoint, or make lace doilies, or play the piano. I've worked hard all my life trying to prove myself as good as any man. Are you going to make me feel bad now that I can do some things a woman can do?"

"Hell, no. Why would I care if you don't know how to do needlepoint? It's no business of mine. I was just surprised you knew how to sew."

"I've been on my own for more than three years. There wasn't anybody to sew or cook for me, so I had to learn." Her gaze focused over his shoulder. "My mother tried, but she just couldn't make me into a lady."

"Ladies are overrated. I'll take my woman over a lady any day."

My woman?

Tyler could have bitten his tongue off for that remark. Where did he get the notion she was his woman? He broke his gaze away from her and frowned as he tried to unbutton his shirt. His left hand seemed to be inordinately clumsy. She finally brushed his hands away and finished unbuttoning the shirt, then helped him slip it off. He thought Nicky must have nerves of steel, and the beauty to go with it. She was sitting with a half-dressed, very randy bounty hunter in the middle of nowhere, looking finer and more enticing than any woman Tyler had ever known. If she guessed what he really wanted to do with her, she probably would go screaming into the night.

Nicky washed his wound with the hot water she'd heated over the fire. Without a hint of discomfort or squeamishness, she held the flesh together as she stitched the wound closed with neat, even stitches. Then she wrapped his arm with a strip of cloth from one of his old shirts, as he had done for her feet, which seemed so long ago.

"You've done this before." It wasn't a question.

"My mama was a nurse in the war."

"Which side?"

"Does it matter?" Her gaze leveled with his.

"No, I guess not. Too many people lost in the end."

"She taught me everything she knows. It was the one thing I actually learned well from her. It's come in handy more than once."

She finished wrapping the makeshift bandage around his arm. "There you go, Calhoun. Good as new. Are you feeling dizzy or woozy?"

"No."

"Good. I didn't think you'd lost too much blood. I'll bet it hurts like hell though."

"You didn't have to do that, you know."

"Where I come from, we say thank you when someone does us a kindness."

"Thank you," he ground out.

"You're welcome. And thank you for...uh...for taking me back? No, that doesn't sound right. Strange as it may seem, I'd rather be your prisoner than Nate and Rusty's." She laughed without humor. "So, um, thanks."

"You're welcome. Did they...hurt you?"

Nicky shuddered a bit. "No, just some groping."

Tyler's fist clenched. Goddamn them for touching her. "I should've killed them."

Nicky's cheeks flamed at his bald statement. She turned quickly and started cleaning up. He grasped her arm to quell her movements. The touch was like a leap of fire from his hand to the pit of his belly to his balls.

"This changes nothing, magpie. You're still going to Cheshire with me."

Nicky shook her head. "No, I won't."

Chapter Ten

Nicky's hope for escape from Tyler came a few days later. They had stopped in a town at the juncture between Colorado, Wyoming, and Nebraska. While rummaging in her saddlebag, her fingers came in contact with something hard, small...a hairpin. Her hopes soared as plans for unlocking her shackles bloomed in her mind. Trying to hide her smile from Tyler, she tucked the hairpin into her pocket and turned. They were in front of a hotel.

"We'll get a room for tonight."

A room? *One* room? He was going to share a hotel room with her?

"B-but, what will they think?"

Tyler suddenly smiled. And it was absolutely devastating. The flash of his white teeth made every wisp of breath whoosh out of her body. Holy crow, he had dimples.

Steady, Nicky.

"Nicole, are you worried about your reputation?" His voice was low, husky. He unlocked the shackles with deliberate slowness, unobtrusively caressing the exposed skin as he removed the metal bands. He was amused. Amused she could possibly be worried about spending the night in a hotel with an unmarried man. At least she thought he wasn't married.

"Tyler, you're not married, are you?"

"No. Never thought a wife would keen to a job like this." His smile was gone.

"Oh."

Nicky averted her eyes, looking straight at his broad chest. A peek of black hair tufted out at the collar of his shirt. Nicky's fingers twitched with the urge to feel that soft, curling hair she had seen in the firelight days ago. My, oh my, but that was the hardest thing she had ever had to do—look at that simply magnificent chest and pretend to ignore it. Just the memory of it heated her cheeks.

He jammed the shackles into his saddlebags with a small grunt. One strong hand grasped her upper arm, steering her toward the hotel. "Let's go."

* * *

The hotel manager blustered at Tyler's request for one room, but he was determined to sleep on a bed that night dammit. His fingers were still curled around Nicky's arm. It was oddly comforting to touch her, even if it was just her arm. His other hand rested on the butt of the pistol strapped to his thigh. She looked faintly amused at the argument.

"This woman is my prisoner. I don't plan on doing anything other than sleeping in a bed. We've been on hard ground for too many days," he said to the pompous little snit behind the desk.

He had never, *ever* let any of his prisoners stay in a hotel with him, but he couldn't shake Nicky's warning about taking her own life if he put her in another jail cell. He told himself that he needed her alive for the double bounty.

"But sir, you said yourself you're not married. I couldn't allow you to share a room. What would people think of my establishment after that?" The bald portly man goggled at Tyler through thick spectacles. He looked about to pass out or have apoplexy.

Tyler leaned in close to the man who immediately shrank back toward the wall.

"Are you telling me that I have to *marry* this woman to sleep in one of your hotel rooms?" he asked through clenched teeth.

Nicky's smirk disappeared. She straightened up and bumped him with her elbow. He glared at her.

"Why, Tyler," she said sweetly, fluttering her eyelids. "Don't you want to marry me?"

His right eyebrow arched up as he regarded her. Her cheeks flushed a dark shade of pink. She was lovely. Her blush confirmed for him painfully that Nicole Malloy was a woman, and not always the hard outlaw she strived to be.

"Are you proposing, Nicole?" he murmured.

She opened her mouth, but nothing came out, so she shut it.

"I've never seen *you* at a loss for words, magpie," he drawled, teasing her, relishing her discomfort.

"I…sure, why not? Will you marry me, Tyler?" she challenged.

Dammit all, she did it again. Tyler was surprised. He sure as hell hadn't expected a marriage proposal. He rubbed his chin with his free hand, the day-old stubble rasping under his fingers.

"There a JP in town?" he asked the hotel manager.

"Two doors down, at the general store." The manager's voice conveyed relief as he mopped his perspiring brow with a crisp white handkerchief.

"Okay, Nicole." He turned to her, grinning. "Let's get married."

Nicky must have thought he'd lost his senses. Her mouth dropped open as she gaped at him. Unwanted tiny shivers of delight made their way down his back as he contemplated her lovely mouth. Tyler leaned over and gently closed it with a thumb. She looked as shocked as if he'd suggested she should run through the streets buck naked.

"We'll be back in ten minutes. Hold a room," Tyler commanded the little man. He jumped at Tyler's voice and nodded enthusiastically.

Tyler grabbed her arm, pulling her toward the door. She stumbled but he stopped her fall easily. She looked up at him and Tyler could see that she was frightened. Bone-deep scared. There it was again. That glimpse of the woman that hid beneath the man's clothes and gruff mannerisms.

"Tyler, you can't be serious." She didn't notice that she had started calling him Tyler when she let her guard down—but Tyler did. He pulled a certain kind of pleasure from it.

"It'll save us a whole heap of trouble. We won't have to tell people where we're going or why. Would you rather spend the nights in every jail cell from here to Cheshire, or sleeping on the ground waiting for those idiots Nate and Rusty to catch up with us again? We'll have it annulled as soon as we get there. Besides, *you* asked *me*."

Nicky's head snapped up as she straightened to her full height. Ah, she was back. The little doe was gone.

"Don't think for a minute this is going to be a real marriage," she whispered through clenched teeth. "Okay, Calhoun, let's go." She took off her hat and tried vainly to finger comb her thick locks.

"The blushing bride?"

She jabbed him hard in the arm with a sharp elbow. As he hissed in pain, his grip tightened on her arm and they left the hotel. The next ten minutes were a blur. The justice of the peace was a sweet, white-haired man who married them in minutes. Tyler heard Nicky say "I do" when prompted. He pulled his mother's gold band out of his pocket and pushed it on her finger.

Like a wooden marionette, she signed her name, Nicole Francesca Malloy, below his, Tyler Francis Calhoun, on the marriage certificate, which promptly went into his pocket. He gave the justice of the peace a dollar and pulled her out of the store.

Tyler's thoughts whirled madly. All he seemed able to focus on was her middle name, Francesca, and his, Francis.

Who would have thought they had almost the same middle name?

Like two halves of the same whole.

He never really contemplated his own wedding, but he was sure Nicky had. A beautiful dress, her family, a loving husband, and a church. None of those even came close to the truth of their wedding over a barrel of crackers, the bride in dirty jeans with tangled hair, and the groom with two six-guns strapped to his thighs and a knife wound in his arm.

Within minutes they were back at the steps of the hotel, and then in the lobby. It was as if nothing had happened.

"Did that really just happen?" she murmured. He felt the same way.

Their gazes locked. Her green eyes wavered slightly. How could he possibly sleep in the same room with this woman?

"Are you going to want to take a bath?" he blurted.

She nodded.

"Send up a bath for my wife," Tyler shot at the desk clerk as he grabbed the key from his hand.

Then they were in the hotel room. Tyler closed and locked the door behind them, and pocketed the key.

Tyler didn't know why he'd gone off and married this woman, but damned if she didn't look like she'd been shot. Maybe she'd hush up now and keep a civil tongue. Tyler's lips curved into a small smile. As if that was ever going to happen with his magpie. Nicky Malloy, no, Nicole Calhoun now, made sure she was heard.

Standing behind her, he had a clear view of her behind. In those jeans, it was a deliciously curvy view. Her legs were long and slender, and her waist looked so damned small. Her chestnut curls were sticking up every which way. His hand twitched as the urge to run his fingers through her hair burst upon him. Tyler tried to steer his thoughts away from that direction. She may be his wife temporarily, but she was first and foremost an outlaw on her way to justice. He cleared his throat. She started at the sound and jumped away from him.

Her gaze locked on his throat. Funny he hadn't noticed before now that her eyes were the color of the ocean when she was frightened. She nibbled her lower lip. Why was she frightened? Because of him?

"Do you...I mean...are you sleeping on the floor or the bed?"

Oh, so that's *what was on her mind.*

"Nicole, you have to sleep next to me. The shackles only reach so far. We'll both sleep on the bed, but don't worry, I always sleep with my clothes on. Your virtue is safe with me."

Her eyes narrowed as her lips came together in a thin, white line.

"Of course. Silly me. The shackles are off for appearances." She crossed her arms and sat down sharply on the stuffed burgundy chair in the corner. "Virtue, huh? You wouldn't know the meaning of the word, *bounty hunter.*"

"Truer words were never spoken."

A loud rap at the door heralded the arrival of the tub. After the hotel boys had filled it with steaming water, Tyler tipped them and then relocked the door. Nicky hadn't moved, sullenly staring at him with a fierce look.

"Use the water now, or I will."

She stood with her arms rigid. "There is no privacy screen in here. At least have the courtesy to step outside."

He made no move.

"Well, then sit by the window and turn your back to me." She was on the verge of shouting. "Leave me some dignity."

Turning the chair away from the tub, Tyler did as she bade, looking out the window as darkness fell over the town—realizing it was the second time he had turned his back to her, something he just didn't do. Ever. He could hear her undressing. The sound of her pants sliding down her legs made his fists clench. The imagination of a man in heat is like a stampede of longhorns. Powerful, sharp, and seemingly unstoppable.

It took every ounce of self-control he possessed to ignore each splash she made. Desire coursed through him like a raging river. He had *never* felt it like this, and it was for a woman who was an outlaw. He cursed himself a thousand times, trying to dismiss her from his mind, but he couldn't. The invisible thread was very short between them now. She was naked, six feet away, and goddamn it all, she was his wife. A sexy, dangerous, tempting wife.

⁂ ⁂ ⁂

It was the first time Nicky had gotten completely undressed in two weeks. She almost groaned as she unwrapped the bindings from around her breasts. The freedom felt wonderful, nearly sensual. Keeping her breasts bound helped her maintain the appearance of a man, although it was beyond uncomfortable.

The water made barely a splash as she entered. She sighed as she felt the simple pleasure from the heat of the water. She couldn't even remember the last time she'd had a hot bath. Normally, she bathed in the cold creek or used a basin of warm water to wash up. Using a sliver of soap, she lathered her hair and herself, keeping a close eye on Tyler. He didn't turn around once. She didn't know whether to be disappointed or relieved.

Nicky reluctantly left the tub and toweled off with the linen provided by the hotel, then dressed quickly in her last set of clean clothes, yanking on her jeans and buttoning her shirt with trembling hands.

⁂ ⁂ ⁂

She hovered behind him, and the smell of her freshly scrubbed skin assailed his senses. He swallowed a groan.

"Your turn, Calhoun."

He stood, and tried not to let his mouth unhinge when he caught sight of his dangerous wife. Somehow, Nicky's breasts had grown considerably larger. She must have had them bound before, and now they were as free as the breeze.

Holy hell!

He had to tear his gaze from her delicious-looking breasts, which sported pouting nipples and eye-popping curves. Her thick hair curled in wet waves while she tried to finger comb it. He felt like grease on a hot griddle.

What the hell was he supposed to look at now?

"I can't find my brush."

Tyler virtually attacked his saddlebag and rooted around for a minute while he calmed himself down. He handed her his brush roughly. A bruise from Nate's abuse stood out on her cheekbone like a flag to his wounded conscience, and her nose was still slightly swollen. God, she was beautiful. How was he supposed to resist her?

"I don't know if it will get through your hair, but it's better than nothing."

Nicky took the brush, and their fingertips brushed lightly, sending a hot lick of flame through them. She plopped herself in the chair he'd just vacated and started brushing her hair.

"Better hurry before it gets cold."

I'm gonna need it cold.

He stripped quickly and got in the water. He washed with his own soap, trying not to remember that Nicky had just been naked in the same tub, lathering her beautiful body and hair and, most especially, those unexpectedly tempting breasts.

⁂ ⁂ ⁂

Nicky tried to concentrate on her hair, but found Tyler Calhoun pushing into her thoughts. She could smell his scent on his brush, wholly masculine and wholly Tyler. She wanted to turn and look at him. *Wanted him.* The realization of her own lustful thoughts hit her like a punch. She heard him stand and towel off. The impulse to turn around grew as big as a house until she couldn't stand it any longer. She turned to peek at him.

He was pulling on his jeans and his hard muscled buttocks were visible, just sliding into his pants. The sight of his bare flesh was so titillating that Nicky had to resist the urge to ask him to turn around. The scars on his back from Hermano's knife were pink against the bronzed skin. So many. Way too many. Hermano would hear an earful the next time he ran into Nicky. Tyler also had a large scar on the right side of his back that looked as if it had been there a long time. Muscles bulged, rippling as he reached down for his shirt. The white bandage on his arm almost glowed against his suntanned skin. Her throat went suddenly dry, her heart rate soared, and an ache settled between her legs. Her pussy was now throbbing and moist and her nipples were hard points against her shirt.

She quickly turned around before he saw her gawking. She tried to mentally slow her heart, but her hands were shaking as she finished brushing her hair.

Why do I feel this way only around Tyler?

"You can turn around."

She stood and half-turned. He didn't have his shirt buttoned and his massive chest was clearly visible. His chest was unbelievably wide, covered with that mat of black curly hair that her fingers itched to feel. The hair tapered down his belly until it disappeared into the waistband of his jeans. Her mind wondered how far down that hair actually went. *Good Lord, she was a near wanton.* In the darkened night, he had been appealing and mysterious. In full light, he was magnificently male, and extremely potent. Her legs stubbornly refused to move.

"You're not dressed," she finally gasped.

And there was that smile again, with white teeth and knee-buckling force. He slowly began to button up his shirt. His pistols were already strapped to his thighs.

"I didn't think a man's bare chest would bother you. And you've already seen me without my shirt, Nicky. You took it off me, remember?"

"But it was dark. And I...ah...well, my brothers' chests didn't look like that."

"Like what?"

He crossed the room in three long strides.

"Um...oh, I don't know...hairy, I mean, they had hair, but not so much of it, and I don't remember...their muscles...and... Is it warm in here?"

He took another step and was right in front of her. She was nose to chest with him. She could smell his spicy soap, could smell him. She inhaled slowly. It was a little heady.

He reached out and tilted her chin up with his thumb to meet his blue eyes. "You look like a girl when you're all cleaned up, magpie."

She felt her cheeks flush. Why did he turn her into such a blithering idiot? Ever so slowly, his callused thumb caressed her bottom lip. The air between them grew heavy, humming with unspoken passion.

She pursed her lips and kissed his thumb. A thousand skitters of desire went down her body and met at the juncture of her thighs. She looked deep into his eyes and saw his desire mirrored hers.

She watched as his mouth descended on hers slowly. When he was an inch away, she felt the hot gust of his breath, then he was kissing her. Her arms wound around his neck and he pulled her flush against him. His lips moved against hers back and forth until his tongue lapped at hers. She opened her mouth and his tongue plundered. Sweeping, dancing, tangling with hers. Her pussy ground into his hard, pulsing erection.

Nicky was losing control. She pulled away to take a breath and opened her eyes to look into the blue eyes of her captor.

Uh oh. Too dangerous, *way* too dangerous. His arms dropped to his side.

"Let's go get some supper." His voice was raw.

Nicky, for once, had nothing to say so she nodded in agreement.

"Before we go, I think you should, ah, that is, you need to...put those bindings back on."

Nicky blinked in surprise. He wanted her to bind her breasts?

"Put the bindings back on? Why?"

"Darling, if you don't know why, I'm not going to be the one to tell you." He took a deep breath. "Believe me, you need to make sure you bind those, or we'll have a lot more trouble than we can handle."

"Well, okay, it will take me a minute. Turn to the window again, bounty hunter."

With a bucketful of doubt in her mind, she wrapped her breasts again, keeping a firm eye on her husband. *Darling?* Where had that come from? And what was wrong with her breasts?

And why the hell couldn't she catch her breath? Her body was burning hot from that kiss. Lord, that kiss. How could she sleep in the same room with him?

"Sure as shooting, we'll have trouble. Especially from me," she thought she heard him mutter.

⁂ ⁂ ⁂

The restaurant was half full. More than a few heads turned to survey Tyler and Nicky as they entered. With her hair down, and her hips swaying as she walked, she was clearly a woman. And the men knew it, damn their hides. Tyler saw their gazes raking her over and anger simmered in his belly. Was that jealousy? Damn, he could do without that feeling. He escorted her quickly to an empty table next to an older couple. The man nodded at Tyler with a friendly smile. Tyler nodded in return. At least some people still had manners.

A waitress warily approached to take their orders, and set a cup of coffee in front of Tyler.

"Evenin', folks." Her voice cracked.

Nicky narrowed her gaze. "I'd like coffee, too," she said, a little too loudly.

"Oh, of course," the young girl squeaked as she hurried off to get another cup.

Tyler grinned at Nicky. She spared him a suffering look.

The conversation between another couple two tables away grew heated. “I don’t care, Edgar. I will not keep silent,” rose the indignant voice.

A red-haired matron stood and practically marched to their table. “As a good citizen of this town, I must insist that the two of you vacate these premises. A woman in men’s clothing who looks as if she’s been in a brawl is shameful enough, but a *bounty hunter* wearing guns and bringing an unwanted element into our fair town is entirely unacceptable.”

Tyler’s mouth tightened in anger. He started to rise and face the harpy, but Nicky’s hand reached out to stop him. She stood at her full height, at least five-inches taller than the woman who clutched her reticule.

“This man,” she pointed to Tyler, “is my husband. I will not have you insulting him or me. What I choose to wear is certainly none of your business, and neither is his profession. We’ll be happily on our way in the morning and not a moment sooner. So, please, go back to your own husband and mind your own business. You *don’t* want to see me angry.”

Her voice had remained steady, deadly. The other woman’s face grew paler and paler until she looked the color of milk. “Well, I...” She stumbled backwards to her husband and hurriedly pulled him out of the dining room.

Nicky sat down again and sighed deeply. Tyler looked at his wife with amazement. She was something all right. No one had ever stood up for him before, especially an outlaw he’d captured. There was no way in hell he could explain it either.

“What?” she said innocently. Tyler shook his head slowly, a grin playing around his lips. “Small-minded people piss me off.”

The waitress returned with Nicky’s coffee. Simultaneously, Tyler and Nicky said, “Steak and potatoes.”

Two of a kind. He caught his breath as Nicky smiled at him. *My wife. Doesn’t that beat all.*

"I wonder who else is going to bother us," she said as she rolled her eyes.

As they ate their supper, Tyler realized that he hadn't wanted a woman this bad since he was a seventeen-year-old with a permanent stick in his pants. Nicky had been pleasant, even charming, throughout the meal as she kept up her ever-present chatter. Tyler had all he could do not to drag her upstairs, rip off those jeans, and bury himself in her sweet body. Every time he looked up, that little pink tongue was out grabbing a morsel off her fork. One positive thing about being on the trail, they ate over a fire, and the lighting was bad. In the bright light of the restaurant, he could see every sumptuous crease in her mouth, her lips, and her tongue. It was making him wild, and hard as an iron bar.

As they headed out of the restaurant to return to the hotel, he kept his hand firmly around her upper arm. Lord, have mercy, she smelled like flowers.

I need a drink.

"If I leave you at the hotel for a little while, are you going to make a ruckus?"

Her brows knitted together. "What are you going to do? Shackle me to the bed?"

"Yeah. I, uh...I have something I need to do."

Her face flushed with anger. "Calhoun, are you telling me that on our wedding night you're going to go poke a *whore*?"

He clamped his hand over her mouth quickly. "Nicky," he hissed. "Keep your voice down. No, I'm not going to see a whore. I need a drink."

He released her mouth and took off his hat. He ran his fingers through his hair, looking frustrated and glaring at her at the same time. She watched him with narrow eyes.

"Fine. You can have your drink, but you'll have to take me with you."

He groaned in frustration. “No.”

“Yes.”

“I said no.”

“And I said yes. If you don’t, I’ll make so much noise, they’ll kick us out of the hotel.”

He ground his teeth together as he debated whether or not the drink was worth the price of bringing his “wife” with him to a saloon. Pure raw need won out over common sense. The whiskey was calling him.

“Put your hair up into your hat. And for God’s sake, don’t talk to anybody. We don’t need a saloon full of men lusting after you.”

She gave an unladylike snort at his proclamation. As she stuffed her hair into her hat, she glared at him. Scooping up a handful of dirt, she rubbed it on her cheeks. She pulled off her new wedding ring and shoved it in her pocket. Tyler nodded his approval. She looked a little bit more like a man now, but still not nearly enough. Unfortunately, it would have to do. Grabbing her arm, they headed toward the Pink Lady Saloon.

“Calhoun?”

“What?”

“Do you remember where you found me?”

“What?” He stopped outside the batwing doors to the saloon, trying to figure out what she was blathering on about.

“In a saloon, remember? I lived as a man for three years. I can drink and play cards with any man, and they’ll never know I’m a woman.”

He nearly laughed at her naïveté. Tyler still doubted her ability to hide behind her male disguise. Then again, he had felt the softness that was hidden by the baggy shirt and jeans, and knew what treasures were hidden beneath those cursed bindings.

“Well?”

"I said, don't talk to anybody."

Giving him a mutinous look, she shook her arm free and stalked into the saloon. Tyler was surprised to see her swagger in like a man. There was no sweet twist to her hips to give her away. When she reached the bar, she turned to look at him with guarded eyes.

Tyler sighed in resignation. He needed a drink. As he ordered whiskey for himself, Nicky sent him another scalding look.

"Whiskey for me, too. On him." She jerked her thumb towards Tyler. Her voice was deeper, like that of a young man.

"Son of a bitch!" Tyler nearly dropped his glass of whiskey as he watched his wife sling back the shot of whiskey like it was water.

She belched softly and quirked up one side of her mouth. "Thanks, Tyler. I needed that."

Tyler's astonishment turned to something else entirely as he began to choke on his own whiskey as it slid down his throat.

With no small measure of glee, she slapped him on the back heartily to "aid" him in his choking fit.

"It's been a while since the old man has had any whiskey," she told the bartender by way of explanation.

Old man?

"Watch it, Nick," he warned softly after he brought his coughing under control. "I'm not old enough that I can't blister your ass for that."

Pouring himself another shot, Tyler turned to assess the crowd that was already in the saloon.

Nicky was slammed into the bar with a thud as a large body bounced into her.

"Watch it, kid."

"Watch it yourself, you drunken idiot," Nicky shot back.

Tyler turned to find a lurching, drunken cowboy staring down at Nicky. His stomach was clenched tightly and he realized that it was fear for his wife.

"You is a mighty small boy to have such a big mouth." The drunk grinned with a cruel twist to his slobbering lips. "Did your pappy here teach you how to fight like a man?"

Before Tyler could make a move, Nicky had pulled one of his pistols out of its holster and had it pressed up against the chunky folds of the man's fleshy chin.

"Do ya want to find out?" Her voice was as deadly as her speed.

"Put that down, ya little runt."

Tyler pulled the gun away from the man's chin and ripped it from Nicky's hand before she could turn it on him, and tucked it back into its holster.

"If you want a fight, you better go find yourself another one." Tyler's voice was suddenly loud in the quiet saloon. "He's just a boy."

"That boy has more curves than a boy ought to," came another voice from the dark shadows of the saloon. "Mebbe it's not a boy a'tall."

A murmur whispered through the crowd as a man stood up from the back of the room and slowly approached Tyler and Nicky. It was Rusty.

Oh, shit.

"In fact, I know this here's a *woman*, and her *bounty hunter*. He shot my pal Nate here after we took her from him. She must be worth a lot a money."

Behind him, another shadowy man limped into the light. Nate.

Double shit.

The murmur of the crowd grew louder. "How much?"

"Don't rightly know, but it must be a lot." Nate grinned, showing crooked, yellowing teeth. "How 'bout it, bounty hunter? How much is she worth to you?"

"I think you had too much to drink." Tyler's hand rested on his pistols ever so lightly. "This here is my little brother, Nick. He's more of a man at fourteen than either one of you will be the rest of your life."

Nicky looked as if she was about to swallow her tongue and his own throat was as dry as cotton. The crowd was growing louder as the mood grew uglier. They didn't have a chance against a saloon full of drunken, greedy men.

Before he could come to a decision on how to get out of this, his wife started a saloon fight.

As Nicky's small fist cracked across Rusty's jaw, she kicked out and her foot connected with a table that sent glasses and whiskey flying at Nate. He crashed into the group that had gathered. In a few moments, it was a melee. Bottles were thrown, chairs were breaking, and fists were flying. Nicky backed herself up to Tyler and they stood facing down the angry crowd together.

Tyler was impressed with the way Nicky had stopped the deadly confrontation, which probably would have ended with his pistols. He never would have thought of it. As he swung and his fist connected with another man's face, he could feel her behind him, giving another drunk the bite of her anger. *Damn, what a woman!*

"We need to get out of here," Tyler shouted.

"I know, let's start moving toward the door."

As they fought their way to the door, back to back, Rusty lunged for Nicky. He knocked her off balance and landed on top of her. Tyler felt the rush of wind as Nicky was taken down. Turning, he grabbed Rusty by the collar just as the man's fist connected solidly with Nicky's cheek.

"Son of a bitch," Tyler snarled as his fist plowed into the other man's face. A satisfying pop told him he had broken the bastard's nose. Rusty was moaning and holding his nose, then Nate was suddenly beside him, poised to strike at Tyler. The fool didn't have a chance after Tyler's fist knocked him out cold.

With a grim smile, he turned back to Nicky. She was unconscious, with a small trickle of blood oozing from the side of her perfect mouth.

"Nicky." His voice was harsher than he intended. She looked so small and hurt lying on the floor that he lost most of his ability to reason. Picking her up gently, he cradled her against his chest and slipped out the door.

⁂ ⁂ ⁂

Tyler sat in the chair, watching. Well, hell, actually he was brooding.

She wasn't asleep, but unconscious, and he found himself watching the rise and fall of her chest to be sure she was still breathing.

It's for the double bounty. There is no *other reason.* No other reason whatsoever.

When she whimpered softly, his gaze snapped to her face. Her beautiful face, now marred with more than one bruise. What kind of husband was he anyway? Letting his wife get the tar beaten out of her by some low-down cowboy. His mama would be ashamed of him. He certainly didn't feel very good about himself right now.

Nicky came to groggily and licked her dry lips. "Tyler?"

"Yeah, I'm here."

She turned and winced noticeably. "Damn, that Rusty has one hell of a right. How long have I been out?"

"Couple of hours."

She rubbed her eyes and glanced around. "This isn't the same room."

"No, I thought it best if we moved to a different one."

Nicky nodded, but didn't question him any further. She could probably barely see him in the lamplight. He was sitting in a chair in the shadows watching her intently.

"What happened to them?"

"They won't bother us again." He'd made sure of that. Those sorry bastards would be picking up their teeth for days.

"Sorry about the fight. Thought it was the best way to go."

"It was."

"What?" she croaked. "Did you just agree with me?"

"It happens every blue moon."

Nicky turned and discovered that one wrist was shackled to the bedpost. "Well, this *is* a nice wedding night."

"Go back to sleep, Nicky."

"What about you? You can't sleep in a chair."

"Don't worry about me. I'm not ready to sleep yet."

As a huge yawn overtook her, Nicky winced then gingerly touched her swollen cheek.

"Ouch." She looked down at herself and wrinkled her nose. "I need to get out of these dusty clothes. I can't sleep like this."

"Fine. Do what you need to do."

"Can you unshackle me so I can at least get comfortable?"

Tyler stood and crossed the room. Careful not to touch her, he unlocked the shackle.

"Take off that sleeve."

Grinding her teeth, she pulled off one sleeve with her back to Tyler. He shackled her wrist quickly before he could trust himself to look at her with her shirt dangling.

"Finish up. I'll be back in five minutes." Then he left the room.

⁂ ⁂ ⁂

Nicky sighed in disappointment, then took off her shirt and jeans. After a moment's hesitation, she reached into her jeans pocket and pulled out the wedding band. She stared at the gold that sparkled in the lamplight, then slipped it on. She held her hand up and cocked her head to the right, studying the ring.

"Nicole Calhoun," she murmured. She sighed heavily at her own girlish fantasies. Reality intruded with the grace of a charging bull. Her husband would be back in minutes.

"I'm not leaving these bindings on again tonight," she announced to the empty room as she unraveled the bindings compressing her breasts. Stretching her fingers out, she snagged her saddlebags from the floor and retrieved her chemise and pantalets. It had been some time since she'd worn both simple cotton garments, and slipping them on felt heavenly. It made her feel like a girl again.

⁂ ⁂ ⁂

Tyler stood just outside the door clenching and unclenching his fists. He had to use both hands now to count how many times she'd been injured while his prisoner. This time, she had done it to save their hides. He had a hard time convincing himself she was the outlaw Hoffman claimed her to be.

As he entered the room again, Tyler found Nicky sound asleep on the bed. He slipped in beside her and immediately regretted it. She was a pile of distractions. She snored softly in her sleep, she was in *women's* underclothes that appeared from somewhere, and her hair kept getting in his face. Sometime after what seemed like hours, he drifted off into unconsciousness, exhausted.

⁂ ⁂ ⁂

Nicky woke early, startled to find herself in a comfortable bed. She realized that somehow her head had found its way onto Tyler's arm. *Oh, right, Tyler*, she thought, *my husband.* His arm felt so firm under her head, she didn't want to move yet, so she stared at the ceiling, wondering how she could have gotten herself into such a strange situation. During the night sometime she had wriggled out from under the covers and snuggled up against him. It was shameful, but not really, since he was her husband after all. He had shackled her to his wrist, and their hands were almost touching.

She smiled, remembering the way he'd woken her that first morning shouting in her face like a howling banshee. She turned to him, full of mischief, ready to scream like the building was on fire. It died on her lips.

In sleep, Tyler was incredibly exotic; his face was softer, almost boyish. Although he still had his pants on, his shirt was unbuttoned, revealing that jaw-dropping chest. She studied his face as he slept. His lashes were black and thick and his cheekbones were prominent, as was his jaw. His cheeks were a little gaunt, but it made his lips look so full, so kissable.

Nicky felt her desire come back like a hammer blow. Her nipples grew taut against her thin cotton chemise. She swallowed hard against the rising tide and took a deep breath, steadying her nerves. There was still the matter of Tyler's wake-up call. She almost giggled aloud. Slowly, she leaned over and placed her lips next to his ear.

"'Morning, darling," she shouted.

Tyler shot straight up in the bed, groping for a pistol. From the expression on his face, he looked ready to throttle her.

"You thought that was fun?" he growled.

He reached into his pants pocket and pulled out the key to the shackles. After unlocking his own wrist, he undid hers and threw the key and shackles on the floor. Nicky was still laughing, tears squirting out her eyes.

"Fun? I'll give you fun," he said as he pinned her arms to the bed.

She couldn't stop laughing. The image of Tyler's surprised expression was too much until he lowered his lips to hers. Nicky's humor disappeared as Tyler's kiss ground her into submission. She moaned softly. His tongue teased her lips until she opened her mouth.

Letting her arms loose, he began to caress her. Goose bumps ran up and down her arms. His hand found her right breast and felt the weight as his thumb grazed her nipple. The peak was already hard and wanting.

Nicky was breathless. Her long buried passion welled up in her and she threw her arms around Tyler's neck, returning his kiss with a ferocity that matched his. The kiss left her gasping, wanting more, wanting him. He pulled away from her. She reached into his shirt, giving in to the impulse to feel his muscled chest. Her fingers gently caressed the thick hair, which was surprisingly soft. When her fingers came in contact with his nipples, he hissed. She pulled her hands away quickly.

"Did I hurt you?"

He flashed her that smile again as he lowered his head to her collarbone, trailing kisses as he untied the blue ribbons on her chemise.

"No, little magpie, it felt good. I'll make you feel good, too."

When he bared her breasts, Nicky tried to cover them, but he pulled her hands away gently. She watched with fascination as he lowered his mouth to her nipple, then all coherent thought was lost. His mouth suckled her, his tongue laved at the taut nub and then he delicately bit it. She drew in a ragged breath as he turned his attention to the other breast, lavishing it with his hot, wet mouth. Nicky was enraptured as she watched him. Could a body have too much pleasure? She wasn't sure she knew the answer, but she knew she was on fire between her legs. She felt the moisture gathering there, knowing that Tyler Calhoun would initiate her into womanhood. And she wanted him to. Dear God, she never wanted anything more than to have Tyler make love to her here and now.

He nuzzled her belly, gently kissing and licking her skin. She was shaking ever so slightly as he began to slide off the pantalets. As he gazed at her body completely nude, his breath caught. He kissed her hips, her thighs, then spread her legs and kissed her center.

She groaned. What in the world was Tyler doing? She started to rise and ask him when his tongue touched her in an incredibly sensitive spot that shot pleasure like a bullet to every inch of her body. Then he did it again and again and again. Nicky's body sang with growing waves of sheer ecstasy as Tyler worked. She floated amongst the clouds, rising to the stars. Suddenly, she held her breath as a tidal wave of rhapsody came crashing over her. Tyler held her legs to absorb the bucking twists.

As she struggled to find her way back from the stars, she felt him rise from the bed, shed his clothes and lie on top of her. His hand reached down between her legs and a finger probed inside her. She would have cried out at the sensation, but Tyler's lips covered hers in a deep, passionate kiss.

His knee gently nudged her legs apart. His body was so hard and she was willing, ready, and so wet. He pushed himself against her and entered in a quick thrust.

Nicky cried out in pain as her innocence was lost.

"Easy, darling, easy," he whispered in her ear. "We're in this together. Just go easy." She started to relax and unclench her muscles as the pain receded. Slowly, he pulled himself in and out. The grimace faded as she felt pleasure instead of pain.

Her tentative movements began to rock with his rhythm. A low moan escaped her lips as he turned his attention to her breasts again. She felt herself spiraling back to the stars as Tyler's thrusts grew harder and deeper. She cried out and Tyler's mouth descended on hers again in a clash of tongues as he arrived at his own shuddering climax.

His kiss turned gentle as he rolled off her, their sweaty bodies sliding away easily. Her eyes remained closed after their kiss. Her chest rose and fell rapidly as though she'd just run from one end of the state to the other. A single tear escaped from her right eye and traveled down her cheek.

Nicky was trying to land. Her entire body was singing in the aftermath of their lovemaking. She felt the tear tickle her cheek. It was a tear for the happiness she'd just experienced, and for the sadness that it was fleeting, not permanent. Regardless of whether this man was her husband, his job was to return her to Wyoming. And Nicky realized even through all that, she had somehow fallen in love with him. She loved his Texas drawl, his wit, his fierceness, his dedication, his pride, and even his warped sense of humor. They all made up the stranger who was now her husband, her lover, her jailer.

She felt his weight rise from the bed. He grabbed his jeans and pulled them on quickly.

"Nicky, I..."

Her eyes snapped open. Was that regret in his voice? Son of a bitch! Her heart winced in pain, but she kept it inside. Not for a moment would she let him see the ragged wound he had just made. He certainly wasn't in love with her, and now after a tumble in bed, he regretted what he'd done. No annulment now. His eyes wouldn't meet hers. They skittered around the room like leaves in the wind, the blue darker from the guilt she saw in their depths. She was angry, even furious, at his behavior. How dare he?

"What, Calhoun?" Her voice was sharp. "Is this where you tell me what a mistake this was? Not to get my hopes up?"

He jumped at her words. Something passed over his face. It couldn't have been pain. That she refused to believe. His beautiful mouth hardened.

"You'd better wash up and get dressed. We've got to get going." His eyes didn't look at the bloodstains on the sheets attesting to her lost innocence.

Nicky stood slowly, unashamed of facing him naked. Her hands bracketed her hips as anger pulsed through her. Goddamn him for cheapening the moment for her.

"I don't care if you regret what we just did. Your pity is unwelcome. I don't need it." She choked back her emotions, determined to be strong. "I told you I hadn't given my body to anybody, that I was a virgin. You know that to be the truth now."

Her voice had gotten lower, huskier. "Don't think for a minute I would have done that with you if it wasn't what *I* wanted."

She held his gaze for a moment then stalked across the room to clean up and get dressed. The pain in her heart was as real as any physical pain she'd ever endured, but she'd be damned if she'd let him see how much his rejection had hurt.

⁂ ⁂ ⁂

Jesus Christ on crutches! He couldn't let her see him shaking. Trembling like a newborn calf. To cover his weakness, he forced himself to use brisk movements as he dressed.

He had just had the most incredible sexual experience of his life with a woman who was an outlaw, and to top it all off, wonder of wonders, a goddamn virgin. Not anymore, he thought sourly. What the hell had he been thinking? Well, he hadn't been thinking. His randy prick had been thinking instead.

He understood her anger. Didn't argue with it a bit. He was angry with himself. Bedding her was the last thing he had planned on doing. So much for any other plans he'd made. They didn't seem to work one iota when it came to Nicky.

He stumbled putting his boot on. Cursing silently he took a quick peek at her. She was pulling her stockings on. Good. Hadn't seen him falling down like an idiot. A lovesick idiot.

Lovesick? Not likely. He was weak from coming his brains out. That was it. He was not, definitely one hundred percent not, lovesick.

Chapter Eleven

They rode in stony silence, their usual jabs and mocking tucked away. The morning was very foggy but Nicky assumed Tyler must know where he was going. She couldn't see a darned thing, but he couldn't see what she was doing either. She had retrieved her hairpin and was busy picking the lock on her shackles. As soon as they stopped for the noon meal, she was going to bolt. It was too dangerous for her heart and her neck to be with Tyler Calhoun. She could still smell his scent on her skin and the ghosts of his callused hands on her body. She tried to ignore her longings, but they were too strong to resist.

Oh, Tyler, why did I have to fall in love with you of all people?

Three hours into their ride, Nicky decided she couldn't be silent anymore. She felt the need to tell Tyler the story of Logan's death, to let him know what it was that had set her off on this run from the law. Deep down, she needed him to believe her story, believe her to be innocent. Believe in her.

"Did you know I grew up with six brothers? Ray, Ethan, Trevor, Brett, Jack, and Logan." She ticked off the names on her fingers. "We were all very close, and fiercely loyal. When we were growing up, sometimes they'd leave me out of whatever they were doing because I was a girl, but most times I could convince them otherwise. They would do anything for each other, or for me."

Tyler didn't turn to look at her, but she saw him straighten in the saddle as though he was listening.

"Jack was the closest in age to Logan and me. Growing up, we were like three peas in a pod, always out getting dirty and having fun with our big brothers, or the ranch hands. I wasn't one for frilly dresses or little girl toys. I was always right in there with my brothers doing whatever they were doing. My mama tried to force me to wear dresses, but she couldn't do it. If she put one on me, as soon as she turned around, I'd take it off, and prance around naked if she took my britches.

"When we got older, my parents didn't want me working around the ranch like a hired hand. They thought I was turning into an old maid because of my behavior. So, on my parents' orders, my brothers started to leave me out completely. They didn't like it much, but as I said, they are fiercely loyal, so they did what my parents wanted. I was bored to near insanity sitting around the house with nothing to do." She paused and took a deep breath. "When Owen Hoffman made an offer for my hand, my parents approved. He was rich and willing, even if he was fifteen years older than me. Who else would want to marry a girl over the age of eighteen who insisted on acting like a boy? Owen did."

"*What*? You were *engaged* to Hoffman?" Tyler shouted.

Nicky glanced at Tyler, noting his disgusted, shocked expression.

"I'm sure there's plenty Owen didn't tell you, Calhoun. Rich men think they own the truth." Her voice was grave. "I want to thank you for this morning. With you, I felt pleasure. With Owen, it would have been rape."

Her fingers were clenched so tightly on her saddle horn her knuckles were white.

"If you want to confess to something, I'm listening," he offered.

Her head swiveled sharply to glare at Tyler with narrowed eyes.

"I should have known you wouldn't even begin to believe me," she said in a tight voice. "You are a bought commodity."

"I'm not bought. I was hired to do a job," Tyler said angrily.

"Six and one-half dozen of the other." She waved her hand in dismissal. "You're still bringing me to my death."

"You'll have a fair trial." Tyler's voice wasn't very convincing.

"Not a chance. Wyoming isn't a state, Calhoun. Frontier law, you know. String them up first, ask questions later."

Her hands were beginning to shake from the effort to be strong, to contain her emotions. She was awash in grief for Logan, grief for the girl she once was, grief for the life she'd never live, and the children she'd never have. Her chest constricted, and she felt like she was breathing through a wet cloth, but she had to go on, to relive it. She needed to vent the heavy pain she'd been carrying around for so long it was like a part of her.

"I convinced Logan to sneak over to Owen's two days before the wedding. I wanted to poke around and find the wedding cake, maybe cause some mischief with it. Some woman had come all the way from Denver just to make it. I know I was being childish, but dammit, I didn't want to marry him. I didn't even like him. Owen was supposed to be out on the north range overseeing some fence repairs, I think. We left our horses on the other side of the ridge from the house and walked from there. I persuaded Logan that we should go to the root cellar first, figuring it was the coolest spot to keep a cake."

Tyler's attention was now riveted on her. His silence willed her to continue.

"There was an open padlock on the door. I thought it was strange, but maybe Owen liked to lock up his food supplies. I should have known, dammit. I knew first hand what Owen liked to do in root cellars, but I was as blind as a rock." She cleared her throat. "When we went in, we found two women and a young boy. They were in tattered, filthy clothes that were stiff with God knows what, and covered with cuts, bruises, and welts. And their wrists, *Jesus*, their wrists were like raw, bloody meat from the shackles that bound them to the wall. They told us Owen had bought them. *Bought* them someplace in San Francisco." A small sob escaped.

"My God, Tyler, he was a white slaver, a sodomite, and a rapist. Logan was trying to get them free and I just stood there terrified, like a bump on a log. All I was thinking about was that I was supposed to *marry* this man. Here these poor people had endured torture, and all I thought of was myself. Logan was yelling at me to snap out of it, to help him. I felt like I was standing in a glass jar watching them."

She swallowed the lump in her throat before continuing.

"After we freed them, we helped them to our horses. I had to carry the boy because he was so weak. His blood nearly soaked through my shirt. It was just so *horrible*, so *unbelievable*, I still felt like I was watching it all happen. We got to the horses as quickly as we could. Then we heard riders coming. Logan and I had an argument about who was staying, but he forced me to take the knife and told me to go. He wanted me to take the two women and the boy to town while he stayed behind to give us time to escape. I ran back to them, but instead of taking them myself, I had them all mount up together on Logan's horse. It was a big gray stallion named Shadow that was seventeen hands high, his pride and joy. The three of them together probably weighed about the same as Logan anyway. Then I heard the gunshots.

"One of the women, Rebecca, looked at me in understanding. She told me to go back to see if I could help him. I felt like a goddamn fish out of water, flopping around, not knowing which way to jump." She shook her head. "I gave her Logan's rifle for protection, and what little money I had with me. They galloped away on Shadow in the direction of town. I crept back across the ridge. Luckily, I was wearing my moccasins and was quiet as a breeze. I hid behind some rocks to see if I could help Logan."

Her eyes were glazed with unshed tears. They felt hot and gritty. Her heart pounded painfully as her mind replayed that awful day in agonizing detail.

"Owen kept calling me to get me to come out or he was going to kill my brother. Logan kept shouting for me to go. I want to say that I listened to Logan, but in truth, it was my fear that kept me hidden. I was so afraid." She paused as a small shudder traveled through her. "I saw it all. They beat him senseless, then Owen shot him in the head. His brother, Bert, found me behind the rock right after Logan was killed. I pretended to faint because it was the only thing I could think of. Then when he started to rip my clothes off, I stabbed him with Logan's knife to save myself. Then I watched them drag Logan's body behind the barn to bury him. In the dirt. With no respect, no loving words. I didn't get a chance to say goodbye to him."

The tears finally spilled over and streamed down her cheeks. The dam of emotion was beginning to break.

"I was so ashamed of what I had done, of my foolishness. I was responsible for Logan's death, over a damned wedding cake, for God's sake. I couldn't face my family, and I knew Owen would be after me because not only had I killed *his* brother, but I knew his dirty secret. I snuck home, got my gear, and left without ever saying goodbye. I've been running and hiding for so long, I can't remember anything else. Except pain and guilt. It was my fault, all of it."

"You saved three people, Nicky. That is nothing to be ashamed of."

"I didn't save them. Logan did."

"What happened to them?"

"They got on the stage and fortunately escaped. The two women made it back home to Nebraska. I've kept in contact with them. I thought it was the least I could do, since I'd failed my brother when he needed me most."

"And the boy?"

"He hanged himself within a week."

Tyler cursed quietly.

"I've never told anyone that story, Tyler." She turned her gaze to him. "It's been inside me for so long. All I ever wanted was to say I'm sorry. I'm sorry, Logan," she shouted to the sky. "I'm sorry."

As her shouts faded into the foggy mist, Nicky's chest began to heave with the force of her sobs. Tyler stopped the horses, then dismounted quickly. After he unlocked the shackles and helped her down off the horse, he cradled her like a baby. Nicky clung to him for dear life. His strong arms were an anchor in the sea of emotion she swam in. Her tears landed on his neck and shoulders like warm rivers of grief as her whole body trembled in its current. He was there and she loved him.

⁂ ⁂ ⁂

Tyler sat down heavily on a large boulder, holding Nicky, murmuring soothing nonsense words. He'd never been one for a woman's tears, but this was entirely different. Nicky was as tough as they came, an exciting, vibrant woman. This sobbing creature was pitiful and upsetting to Tyler.

Shackled. Tyler closed his eyes tightly. He'd shackled her just like that pig Hoffman. He felt disgusted at himself. She had looked at him with such an intensity of soul-deep grief that it truly frightened him. She had relived something buried deeply, which had festered inside her, and clamored to be purged. He didn't want to believe her horrific story, except perhaps that her brother was killed by Hoffman and, though her grief was real enough...could there still be a ruse?

Tyler was torn between stopping those God-awful tears and kissing her breathless. Her thick curls were tickling his chest, whispering caresses on his neck and cheek. She was so warm and alive, and so needy. As if in answer to his body's rising awareness, she started kissing his neck. Her small kisses were like oil on a fire. His groin was pressed up against her hip. And she'd left her breasts unbound. One lay against his chest, the other his arm, and they felt like branding irons. He was stupidly pleased to notice that she had put the wedding band back on her finger. It looked comfortable on the slender digit.

He groaned and caught her mouth in a passionate union. His fierceness startled him, but she answered it equally. He dragged his lips from hers, looking down into her tear-stained face. Her eyes were drowsy with passion. She was, incredibly, smiling at him.

"It's still there," she whispered.

"What?"

"The fire. I thought it might have burned itself out after this morning. I was wrong."

"Oh."

She suddenly blushed. Her awareness brought him back to earth. This was far too comfortable. He stood, setting her feet gently down on the ground. He led her to her horse and shackled her wrists again, averting his eyes as he worked.

After he mounted his horse, he urged both forward.

"We'll stop in an hour or so and eat," he said, voice tight.

Was there ever a woman who could match him? Who stood as strong and proud as he? No, never. Nicky was uniquely like him, his soul mate, his kindred spirit, his other half. The invisible thread had pulled them together at last. He was in love with her.

Jesus help me. What the hell am I supposed to do now?

When they stopped to eat, Tyler headed for a nearby stream alone after securing the horses' reins to a tree. He needed to fill the canteens and dunk his head. The memory of Nicky's body pressed up against him was just too vivid, too hot. When did he lose control? It was unacceptable. Things had to smooth out, to revert to normal. His sanity depended on it.

⁂ ⁂ ⁂

Nicky watched Tyler stalk away. He had scowled blackly since their kiss earlier. His handsome face had never once turned her way. Just as well. She slipped the hairpin in the lock of the first shackle. She wriggled and twisted it as much as she dared. It wasn't working. Perspiration dotted her brow as she tried desperately to free her hands. Her heart was thundering in her ears and she imagined she heard Tyler's heavy footfalls coming back.

"Pleasepleasepleaseplease."

Just when she thought the hairpin would break, she heard a "click" and the cuff popped open. Staring at her free hand with her mouth unhinged, she realized precious time was slipping away as she sat there and gawked. Maneuvering the pin to free the other hand, she kept darting furtive glances toward the direction Tyler had gone. A second "click" and her other hand was free. Gently, she placed the shackles on Tyler's saddle. After untying Juliet's reins, she slowly trotted away, breaking into a gallop as she fled to freedom.

⁂ ⁂ ⁂

Tyler raised his head from the cool water and shook his head, spraying droplets of water all over his shirt. He ran his fingers through his wet hair, wringing the moisture from it. He was surprised Nicky wasn't bellowing to be let loose. Maybe she needed to dunk her head, too. He shivered from the memory of her wet hair after her bath last night.

"Enough."

It was time to think with his brain again instead of his nether regions. This woman was still a wanted outlaw, regardless if he was in love with her. Never once did he ever feel remorse for the outlaws he dragged back for a bounty. Why the hell did he ever take Owen Hoffman's offer? He didn't know how to control his rampaging emotions, because he hadn't let himself have any for twenty years. He felt like he was pulling and yanking on that invisible thread, trying to stretch it back out between them. Like a wolf gnawing on his leg to free himself from a trap.

He filled both canteens and stomped back to the horses. At first he couldn't believe his eyes. Only his gelding Sable stood there, whinnying softly. He blinked, trying to comprehend what he saw. The shackles sat atop his saddle. She was gone.

Nicky was gone.

She couldn't have more than a few minutes head start. He jammed the shackles into his saddlebag, swung the canteens onto the saddle horn, and threw himself into the saddle.

He spurred his horse forward, glad to have such a large, fast beast. *Damn her.* How did she get free? He felt angry, betrayed, and somehow...hurt. *No.* No woman was going to turn him into a simpering fool. It was the goddamn frigging bounty that mattered, not Nicky.

He could see the fresh hoofprints in the damp, scrubby ground. The fog was making it impossible to hear anything, though. He cursed himself up and down for letting her out of his sight. No prisoner had ever escaped from him before, but then again, Nicky was no ordinary prisoner. She was his wife, his lover, his heart, his soul.

And she had just left him. And taken every scrap of warmth with her.

⁂ ⁂ ⁂

Nicky hunkered down as low as she could in the saddle. The cold wind whistled through her ears as she fled from the man she loved. She had to smash her hat down on her head to keep it from flying off as her curls flapped like a flag. Her heart was trip-hammering in fear and elation. She had done it. Escaped from Tyler. She ignored the sadness that threatened to tear her heart from her chest...she'd deal with those emotions later.

She was headed east toward Nebraska, or so she thought anyway. This darned fog gave her no help. Suddenly Juliet's hooves were silent. It took a moment for Nicky to realize that the ground was gone and they were flying over the edge of a precipice. The ground rushed up at them with dizzying speed. Nicky let out a short scream before they landed, and then all was black.

⁂ ⁂ ⁂

Tyler thought he'd heard something, but couldn't pinpoint the noise. As he approached the ravine that marked the border between Wyoming and Nebraska, he pulled Sable to a halt. He needed to determine which way she would go. East, definitely not west. That would lead her back toward him. He turned his horse and started to spur him forward when he saw hoofprints on the ground in front of him, facing the ravine.

"What the hell?"

She couldn't have jumped it. It was twenty feet wide at this point. Still...he dismounted with a curse. If she had, there was no way he'd catch her today. Sable couldn't make that kind of jump. He knelt to examine the tracks when his eye caught something in the ravine.

Nicky.

Oh, Jesus.

Cold, raw fear coiled in his stomach.

He picketed Sable quickly since there were no trees close by to tether his reins, then tied a rope to his horse's saddle with trembling fingers. He clambered down the side of the ravine and saw her sprawled flat on her back, arms and legs every which way, deathly still. Her horse was near death; the poor thing had two broken legs, and was wheezing slowly.

He forced his legs to move to Nicky. There was blood on her forehead and her lip was split. He could see her left arm was twisted at an unnatural angle. He knelt down on the damp sandy ground, and slowly lowered his ear to her chest.

Please God, don't take her from me.

She was breathing and had a heartbeat. Relief flooded through him like summer sunshine. *Alive. Nicky was alive.* After laying his jacket over her still form, he climbed back up to his horse and retrieved his saddlebags, a canteen and his rifle. He almost jumped back into the ravine off the rope, anxious to return to her, but her horse would come first. Patting the mare's head as he slipped Nicky's saddle, bedroll, and saddlebags off, her soulful brown eyes regarded him, pleading with him. With a clean shot, he put her out of her misery. The gunshot sounded stilted in the fog. He grabbed Nicky's saddlebags and hurried over to her.

Tyler took a pair of stockings and Nicky's book to secure her arm in a makeshift splint. It would have to do until he found a sturdy piece of wood, or until they could get to a doctor.

He slowly felt her legs, arms and ribs for any other injuries. He let out a sigh of relief when he couldn't feel any.

He laid out her bedroll quickly, and gently set her on it. He stared down at her a moment, willing her to waken. Tyler wondered if she ever would. What would he do then? Disgusted with his morbid thoughts, he pushed them aside. Grabbing a cloth, he poured some cool water on it, carefully wiping the blood from her face. She was pale as milk and had a deep gash near her hairline that was bleeding. He pressed a clean cloth against it, dismayed at his reaction to blood. It wasn't just any blood, though, it was *her* blood. He forced himself to continue.

Stop being such a nancy-boy.

Hardening his resolve, he began to bandage her wounds. After overcoming his tremors, he looked at his handiwork and decided he could make a halfway decent nurse. Glancing around, he realized that they were too near Nicky's horse. He'd have to make camp away from the carcass and away from any predators that might be drawn to the scent of blood. He'd do anything to protect his wife.

Chapter Twelve

It was twilight when Nicky slowly came into consciousness to the sound of a crackling fire. The warmth of the flames tickled her cheeks like a caress. And then there was pain, searing pain in her arm and her head, and a thousand other small places on her body. She groaned, but it sounded more like a kitten's mewl. The memory of the fall hit her like a blow to the chest. *Juliet.* She struggled to open her eyes, but even blinking was agony. When she finally succeeded, her eyes refused to focus. She could see a dark shape cooking over the campfire.

"Tyler," she croaked, barely above a whisper.

He started at the sound of her voice, his eyes incredulous. Setting down his skillet, he approached her, reaching out to feel her forehead with one callused palm. His hand then caressed her cheek.

"You're awake." His voice was low, grave. "I had my doubts there, magpie. How do you feel?"

"Like I was in a stampede."

Turning, he took his canteen and poured some fresh water into a tin cup for her. Ever so gently he lifted her head and placed the cup to her lips.

"Drink."

She tried to drink deeply, suddenly aware she was parched. Tyler pulled the cup away.

"Not too fast. You've got to go easy. Your stomach has been without food for too long."

"How long?"

"Four days."

Her heart began to beat faster as the pain in her head grew to a throbbing crescendo. She goggled at him. He had taken care of her for four days?

"Juliet?"

He shook his head and avoided looking at her directly. "I had to let her go. Both her front legs were broken."

Tears sprang to her eyes. *Oh, Juliet, I'm so sorry*, she wailed inside. The tears went unshed as she met Tyler's gaze. He looked positively worried. His brow was furrowed as he took in her pale face.

"Tyler...I...thank you." She didn't know how to convey her gratitude. It still felt awkward to say thank you to the bounty hunter that had captured her even if he was her husband.

"It was a dumb thing you did, Nicole. Running like that in the fog, over unfamiliar ground. You're lucky you didn't break your neck instead of just hurting your arm and slicing up your head. You're not much of an escape artist."

His voice was soft, instead of harsh. She tried to smile at him.

"I had to check your arm myself, used your stockings to wrap it up tight so I could move the camp farther away from the horse's carcass. I waited, but then you didn't wake up. I needed to make sure it wasn't broken." He looked at her grimly. "It looks like just a sprain. You were lucky."

Nicky glanced at her arm. Tyler had redone the setting in the meantime, so her arm was bound to a makeshift splint with her stockings and strips from a shirt. That's when she realized she only wore her chemise under the blanket. For all intents and purposes, she was naked. That felt even odder than the fact

Tyler took care of her. He was obviously the person who removed all her clothes in the first place. Nicky forced herself not to blush.

"Let me finish cooking and you can get something in your stomach." He returned to the fire and picked up the frying pan he'd been using. The silence was comfortable between them as the sounds of the night began to play their age-old song.

"Tell me about your life," she murmured, eyes closed.

"Why?"

Nicky opened her eyes to study her husband's face. The flickering firelight danced across his handsome features, making his blue eyes look like fathomless pools.

"Well, you are my husband, and I want to know. Besides, you have an advantage. You have 'a file' on me."

His scowl didn't vanish—if anything, it deepened at her attempt at levity.

"Come on, Tyler," she cajoled. "Please?"

His face softened as he exhaled the breath he was holding. "Not much to tell."

"Then it shouldn't take you long."

"Pushy witch."

"You're from Texas?"

"Yeah, from near Houston." He paused while she waited patiently for him to continue. Nicky realized she was treading on dangerous ground, so she stepped lightly, praying that he'd open himself up to her.

"My pa was a sheriff. I grew up walking, talking, hell, *breathing*, as a future lawman. He took me with him when he could. Most of the time, they were small-town problems—nothing dangerous. My ma was so scared I'd get hurt, she clucked like a mother hen when I'd saddle my horse to go out with my pa."

"Any brothers or sisters?" she asked when he paused.

"No. Had a sister, Lily, who died when I was five and she was seven. Rattlesnake bite. She was hiding from me behind the woodpile. She liked to outsmart her little brother." He kept his eyes on the fire as he spoke. "Ma never really got over her death, so she tried to smother me. I pushed her away."

Nicky reached out and held his hand with her good arm. He didn't pull away, but he didn't close his long fingers around hers either.

"When I was around ten, Pa and me rode out to the McMillan farm. There was a report of a missing milk cow so he let me come—it probably just wandered away, right?" His lips twisted into a sneer. "Little did we know that an outlaw on the run had killed her for food. We found her carcass butchered a few miles from the farm. The son of a bitch was hiding and panicked when he saw us. Without a word, he shot my father dead in the back."

Nicky couldn't contain her gasp. What a thing for a ten-year-old child to witness. At nineteen, she had been an adult, and still she felt the pain of Logan's death as if it was yesterday. The pain must have been unbearable for a child.

"I turned to see him walking toward me...guns drawn. I tried to wrestle my pa's gun from the holster, but I wasn't quick enough. He shot me, too."

Nicky's hand squeezed reflexively around Tyler's as she mourned the childhood that had been taken away from him so cruelly. The old scar on his back was explained. The wound of a child thrust into manhood. And she'd been responsible for the newest scars inflicted by Hermano.

"Lucky for me, it went straight through and buried itself in my father's body. After that bastard ran, I crawled to my horse and rode back to the McMillans' house. I lived, but it was three months before I got out of bed. The only thing that kept me alive was revenge. I was gonna find that bastard and kill him."

The hatred in his eyes chilled Nicky to the bone. Had he lived so long with that emotion that it had stained his soul?

"It took eight years until I found him, not as a lawman, but as a bounty hunter. He was worth three hundred alive, half that dead. After I was done with his worthless hide, I was lucky I got the hundred and fifty. From then on, I drifted from bounty to bounty. Built my reputation as the best." He finally slid his glance to Nicky. "Only the best to find the best."

The look in his eyes was predatory in the firelight. She needed to break the spell he had woven with his tale of death and misery.

"What happened to your mother?"

He turned his gaze back to the fire. "She died of grief within a year. Once I was finally healed, it was like she had given up. I was on my own after that."

Nicky's brows furrowed. "You were on your own at the age of eleven?"

"I was almost twelve by that point, but I was big for my age. People thought I was about sixteen."

Nicky mumbled under her breath, "I don't doubt that, you're still big."

"I worked the range, just like you. Taking jobs when I could, learning all I could from anybody who could teach me."

"Sounds like a lonely life, Calhoun. The ring?"

He nodded. "It was hers. The only thing I had left from her."

Nicky took a deep breath, biting back the sound of grief she wanted to express for the child Tyler had been. "I'm sorry for what you had to go through as a child. No wonder you're as tough as you are. You couldn't have survived without it. I don't know how I've survived on my own for the past three years."

"You're tougher than you look, Malloy." His mouth quirked up at the corners in a semi-smile.

"That's Mrs. Calhoun to you, mister," she teased. The minute the words were out of her mouth, she regretted them. His face immediately transformed back into the stoic mask she was so used to seeing. He had closed the door again. She sighed and tried to find a comfortable position on the hard ground.

"I miss my family with an ache," Nicky said after a few minutes of silence. "It's been over three years since I saw them, and now," she shrugged, "I'm sure they're ashamed of me. After all, they think I'm a thief and a murderer."

She sighed as the enormity of the last three years settled on her shoulders. "When you've lost so much, it seems near to impossible to get any of it back."

It was then that Tyler finally squeezed her hand. It was a lightning bolt of hope that coursed through her bruised body and heart.

They ate Tyler's simple meal in silence. He helped her when she couldn't help herself. Nicky tried not to be embarrassed, but it was hard to be beholden to anyone. Tyler shoveled the food in like he hadn't eaten in days while Nicky picked at hers. When they were finished, he stacked the plates beside the fire.

"You'd best get some rest," he ordered as he stood up abruptly. "I'm going to scout around to make sure there's no trouble. You never know if Nate's foot or Rusty's face will heal enough to come after you again. Woman, you sure do inspire men to chase you."

As he walked away from the circle of firelight, Nicky felt her heart squeeze a little tighter. How could she have fallen in love with such a complex, haunted man? The bond between them had grown stronger no matter how hard they fought it. There was a reason they were drawn together, two kindred souls in pain, lonely and suffering. They had found each other, and circumstances were pulling them apart, to shatter into pieces.

⁂ ⁂ ⁂

Tyler walked in the darkness, and took a deep breath to clear his mind. What in the hell prompted him to tell her things he'd never told a soul? And why couldn't he picture his life without her now? Somehow, God help him, he had come to love this woman more than he ever thought possible. And soon, he'd have to let her go because he couldn't bear to watch her die, along with his heart and soul.

He walked on blindly, running from his heart, his destiny, his wife.

* * *

The bright sunlight pricked at his eyelids, forcing his short slumber to an end. Tyler'd had a hell of a time going to sleep and it felt as if he'd just closed his eyes moments before. A weight had settled on his left shoulder. He opened his eyes and was pleasantly surprised to see his wife's head resting on him.

Her face was tilted slightly toward him. Without thinking, he leaned forward and kissed her on the neck just below her ear, inhaling her unique scent.

"Tyler."

Her eyelids slowly opened. Oh, those beautiful green eyes. "How do you feel?" His voice was tinged with sleep. He muffled a yawn against his hand.

"Much better."

"You sure?"

She smiled deeply so her eyes crinkled up at the corners. His heart lurched as he bathed in the glow of that smile. How could this have happened? He had truly lost his heart to this woman.

She ran her tongue along her lips, the gesture provocative in her innocence. His blood began to thrum in his ears as his awareness of her potent sexuality began to take its effect. He had tried to ignore her nude body as he washed and tended her for the past four days. It was damn hard too. Now she was awake and nearly naked under those blankets. He was as randy as a young buck snorting after a doe in heat. *What madness.*

"You want some water?" He started to rise, but her gentle pressure stopped him.

"No, stay. I like this."

She snuggled into the crook of his shoulder, resting her injured arm on his chest. He was relieved to see color in her cheeks and a sparkle in her eyes. She reached up with her hand and slowly caressed his stubbled cheek. She traced the outline of his lips with the tip of her slender finger. A shiver of anticipation raced through Tyler at her touch and his groin began to throb more insistently.

"Doesn't that hurt your arm?"

"No, it's okay. I'm being careful."

Nicky touched the buttons in his shirt and looked at him with one eyebrow raised. His large hand gently pulled hers away, unbuttoning and then shedding his shirt. Nicky stared at his chest with wide, hungry eyes. He knew what she saw, but it wasn't that different from any other man. She focused on his navel, just visible over the waistband of his pants. She slowly traced the perfect circle with her finger. Goose bumps broke out on his arms and his nipples hardened instantly. Her finger followed the trail of goose bumps and felt the hard nubs of his nipples. He grasped her wrist tightly, stopping the meandering finger.

"Nicole." His voice was barely reined. "What are you doing?"

She looked up at his face. His jaw was clenched so tightly that his pulse throbbed at his temple. Her eyes reflected passion so fierce it was almost a physical blow. She smiled slowly, knowingly. She pulled her wrist free, then licked the tip of her finger and rubbed it over the hardened male nipple. He hissed and closed his eyes.

"We can't...I mean, you're hurt," he ground out.

Nicky raised her head and placed her lips ever so gently on his nipple. He wanted her. God, he wanted her so badly it was painful. She didn't know how desirable she was, how her soft touches were driving him past the point of no return.

She kissed her way up his chest to his neck, then his cheek, then his mouth. Her tongue licked his lips from one side to the other, gently nibbling on the corners. He groaned. It was a deep guttural sound. She responded with one of her own. Tyler felt his control snap like a dry twig. He opened his mouth to her probing tongue and devoured her in an endless, breathtaking kiss. His body cried out for her. She dug her fingers in his muscled back as she pressed up tight against him.

He trailed kisses down her jawbone to her ear, light flicks of his tongue on her earlobe and down the side of her neck. She tasted like honey, so sweet. He paused as his lips reached her collarbone. She was shaking.

He raised his eyes to look at her. "Are you sure you want to do this?"

In response to his question, she reached down and squeezed his hardness, once. It was enough. He looked at her chemise, the dark outline of her nipples visible through the fabric. He reached out and caressed her breasts, the nipples instantly hard pebbles of desire.

"Help me," she whispered.

He pulled the blankets back completely, slipped the chemise carefully over the splint, then up and over her head. She was nude. Beautifully, deliciously nude. He stared at her, drinking in the long, creamy legs, her flat stomach, her full breasts, her mane of softly curling hair, and her face. Ah, her exquisite face.

"What are you doing?" She sounded concerned.

"Looking. You are so goddamned beautiful, magpie." His voice was hoarse.

"Only to you."

He shook his head and smiled slowly as he ran his hand up her calf to her thighs and stopped at the junction of her legs to that soft place. When one finger touched her there, she jumped, startled by the sensation. He moved his fingers against her, stroking, caressing, teasing. His mouth found her already hard nipple and she gasped. Tyler licked, nibbled, and suckled at one breast, then the other. He wanted to pleasure her. His hand worked like magic to bring her to a climax. She stiffened, crying out as his fingers plunged in her.

He gently kissed her closed eyelids. They fluttered open, her pupils wide, the green darkened with passion. She fumbled for his jeans, but he stood and took them off. Nicky stared at his maleness. It stood straight and large in a dark patch of black hair. She reached out and closed her hand around it. He felt himself sway under her inexperienced fingers as she ran her hand up and down his staff.

He lay down quickly, out of her reach before he lost control, nudging her knees open. He paused at the entrance to her womanhood, panting, wanting to look in her eyes as he plunged into her. She stared back at him and her mouth formed the word *Tyler*. Her hand grasped his hip to guide him. When he was deeply inside her, he knew the ultimate ecstasy. The pleasure was nearly enough to kill him. He was glad she wasn't a virgin any more for he had no restraint. It was almost too much. Her moist tightness enveloped him as pleasure ricocheted through his body. He fought to regain control then began to move in and out slowly. She rose to meet him, consumed by her own passion. She moaned his name as he pushed deeper. Suddenly, she pulled her legs back, opening herself completely to him.

"Oh, Nicky." It was more of a prayer than anything.

"Nicole," she corrected him breathlessly.

"Nicole," he moaned as he moved in her faster. She quivered around him as she reached her peak again. As her fingers dug into his side, he felt his own climax building. He claimed her mouth in a reverent kiss as he spilled his seed into her. His beloved wife, Nicole.

⁂ ⁂ ⁂

After they made love, they made love again. They spent the morning teasing and pleasuring each other. If she had her druthers, and a hell of a lot more energy, she'd never stop making love to him. She felt weaker than a new foal. As it was, he was doing all the work pleasuring her. Nicky felt a twinge of guilt, but pushed it aside. He was certainly gaining his own pleasure too.

As they lay in each other's arms, Nicky's stomach rumbled noisily.

"I see you need to be fed. It's nearly noon, no wonder you're hungry." His smile was potent as Nicky melted under her husband's gaze.

After a quick kiss, he stood up and pulled on his clothes. Commanding her to sleep, he went to rustle up some game to eat. She smiled at his concern. Tyler Calhoun turned sweet. Who would have thought?

She dozed on and off, but she felt a niggle of doubt when Tyler didn't return. Awkwardly, she dressed herself and rose to her feet. After a few shaky steps, she looked around the ravine, but saw no trace of him. The doubt turned to concern. She eyed the rope hanging down the side and shrugged. With a bit of struggle, she climbed to the top of the ravine using only one hand. Her sprained arm throbbed some, but it wasn't too bad. It was her body's weakness that surprised her.

Winded, Nicky sat on her knees until she caught her breath. Tyler's horse grazed on the thin brush. Her saddle sat on a rock, and hanging from the side was her gun belt, the pistols tucked into the holsters. She stared at it, her heart doing double time. He obviously hadn't expected her to climb up here. She licked her lips and approached the saddle. A cool breeze caressed her face as she reached out her shaking hand to the gun belt. Jack's initials gleamed in the sun on the handles of the Colts. J.M. That's why she'd picked the name Jesse Miller. Her alias had to match the pistols.

Oh, Jack, I miss you, all of you. I want a normal family again. I want Tyler. I want to have Tyler's babies.

"Go ahead and take 'em," said Tyler from behind her. Like a streak of lightning, she grabbed the pistol and whipped around toward Tyler with an instinct born of being on the run, a surge of adrenaline coursing through her veins. Tyler didn't flinch from the gun barrel, but his eyes looked like blue ice.

"Tyler, you scared me," she said shakily as she lowered the pistol and replaced it in its holster.

"I see you're feeling better." His cold eyes raked her up and down with a slight sneer to his lips.

She nodded silently, shifting from foot to foot. Where was the Tyler that had made such sweet love to her? This cold-eyed stranger had taken his place again.

"I said, take 'em." His voice was even colder than his eyes. "You'll need them. I'm not taking you back to Cheshire."

With that he turned on his heel and shimmied down the rope into the ravine again. Scowling, she followed her husband, slowly descending to the ground using her one good arm.

Ignoring her body's protest, she was fueled by confusion and hurt caused by Tyler's behavior. What was going on?

Tyler had snared a rabbit and was readying it for cooking as Nicky approached him.

"What do you mean, you're not taking me to Cheshire?"

His gaze shifted to hers for a brief moment. She gasped at the deadness in his eyes. Her confusion began to turn to anger.

"Tyler," she said more forcefully. "Are you letting me go?"

"Yes, woman, are you dense?"

For a full minute, Nicky merely stared at him while he worked. She couldn't speak just yet. Her mind whirled with a thousand questions. And she was trying desperately not to hit him upside the head.

"What about us? I mean, we're married in every sense of the word."

"Not every sense. I'll have it taken care of when I get back to Houston."

"Calhoun, you...you just can't do that. You're going to just cut me loose? Thanks for the tumble, but so long? I don't think so."

She was absolutely furious, and felt as if her heart was tearing in two at the same time. She yanked on his shirt to try to make him stand and fight. It was like pulling on solid rock.

"Stand up."

He did as she bade, rising to his full height, staring down at her. Only the telltale twitch in his cheek spoke of his inner turmoil. Was it only a short time ago that they had lain in each other's arms?

"You will not just let me go. You will help me prove my innocence and then, and only then, will we decide what to do about this marriage." Tyler's expression did not change. "What's the matter, Calhoun? Afraid?"

His jaw tightened as he extracted her hand from the front of his shirt.

"Look, you want to go, so just *go*."

"What are you talking about?"

"Nicky, I'm not a fool. Don't treat me like one."

Nicky wanted to scream in frustration. "Tyler, are you angry with me? Please, tell me what's going on." She tried to touch his arm, but he stiffened and pulled away from her.

"You can't bear for me to touch you now? This morning must have meant a helluva lot more to me than to you, Calhoun." She couldn't completely disguise the hurt in her voice.

"What do you want me to think? You try to run away again even before you're fully healed from the last try, then you pull a gun on me, and somehow you plead innocent."

"Run away? *Run away*?" she parroted. "Is that what you think?"

Tyler's silence confirmed her question.

"Jesus, you think very little of me, don't you?" She squeezed the words out of her throat. "Tyler, I was not running away. The pistols used to belong to my brother, Jack. I was...wishing I could be part of my family again. To feel loved, to feel wanted. To have a future beyond the next ten minutes. To not have to know people like Hermano. To stop running."

She hugged herself with her good arm as she walked a few feet away from her husband. She kept her back to him so he wouldn't see the pain she knew was shining in her eyes. She couldn't completely blame him for his accusation since she had tried to run away more than once.

"I have a proposition for you, Tyler. You come with me to North Platte, Nebraska and meet the two women I helped to escape from that bastard, Owen. If you still don't believe me, then take me back to Cheshire. If you do..." Her voice trailed off. "Then I don't know."

"Why?"

"Why what?"

"Don't you want your freedom? Why do you want me to go with you, to help you?"

Because I love you. Nicky's mouth opened to speak, but she couldn't voice the words her heart was screaming so loudly. How could she tell him she loved him? He obviously didn't feel the same way, and she wasn't about to put her head in that noose. She turned back toward him.

"Because I can't do it alone. And I need you to believe me." She opted for a partial truth.

The sincerity in her voice apparently made Tyler hesitate from his resolve to rid himself of his wife. After a moment of studying her face, he spoke.

"All right. To North Platte then. And no tricks."

Her anger licked at her again. It was just like him to assume she was going to try something underhanded. She could've saddled his horse and been halfway to somewhere else before he came back. But she hadn't...couldn't.

"Agreed. And no shackles either."

She smiled then, relishing the anger that passed over his face. She'd show Tyler Calhoun what she was made of...and hoped he'd love her for all she was.

Chapter Thirteen

He ate the food, but didn't taste it. He was silently licking the wounds she'd intentionally, or unintentionally, inflicted upon him. After they ate, they began to gather everything up to leave the ravine. Each time their hands accidentally brushed, Tyler thought he saw Nicky flinch. Each flinch was another injury to his heart.

As they climbed up and out for the last time, he tried not to think of the wonder and heaven he'd found in that dirty ravine. He tried not to think about the injured woman who was climbing up with one good arm. Tyler was climbing up behind her, and he tried not to stare at her behind and remember how it felt to caress it, kiss it. *Get a hold of yourself, Calhoun.*

As he brushed himself off, he watched her approach her saddle. He could sense her hesitation.

"I hate to leave it behind," Nicky said, biting her lip.

"Do you expect me to carry it on my head or strapped to my back?" Tyler's voice was laced with sarcasm. He was angry and hurt and she was the nearest target.

"You don't need to be so mean about it. I've had this saddle for more than ten years. My papa had it made especially for me."

Tyler rolled his eyes in frustration. "I'll buy you a new one."

She shook her head and frowned at him. “It’s the last tie to the girl I was. When I leave it behind, I’m leaving Nicky Malloy behind.”

Tyler gritted his teeth together and swallowed the sharp retort. He needed to stop taking his anger out on her. It wasn’t helping their situation at all. “You’re not Nicky Malloy anymore. You’re Nicole Calhoun.”

“Nicole Calhoun,” she repeated as if tasting the name. “Yeah, I guess I am...for now, right?”

Tyler didn’t respond to her jibe. He didn’t expect her to stay with him, didn’t dare voice the little thought running through his brain. *Nicole Calhoun, always.* He loaded their saddlebags onto Sable. “Are you ready?”

Her gaze jumped to his broad back and she narrowed her eyes. “In a hurry to get rid of me?”

He ignored her.

“You can’t ever give a little, can you? Give someone a little, they take a lot.”

Back off, magpie. There is no future for us.

She turned and approached him with sure steps. “This is from the man who hunts killers and thieves. You know what you’ve seen, but you don’t see *me,*” she stated, poking him with her finger sharply.

Almost against his will, he looked her in the eyes. She was angry, but he also saw pain and fear. He had put a good deal of that pain there, but he couldn’t take it away. She wasn’t meant to be with him for the rest of her life. It just couldn’t be.

“Are you ready?” he repeated softly.

She mounted Sable easily, without answering him. Tyler swung up behind her and kneed his gelding forward.

Nicky turned around once to look back at her saddle. Tyler thought of it all day as they rode deeper into Nebraska. She was

Nicole Calhoun now, for better, or for worse. And he thought the worse was definitely coming. And coming fast.

⁂ ⁂ ⁂

Conversation between Tyler and Nicky was strained, to say the least. They simply didn't know what to say to each other without causing tempers to flare. When they stopped for a short break, Tyler fashioned a sling for her from one of his shirts. He could see the pain lines around her eyes, and wanted to help ease it. She had looked surprised by his act of kindness, damn it all.

After filling their canteens in a stream, they continued on their journey. He wanted to keep her at arm's length to make their final parting a little easier, if that was possible, yet here they were dangerously pressed together on his horse. Her behind rubbed his groin provocatively with the sway of the horse, inciting lustful urges he was helpless to control.

"Tyler?"

He grunted in response. The effort to ignore her body pressed up against him was wearing down his resolve to keep his distance from his wife. And every time he breathed in, he smelled her hair. She had gathered it up in her hat to keep it out of his eyes—he had been amazed it still fit—but he could still smell the sweet scent. He just didn't have the energy to talk.

"Thank you."

Silence met her gratitude.

"I mean thank you for helping me, for going with me...for trusting me."

Tyler cringed inwardly at her words. Did he trust her? Or did he simply want to believe her? His feelings for her were still so new, so fragile. He hadn't trusted anybody in a very long time. He was in love with his wife, but he didn't trust her. What kind of man could love without trust? It was something Tyler wanted to get control over, even as it spun hopelessly out of control.

He had gone so far as to strap her gun belt on her hips before they set off from the stream. She had looked at him with the oddest expression in her eyes, a mixture of sadness and confusion. The guns weren't loaded, and so far, she had made no move to remedy that situation. He didn't know whether or not he was relieved.

She sighed as she snuggled back against his chest. In a few minutes, he realized she was asleep. He knew she wasn't fully recovered from her fall, but she insisted on setting off to North Platte immediately. Nothing he said could dissuade her. He snaked an arm around her waist to prevent her from falling and continued east.

⁂ ⁂ ⁂

"Nicky?"

Tyler's voice was in her head, insistently whispering. His lips grazed her ear. She shivered as the goose bumps danced down her neck like a parade.

"Wake up, Nicky."

His tone was sterner, and her eyes flew open. His heavily muscled arm felt like a steel band around her waist, warm and safe.

"We're stopping for the night." His voice was now gruff with frustration.

"Where?"

"Here."

She straightened up quickly and knocked Tyler's nose soundly with the brim of her hat. His muffled oath startled her.

"Sorry, Tyler."

He grunted at her as he slid off the horse, then helped her down. For a brief moment, she sensed he wanted to do more than help her dismount, but he turned away quickly to make camp.

After building up a small fire, they ate a supper of beans and biscuits in silence. She felt uncomfortable, miserable, and tongue-tied. Her arm was aching as much as her heart.

"Tyler..."

"Nicky..."

They both began to speak at the same time. Nicky emitted a short sound that could have been a laugh.

"Go ahead."

"No, you first."

"Are you sure?"

"Yeah, go ahead."

"Umm...I forgot what I was going to say."

"Me, too."

Tyler rose quickly, and went to fill their canteens, leaving the bedrolls to Nicky. He took the easy way out and left the decision up to her. Nicky eyed the blankets with a frown. She knew what he was about. *Coward.* Well, she'd show him a thing or two.

⁂ ⁂ ⁂

When he returned with the canteens, he found the bedrolls neatly fitted together beside the campfire. He hid the smile that rose to his lips. He had hoped for it like a fool, but not too hard, for he didn't want to be disappointed. She was already covered with a blanket, and her back was to him.

⁂ ⁂ ⁂

She knew he had returned, but she decided to play possum and pretend she was sleeping already. In truth, her entire body was aware the second he laid down next to her. Her desire rose inside her like a flower reaching for the sunlight. She heard him sigh. Something was weighing on his mind, too.

⁂ ⁂ ⁂

Tyler reached out to touch her hair. It was an unconscious gesture, and he pulled his hand back at the last second. *What are you doing?*

⁂ ⁂ ⁂

Nicky debated rolling over and opening her eyes. She knew he wasn't asleep. He was probably in the same predicament as her. She wanted to touch him so desperately, it was nearly painful. One of them had to swallow their pride. *Touch him.*

⁂ ⁂ ⁂

Tyler resigned himself to a sleepless night next to his wife. He wanted her so badly, he was almost shaking with need. He felt like a man possessed. *Touch her.*

Nicky turned and wound an arm around his neck as he reached out for her at the same moment. She pulled his lips to hers for a long, breath-robbing kiss. It wasn't tender or romantic. It was elemental, consuming, almost bruising.

"Love me, Tyler," she whispered brokenly.

He hadn't even needed to hear the words. Thus began a sensual dance between them as clothes were quickly shed and heated flesh slid against heated flesh.

Their mating was fierce and frantic. As if a day without contact, or too much contact, had left them with a burning need to fulfill. Their passion was an expression of their love, the fragile bond that was stretched to its limit by all they had yet to face.

Without speaking a word, they reached for the stars together. After an explosive climax, they lay together, entwined arms and legs wet with sweat. Tyler tucked her spoon-like to his chest, then covered them with their blankets.

⁂ ⁂ ⁂

Nicky had never felt so safe, so warm, so secure. She wished she felt loved, too.

I love you, Tyler.

⁂ ⁂ ⁂

I love you, Nicky.

The words remained unspoken.

⁂ ⁂ ⁂

For the next two days they barely spoke a word in conversation. Each night their passion burned brighter than the sun, scorching them both with its intensity. They clung to each other with a fever that raged out of control. Desperately trying to hold on to something that was sliding through their fingers. The invisible thread between them was stretched taut, ready to break apart, and take them along with it.

They'd stopped at the first ranch they came to, and Tyler made arrangements with the owner to purchase a horse and saddle for Nicky. Sable was strong, but it wasn't fair to push his horse so hard with two riders. And, above all else, the sweet torture of having her sit in his lap every day was slowly driving him mad.

Leaning over the corral fence, Nicky and Tyler were eyeing a dozen horses that were milling around. Nicky had immediately spied two different horses she liked; one was a gray gelding, the other a buttermilk mare.

"I can't decide. They're both beautiful."

"Not as beautiful as you," he said softly, nearly under his breath.

Nicky turned and eyed him. "What?" She wasn't at all sure she'd heard him correctly. Did he really just call her beautiful? Her? Gangly, ungainly, boyish Nicky?

He raised one black eyebrow at her, a hint of a smile playing around his lips. "I said you'll have to pick one, beautiful."

No one, *not one person*, had ever called her beautiful. Not even her mother. In fact, she'd been called horse girl, freckle face, scarecrow, and other worse select phrases for such a tall, unfeminine person such as herself. How could he possibly think she was beautiful?

"Don't call me beautiful," she nearly snapped at him.

He narrowed his gaze. "Why not?"

"Sweet-talking me is not going to solve our problems, Calhoun," she said tightly. She was busy trying to hold back the tears that threatened at the callous way he was trying to charm her.

Beautiful, my butt!

"Sweet-talking? Since when have you known me to sweet-talk anybody?"

She opened her mouth to speak, but couldn't think of a single retort. He had a valid point. No one could ever accuse Tyler Calhoun of sweet-talking anybody.

"Then why did you just call me beautiful? Twice?"

He regarded her thoughtfully before shaking his head.

"I'm not sure who told you different, honey, but you're not only beautiful, you're incredibly sexy. Anybody that doesn't think so must be blind as a bat."

"Me?"

"You, Mrs. Calhoun." This time he smiled—*really* smiled—at her.

"I...I, um, thank you, Tyler." She hid her nervousness by gripping the fence tighter.

They were silent for a few moments as Nicky absorbed Tyler's words.

"Back to the horses. We don't have enough to buy both, so you'll have to pick one," he said.

I already picked one, but he doesn't want to keep me.

"I don't want both of them. I only need one."

"I only need one, too."

"I don't know if I'll ever understand you, Calhoun." She sighed. "Are we talking about horses here?" She couldn't grasp his train of thought. First he called her beautiful, and now this.

His gaze moved to hers. "I don't know what to do." *About us* remained unspoken.

She studied him silently. He seemed to be trying to reach out to her. Could it be that he felt the same way about her? Her heart did a little dance. Surely not.

"Neither do I." She turned to focus her gaze on the horses. *But I know what my heart tells me.*

"I plan on staying with you until it's over. One way or the other."

His words caused a shiver of unease to sneak up her spine.

"One way or the other?" She was afraid of his response.

"Yeah, either we go our separate ways after all this is over, or...we stay together and try to make it work."

"What do you want?"

He sighed as his callused hands twined together in front of him on the corral fence.

"A bounty hunter's life is about as hard as it can be. The wife of a bounty hunter is set up for heartbreak from the get-go." He paused. "Can't say that I've ever been so confused in my life." He just couldn't cut her loose yet...not yet. He had to stay with her a few more days.

"Me either."

He grinned wryly at her, then reached out and brushed his thumb along her jaw softly. "I've never even dreamed of running into someone like you, but here you are. Why can't things ever be simple, magpie?"

"Don't know the answer to that one. I've been pondering that question for some time now." She leaned into his hand as he continued caressing her face. It felt heavenly.

"Let's call a truce for now."

"Okay by me."

"I like this agreeable wench. You should do that more often."

Ever so slowly, he leaned down and brushed his lips lightly over hers. Sealing the pact.

"How about the horse, Mrs. Calhoun?"

She shook her head to clear the cobwebs. "I think I want the mare."

"She'll go nicely with that mass of locks atop your head." He tugged on the curls peeking out from underneath her Stetson.

"My what?" She laughed. "My hair? What have you done with the real Tyler Calhoun?"

He smiled sadly at her. "You'll be the height of fashion. Imagine women everywhere buying a horse to accent their newest dress, or the color of their hair. You'll be famous."

She punched his arm.

"What will you call her?"

Nicky looked at the horse. "Ophelia."

Tyler threw back his head and laughed. Shakespeare, of course, what else?

⁂ ⁂ ⁂

As the owner of the ranch approached them, Tyler walked over to meet him, still chuckling. The stranger was well built, in his thirties, large enough for Tyler to be on his guard. He wore weathered-looking jeans, a light blue shirt, and a dusty black hat. His brown eyes were piercing.

"She wants the buttermilk mare. How much?"

"How about forty for the horse and saddle? My wife died about two years ago, and I'm glad somebody can use her saddle. It's too small for me or my men to use."

"Sounds fair to me." Tyler reached into his pocket to pay the man.

"Before you leave, there is something I need to tell you," the rancher began. "About the woman you're with. Is she really your wife? She looks familiar to me."

A sense of unease began to squeeze Tyler as he listened to the rancher speak.

⁂ ⁂ ⁂

Nicky reached out to the mare and petted her silky nose. The mare nudged her gently.

"Hey there, girl, wanna come with me?" A fragile happiness had wrapped itself around her like a warm coat. She almost felt hopeful about her marriage. It was the first shaky step toward their future that was still so uncertain.

"I'll tell you a secret, new horse of mine. I love him, girl. That's never, ever going to change. Even if he is a pigheaded bounty hunter." She smiled at the horse conspiratorially. "And he said I was beautiful? Can you believe it? I can't."

She glanced at Tyler, who was deep in conversation with the rancher. His face was set in stone.

What was going on?

⁂ ⁂ ⁂

Tyler eyed the man, keeping his cool mask in place. "What do you mean she looks familiar?" The words were clipped as he forced them through his dry throat.

He puffed out a sigh. "I've seen her on a wanted poster, mister. It's none of my business, but I think you oughta know she's on the run from the law."

Tyler's lips came together in a frown. He debated whether or not to tell the man he knew very well who Nicky was.

"I'm a bounty hunter, mister. I know who she is—a murdering thief. I tell people I married her to shut her up, keep her in line. Less suspicious when a man and a woman are traveling together."

The man nodded in agreement. "Not too many women tromping around in jeans though."

"I don't give a shit about her clothes, or what she looks like. If she got away, I'd be out a good bounty." Tyler continued with his pretense in his coolest bounty hunter tone. "It's the bounty I'm after. And I'm not about to let anyone take it out from under my nose. Making myself clear, mister?" He touched the butt of his pistol deliberately.

"No problem here, mister. Just was being neighborly." The rancher held up his hands.

"Just wanted you to be clear." Tyler held out the money. "Here's the forty for the horse and saddle. Need to make sure my bounty arrives alive."

With a sense of fatalism, he knew, just *knew*, she was listening. He swiveled his head and saw her. He saw the pain and anguish etched into her lovely face and eyes. Oh, God, how much had she heard?

"Come with me and we'll get that saddle." The rancher led Tyler toward the barn. Tyler tore his gaze away from his wife, aware that what he had just done may have caused irreparable damage to his fragile relationship with her. And he wanted to take it back, to magically pull those words out of the air, out of her memory, out of his.

What have I done?

⁂ ⁂ ⁂

Nicky felt all blood drain from her face. If Tyler had plunged a knife in her heart, he couldn't have hurt her any more than with his cruel, cold words. How could something with no edge be so sharp as to rip her apart? She glanced down at her chest, expecting to see blood, if not her very soul, leaking from her body.

Her eyes were full of unshed tears as she watched the two men walk away. When they were out of sight, she fell to her knees and tried to breathe. Oh, sweet Jesus, she had never felt such pain. With a start, she realized the low, keening sound she heard was her own. It was the sound of a soul in ultimate pain, of a heart breaking. The pain was so deep, so intense, she thought her heart would stop beating completely. To her shame, it was even worse than when Logan had died. She had thought, hoped, dreamed he had truly wanted her for his wife. And now, she knew for sure, it was all a game. She was still his bounty, nothing more.

I plan on staying with you until it's over.

Yes, he meant to stay with her until he got his bounty. Until it was over for good. *One way or the other.*

That night when they camped, she placed the bedrolls on opposite sides of the fire. She hadn't spoken a word to him since they'd bought the horse. Tyler Calhoun was never going to bed this wife again.

Chapter Fourteen

They arrived in North Platte the next evening. Nicky told him where to find Belinda and Rebecca's house. The two women had shared residence since their harrowing ordeal in white slavery. Nicky had located them shortly after their escape to be sure they were all right, and formed a permanent friendship with them. They stopped the horses in front of a two-story blue house with lace curtains and a white picket fence.

Looks like a home, thought Nicky wistfully as she tried to dismount, but Tyler quickly swung out of his saddle and approached her. She was still wearing the sling and her arm was tender and awkward in the splint.

"Let me help."

Grasping her waist he lifted her from the mare. As her feet touched the ground, she looked up into his unreadable blue eyes.

"This is familiar," he murmured.

His words sent a wave of desire down Nicky's body. He bent his head and brushed her lips gently with his own. She closed her eyes, her body unconsciously swaying toward Tyler. Amid the confusion of her body's reaction to his kiss, her mind was swirling as well. Did he? Didn't he? Did she? Didn't she? She opened her eyes and frowned at him.

"We sure do get ourselves all twisted up, don't we?" He paused. "Nicky, about what you heard yesterday. You know I was trying to protect you, don't you? He recognized you, magpie." His voice was thick as he stared into her eyes in the growing darkness. "I didn't want him to go after the law or, God forbid, try and take you in himself. I didn't know him well enough to figure out what he'd do."

Nicky mutely stared up into his darkened face. Was he really telling the truth, or trying to keep her on a short leash? Did he? Didn't he?

"Let's go." He dropped his hands from her waist and started toward the house.

Nicky followed, watching as his long legs carried him up the six steps to the front porch. In the darkening twilight, he was a foreboding figure. He turned to look at her questioningly. Without a word, she followed him up the steps, willing her heartbeat to slow down. Now was not the time to get cow-eyed over the man who considered her a commodity, not a partner.

I am a bounty, nothing more.

Tyler raised his hand and knocked on the door. As they waited, the silence was markedly uncomfortable between them. Tyler turned and looked at Nicky. She was startled to see the depth of his exhaustion in the purple rings that seemed to be permanently fixed under his eyes, which she was sure mirrored her own. Neither one of them had slept much since he'd captured her, but it was more than lack of sleep, so much more.

A tiny woman with nearly white-blonde hair, who looked to be Nicky's age, timidly opened the door. She eyed the two of them warily through the small crack with enormous gray eyes fringed by layers of dark blonde lashes. She looked like a beautiful doll.

"Yes?"

Nicky pulled off her hat, letting her curls loose. "Rebecca, it's me, Nicky."

Instantly, the wariness vanished from her face, and pure joy replaced it. She flung the door open and stepped forward to embrace Nicky. The petite blonde was wearing a lavender confection of a dress with ruffles and lace.

"Oh, Nicky, I'm so glad to see you. It's been so long." She stepped back to gaze at her friend and raised one blonde eyebrow when she spotted the sling. "Please, come in."

She glanced at Tyler suspiciously, then turned to Nicky with questioning eyes.

"It's okay," she hesitated. "This is my husband, Tyler."

Rebecca's eyebrows rose in surprise at Nicky's unexpected nuptials, but grinned at both of them as she ushered them inside. "My, you are tall. I'm going to get a crick in my neck looking at you."

Tyler grinned down at her and tipped his hat.

"Belinda," she called. "Come down. We have guests."

After an equally petite brunette wearing a yellow dress made her way down the narrow staircase, Nicky hugged her, too. Tears stood in the three women's eyes as they held hands. They had shared something ordinary people don't, a bond that would last the rest of their lives.

"It's so good to see you, Nicky," Rebecca murmured.

"You, too," said Nicky huskily. "I can't believe it's been six months."

"Too long," Belinda chimed in.

After another careful hug, the three finally let go of each other.

Nicky, Tyler, and Rebecca went into the parlor, while Belinda went to make coffee. Tyler's massive size dwarfed the room and his hostesses. While Nicky was tall, these two were just barely over five feet, and Tyler looked like a giant. He smiled at Rebecca as he sat on the settee next to Nicky. She sat stiff-backed, her eyes narrowed at her husband without acknowledging that what she was feeling was jealousy. He scowled at her. She scowled right back.

"So Nicky, what brings you to us?" Rebecca questioned.

"I need your help," Nicky said.

"Of course. Anything." Rebecca's gray eyes reflected concern as she reached out to cover Nicky's hand with her own.

Tyler broke in before Nicky could speak. "I want to know what you can tell me about Owen Hoffman."

Rebecca jumped as though she'd been bitten. One hand fluttered like a small bird to her mouth as the color drained from her face. "Hasn't Nicky told you?" Her voice was barely audible.

"Yes, ma'am, she has, but I need to hear it from you and your sister," Tyler replied, gentling his voice.

"Belinda's my cousin, but we're as close as sisters." Rebecca's eyes were wide, her voice jumpy.

"Just tell me what you can remember."

"Please, Rebecca, I need you to tell him everything," Nicky pleaded softly.

Rebecca nodded, then took a deep breath and slowly began to tell her heartwrenching tale. She told of being on holiday in San Francisco with her family, and taking a walk with her cousin, Belinda. They were kidnapped, bound, and gagged. Before they knew it, they were in some seedy place in the Barbary Coast, the drinking and gambling pit of the city. The boy, Jacob, had been there when they arrived. Rebecca thought that perhaps his family had sold him for money. Her voice cracked occasionally as she spoke. Nicky felt the bile rising in her throat anew at the horrors the two women and the boy endured, that were forced upon them by their kidnappers.

Belinda came in with a tray of coffee that Nicky took from her shaking hands. Dismay was evident on her delicate face as she was forced to relive the ordeal through her cousin's retelling, but she sat next to Rebecca and held her hand tightly. They looked like two frightened birds in their brightly colored dresses and matching gray eyes. Belinda began to add her own observations to the story. A rancher purchased the three of them within a few days, and they were transported to Wyoming in a carriage with blackened curtains, bound hand and foot.

They had been in Owen's root cellar for two weeks when Logan and Nicky found them. The twins had saved them from more savage humiliation at the hands of the rich man. Nicky cursed silently as her hands itched to curl themselves around that perverted son of a bitch's fat throat.

"When we returned to North Platte, we vowed that we'd never reveal the details of this nightmare. Poor Jacob, when we arrived here, he couldn't... Well, the first time Nicky came to us, he thought she was there to bring him back to Wyoming, back to that place. It wasn't Nicky's fault, mind you. He just didn't understand no matter how many times we tried to explain it to him. But how could he possibly understand? He was a child. He just couldn't go on, so he, well, he decided to end it in his own way."

Nicky squeezed her eyes shut as the memory of finding Jacob hanging from the attic rafter flashed vividly in her memory. Another person dead because of her. So much pain, so much suffering, so much guilt. Tyler reached over and laced his fingers with hers. Nicky opened her eyes and stared at their intertwined hands.

Rebecca continued. "We were able to go on as spinsters, and open our own seamstress shop. To this day, we haven't told a soul of our experience. And the only reason I did it today was because Nicky asked. Without her and her brother as our guardian angels, we wouldn't be alive today."

⁂ ⁂ ⁂

Tyler had carefully studied the two women while they spoke. He trusted his gut instincts when it came to people. Still...there was always doubt when Tyler was forced to trust someone, anyone, even his wife.

Rebecca must have sensed Tyler's disbelief as his blue eyes probed her and her cousin. She stood, her spine nearly snapping as she straightened, and walked over to him. She rolled back the sleeves of her pretty lavender dress, exposing deep, ugly scars on her wrists and arms.

"You can't be bound for weeks and not have any marks," she whispered, conveying to him that her scars only began at skin level. Those buried within her heart and soul would probably never heal completely. Her shaky hands pulled the sleeves back down as she sat next to an equally pale Belinda.

"You didn't believe Nicky," Rebecca stated.

Tyler didn't respond, but he inwardly winced at her honesty. God Almighty, how did he get saddled with such point-blank women? Nicky slowly withdrew her hand from his as her friend spoke the brutal truth out loud. He didn't believe her or trust her. How could she possibly think he loved her?

"You thought her an outlaw and who knows what else...you didn't believe her, but you *married* her?" Rebecca's incredulous voice swept over him along with a wave of shame. She studied him with shrewd eyes.

Nicky cleared her throat, breaking the tension momentarily.

"Actually, we started off at odds. Tyler is a bounty hunter hired by Owen to bring me back to Wyoming," she said, voice low.

Startled gasps from Rebecca and Belinda met her statement. Belinda looked about ready to faint. Rebecca looked like she wanted to find the nearest skillet and backhand his head.

"He married me to save me some embarrassment, and so I didn't have to spend any more nights in a jail cell." Nicky looked at Tyler with her own unreadable expression. "Somewhere along the way, we stopped being enemies, and started being...friends."

"Any more nights in jail?" Rebecca repeated, with a delicate lady's snort. "Just what in the name of all that's holy is going on here?"

Tyler didn't respond to his wife's look. He didn't think he could, so he stared at the pretty patterned carpet beneath his dusty boots. Somehow, these two women had convinced him that Nicky's version of her brother's death was true. Logan had given his life for these three women and one innocent boy. How could she call him her friend after he did all he could not to believe her? And still, she was with him. He shook his head slowly.

"How did you hurt your arm, Nicky? And your face. It looks like you've been fighting," Belinda said.

"Horse threw me," she answered lightly. Tyler heard the undertone of tension in her voice. "I wasn't looking where I was going and found a gopher hole. And, ah, my face, well, we had a little trouble along the way."

Tyler nearly snorted at her description of a "little trouble". He had to do something for her. She deserved to be free. He didn't know how to make up for his words to the rancher that had cut her so deeply. He just didn't know what to do. *Dammit, how am I going to fix this?* It was easier this way, he told himself. She hated him already, so when he left her in a few days time, it wouldn't be as hard on her. He kept trying to make that thought stick, but all he could remember was the pain in her beautiful face when she heard him call her a bounty—nothing more than money in the bank.

But he could help clear her name. And dammit, that's what he was going to do. He could give her back her life, even if she lived it without him.

⁂ ⁂ ⁂

Tyler crouched down on one knee in front of the two cousins, holding his hat in his hands like a penitent speaking to his preacher. Nicky couldn't help but notice the appreciative looks Rebecca and Belinda gave his handsome face and form, even if Rebecca was shooting daggers out of the other side of her face. Nicky's stomach lurched with the unknown feelings of jealousy. Both of them were far prettier and feminine than she. She was dismayed to remember that she was a tall, gangly thing, with arms that were too long, callused hands, cursed curls that wouldn't behave, and ugly freckles splashed across her face. What man would look at her and her beautiful friends in the same way? *None,* she answered herself. Why, she even smelled like a horse.

"You ladies have to repay the favor to Nicky. You'll have to come back to Wyoming with us and clear her name."

The room was deathly silent after Tyler's proclamation. The night songs of the crickets could be heard faintly through the closed window. Nicky stared at Tyler with her mouth unhinged. Rebecca narrowed her eyes, and Belinda shrank back a little bit further into the settee.

"I'll guarantee your safety, ladies. Nothing will happen to you." Tyler's voice was firm and sincere. "If you tell your story, and Nicky tells hers, she might be a free woman. Otherwise, she'll have to spend the rest of her life with men like me chasing her."

Nicky was both angry and elated. She was angry at Tyler's obvious manipulation of her friends, and elated that she might, just might, be free. Free to have a life with Tyler, to have children of her own, to stop running and hiding, to see her family again. Oh, Jesus, if he was wrong, and took that away from her, the devastation would be more than she could bear. Should she hope for it, or not believe it at all and save herself the pain later?

Rebecca sighed heavily, then looked at Belinda. After a moment, she turned to Tyler and nodded. "For Nicky, we would do anything. We owe her more than we can ever repay her in a lifetime."

He smiled broadly. Nicky knew the power of that smile, and it wasn't lost on the cousins either. She curled her hand into a fist. How could he shamelessly charm them? What did she mean to him? An obligation to be fulfilled? A bounty to retrieve? If they returned, and the sheriff didn't believe her, he'd still get his reward. She decided not to plan on hoping for the best, it was safer that way. She couldn't count on life being rosy for her, ever.

A coldness settled over her like a blanket as she watched Tyler discuss the travel arrangements with Rebecca and Belinda. No matter what happened, Tyler would be covered.

⁂ ⁂ ⁂

That night, as Nicky was finishing up her bath, Rebecca asked her quietly if she and Tyler needed separate bedrooms. She must have sensed the tension between them, and didn't know what to make of it. They obviously had feelings for one another, but the situation they were in was precarious at best. Nicky paused a moment, and then shook her head with a grimace.

"No, better put us in one. He barely lets his prisoner out of his sight."

Rebecca looked shocked at Nicky's words. "Prisoner? Pshaw, Nicky, he's doing all he can to help get your good name back, and you think he still thinks of you as his prisoner? Every time I see him look at you, his eyes get soft and...dreamy. I daresay that man loves you."

A ray of hope shone briefly into her soul, but she shut the door before it could sneak in any further. Although she wanted to believe Rebecca with every bit of heart she had left, Tyler was not likely to ever look dreamy, especially about her. And his cruel words to the rancher just proved he was after one thing only. The bounty.

Deep down inside where the most fragile part of her heart lived, she was confused and a little lost. Why did he want to clear her name? Did he really want a future with her? Or was he just using her?

"One room, Rebecca."

"Okay, Nicky, but mark my words, that man is in love."

After she helped Nicky slip into a nightgown over the splint, Rebecca led her upstairs to a comfortable guestroom. She crawled into bed, promising her friend she'd see a doctor in the morning to check her arm. The nightdress was so soft it felt almost unreal. She could hardly even remember what one felt like up until now. Her life had held nothing soft for more than three years. Her burning eyes closed with unshed tears as Rebecca left the room quietly. Her last thoughts before slipping into unconsciousness were of Tyler's smile, his touch, his kiss.

⁂ ⁂ ⁂

Rebecca found him on the porch, cleaning his rifle with ruthless fastidiousness.

"Mr. Calhoun? Your room is up the stairs, second door on the right. Nicky's already in bed. Poor thing was completely exhausted."

Tyler stopped his task, ready to be berated by yet another female bent on changing his life. He could almost hear her thoughts ready to bust out and smack him.

"She insisted on one room. Said something about a prisoner not being out of your sight."

He thanked God it was dark or Rebecca was sure to see Tyler's cheek color as he softly cursed. "She has every right to be angry and suspicious, ma'am. I haven't given her reason not to be."

"At least you're honest, Mr. Calhoun. I respect that in a person." She softened her tone. "Sooner or later you'll have to tell her that you love her."

Tyler cleared his throat. "Do I?"

"Do you have to tell her, or do you love her?" Rebecca's keen gaze watched him closely.

"Do I have to tell her?" His voice was low, painful, almost a whisper.

"Yes, you do. She needs to hear it."

"I'm not a man of flowery words, Miss Connor."

She sat beside him on the bench. "You don't need flowery words, Mr. Calhoun. A woman needs to know her husband loves her."

"She's the first person I've cared about in a long time," he said as he stared out into the darkness. "But I've made too many mistakes already. I've been doing a lot of soul searching, and I just can't subject her to life as the wife of a bounty hunter. If you knew how many times she's been in danger the last month, your hair would turn gray, and the minor 'trouble' was not minor. Jesus Christ, my pardon for that, she's been hit by other men more than once this trip, and I couldn't stop it. No, it's no life for a woman even if I love her more than life itself. I'm just not good enough for her."

"She's pretty tough. Resilient, too."

He shook his head. “Believe me I know, but I can’t stand the thought of her being in constant danger. There are men who would love to get their hands on me, just to torture me to death. If they got their hands on my wife, I’d go plumb *loco*.”

“You’re not willing to make a new life with her then? Give up the bounty hunting for good?”

“I would give it up in a second. In fact, I think I already have. But that doesn’t mean those men I’ve captured would. I’ve put quite a few of them behind bars, and they won’t be behind them forever.” He ran his hand down his face. “I couldn’t take the chance of losing her.”

Rebecca frowned. “You’re going to lose her anyway if you continue on this path. Love means taking chances. If you don’t, you’ll live the rest of your life regretting it. She won’t accept anything less than all of you—heart, body, and soul. So you’d better think long and hard about your cowardice.”

There was a tension-filled pause as Tyler absorbed Rebecca’s bald statements.

“If you were a man, I’d either call you out or beat you within an inch of your life for calling me a coward.”

Rebecca didn’t seem to be cowed by Tyler’s words. She rose from the bench and bracketed her hips with her dainty hands.

“The truth is always a bitter pill to swallow.” With that, she spun on her heel and walked back into the house.

Perfect. Another woman telling him what to do. How the hell was he supposed to tell Nicky he loved her when she thought all he was after was her bounty?

Tyler sat on the porch for a long time. He wondered why he’d told Rebecca that he loved Nicky. He hardly wanted to confess it to himself. He’d only known her a month, and she’d already turned his life upside down. A bounty hunter in love with an outlaw. What irony. If he could help Nicky get free, then maybe... No. His line of work wasn’t for a wife, even someone as tough as Nicky. She deserved a second chance at a normal life, a home, children...and a husband. His heart did a giddyup at the thought of Nicky in bed with another man. *Like hell.*

He wanted to be with her as much as possible these last few days. Savor what he could, while he could. There wasn't always going to be a tomorrow to pin his hopes on. He could store the memories he had, and take them out of his heart on rainy days to remember, to treasure.

He finally rose and went upstairs. When he entered the room, he heard Nicky's even breathing as she slumbered a few feet away. Without another thought, Tyler shed all of his clothes and climbed under the blankets to be close to his wife. The only things he wanted to do was hold her, comfort her, and keep her safe. She was soft and warm like a kitten, and nuzzled up against him instantly.

"Tyler?"

He raised his arm and she was enveloped in his embrace. Her soft curls caressed him, her breath on his chest tickled. He leaned down and kissed her forehead gently, and closed his eyes.

"I love you, magpie."

Chapter Fifteen

Rebecca was up at the crack of dawn fetching Dr. Miller to look at Nicky's arm. She roused her friend quietly, trying not to disturb the man beside her.

"Land sakes, he doesn't have any clothes on," she whispered under her breath. Tyler chuckled into the pillow at her discomfort.

Nicky dressed hurriedly and went downstairs to see the doctor. She hadn't wanted a confrontation with Tyler so early in the morning, especially when she realized she'd spent the night in his arms. Arms that were warm, inviting, and promised a future that she didn't know she could ever hope for with a husband who she didn't know she could believe in.

Dr. Miller was a middle-aged man with sandy-blond hair with a few salt and pepper strands mixed in. He chatted with Nicky about his wife and three children as he examined her arm thoroughly.

That's what I want, thought Nicky miserably. *I want a husband who will brag about me to perfect strangers...I want children.*

He complimented her on the splint. Nicky barely controlled not rolling her eyes. Leave it to Tyler to do it without any mistakes. The doctor confirmed that it was indeed just a simple sprain, not too severe, and was healing properly. In another week, she could remove the splint completely.

Nicky thanked the doctor as Rebecca escorted him to the door and paid him. Then they went into the kitchen for some coffee.

"Do you think he went back to sleep?" Rebecca queried, glancing at the ceiling as they sat down at the table.

"If he wasn't, he'd be tearing down the stairs looking for his bounty."

"Nicky Malloy, don't put yourself down so. Any fool can see he loves you."

Nicky winced as her heart fluttered, hoping, no, *praying*, that Rebecca's words were true. "It's Calhoun, not Malloy."

Rebecca smiled. "Bother, I forgot that. He is your husband and he loves you. If you don't believe me, march up there and ask him yourself."

Nicky regarded her friend in horror. How could she even suggest such a thing? She shook her head vehemently.

"I couldn't. I couldn't just blurt it out. What would I say? Tyler, do you..." She paused.

"Do I what?" came the familiar deep tones of her husband's voice.

Nicky nearly flew off the chair in fright and embarrassment. She clutched at the table for purchase with her good hand. It was the only thing keeping her vertical as she gazed at Tyler. He looked absolutely striking in a clean black shirt and pants. His hair was finger combed with small curls escaping the black waves here and there. He had shaved, and his strong jaw nearly shone. And he was smiling, just a hint of one, but it was there. That man had no right to look so gorgeous. The air was positively pulsing with emotion as they regarded each other across the kitchen.

Rebecca excused herself and quickly left the little kitchen. Neither one remarked on her leaving the room.

"Do I what?" he prodded.

"Do you really think it's necessary for all of us to go to Wyoming?" she hedged.

His smile broadened, weakening her knees even more. No one had the right to look like that first thing in the morning. Made a body as limp as a dishrag.

"Is that really what was on your mind?" His eyes searched her face. She writhed under his penetrating gaze.

"Of course. Coffee?"

Tyler studied her quizzically before he sat down. "Sure. The arm looks great. What did the doc say?"

"A sprain, just like you thought. I need to wear the splint another week."

She poured a cup quickly, sloshing the hot liquid onto the table. Cursing silently, she reached for a rag to wipe up the mess.

"I'm surprised you didn't come looking for me." She sat opposite him and lowered her eyes to her coffee cup, but the black steaming depths told her nothing.

"Actually, I was sorry you weren't there for other reasons," he said. Nicky's heartbeat ratcheted up a notch as she remembered their passionate lovemaking. "Besides, I could hear your voice down here. I knew you were with the doc, remember?"

His last statement was like a pinprick in a soap bubble. She could almost feel herself visibly sag. Of course, he knew where she was all the time. His prisoner was always within sight or hearing.

"Back to the subject of Wyoming." She willed her voice to be steady. "Why didn't you tell me what you were going to do?" Her green eyes rose to meet his blue gaze.

"I didn't know what I was going to do until I did it."

"I still wish you'd have discussed it with me before you bullied them into going."

His eyes narrowed. “I didn’t bully anybody.”

“It should have been my choice. Not yours. Who are you to make the decisions about my life?”

He took a long gulp of coffee. “You are my wife, Nicole. That gives me every right under the law. What put the bee in your bonnet?”

“Me? I’m not the pushy one, smiling and flirting like a lunatic to get those two ladies to agree to your harebrained scheme.”

Tyler’s mouth thinned into a white line, as the telltale muscle twitched in his cheek. “I was not flirting. I was trying to help save your neck.”

“Hah! And soon we’ll see pigs sprouting wings and flying around barnyards.”

“You’d better watch that mouth, Nicole.” As the words left his mouth, she felt exactly as she had when he’d said them before. It seemed like a lifetime between then and now. “Or I’ll gag it shut.” He stood to his full height, glaring down at Nicky, who was glaring right back.

“Who’d have thought the mighty bounty hunter would have to resort to his manly wiles?” she sneered.

“Manly wiles? Woman, are you crazy?”

“Yes, I’m crazy,” she shouted up at him. “Crazy to have ever trusted you, crazy to have brought you with me, crazy to think you would give up a fortune for me, and crazy to think you could ever love me when the world is full of beautiful women like Rebecca and Belinda.” She clapped her hand over her mouth as she realized what she’d said.

Tyler’s face relaxed as he sank back into his chair, and a grin began to play around his lips. “You’re jealous, magpie.”

“I am not jealous,” she denied vehemently. “I just don’t want to see my friends used.”

"You are jealous, and you're using it as an excuse to fight with me."

"For the last time, I am not jealous."

"You have nothing to be jealous about, Nicky. Rebecca and Belinda are sweet ladies, but nothing more. I don't have room in my life for lace and frills."

"What do you have room in your life for?" she said before she could stop herself.

He stared at her long and hard. "I don't know," he finally answered.

She wrapped her arms around herself in a hug as she regarded him warily. "I don't like the idea of going back to Cheshire." She looked off into the distance. "Even if it means the chance to see my family again."

"I think if your friends tell their story, and you tell yours, the sheriff in Cheshire should help us clear your name."

"What if he doesn't?" she snapped as her gaze swung back to his. "What if he doesn't?" she repeated in a whisper.

"He will. Trust me."

She stood abruptly, clearing her cup from the table with a swipe. It clattered in the sink as her hands shook. Suddenly, he was behind her, turning her to draw her into his warm, strong arms. She wasn't crying, but she was trembling, and his embrace never felt so good. Nicky tried not to melt into his arms, but she was so frightened, her heart overrode her head and she wrapped one arm around his wide back. Her nose was pressed up against his shirt. He smelled so clean, so safe, so...Tyler.

"I'll never let anything happen to you." His voice resounded through his chest to her ear. "Even if we have to become the Calhoun gang."

She looked up into his blue eyes, which radiated sincerity. *He's telling the truth.* A surge of raw emotion accompanied her realization.

"Tyler, if only I could believe it. Safe forever." She shook her head sadly. "I'll never be safe from Owen. You see, I know his secret. He'll see me dead one way or another."

Tyler stared down into her eyes. She felt so different from the wildcat he'd found in a saloon so long ago. "He won't hurt you with me by your side, magpie. I won't let him."

Slowly, he lowered his lips to hers. It was the gentlest kiss he'd ever given her. Light, like butterfly wings. Nicky felt her body sway under his gentleness. She sighed softly as the pressure of his kiss grew stronger. The clash of lips and teeth deepened to tongues as the kiss flared out of control like wildfire. She couldn't let go of him, his embrace, his passion, until she heard a startled exclamation from the kitchen doorway.

Nicky dragged her mouth away from him forcibly and they both turned to see Rebecca and Belinda. Rebecca was smiling broadly. Belinda was blushing furiously.

"Does anyone want breakfast?" asked Rebecca.

Chapter Sixteen

After a week's preparation, they left the Connors' house together. The doctor had removed Nicky's splint, wrapped it in a bandage, and declared her fit to travel. It was a little tender and ached after each day's ride, but it wasn't too bad. The bandage helped keep it secure.

The cold bite of late October was making its presence known as the small group made its four-day journey to Wyoming. Rebecca and Belinda rode in a wagon. Tyler had switched to riding his horse, and he finally let Nicky drive the wagon. After three days of travel, her hands were nearly frozen, even with her thickest gloves on, but she was nothing if not stubborn, so she drove the wagon without complaint.

Nicky knew they were getting close. She had been recognizing landmarks for the last several hours. Each clop of the horses' hooves was like a small blow to her heart. She felt as if they were approaching a point of no return, but she wasn't sure if it was close to death or to life. Her stomach was tied into an unbreakable knot of tension and fear.

Tyler rode his horse steadily beside the wagon of women, regardless of how slow the pace. She had heard a few snickers from men in the town they'd settled at the first night. Words like "harem" and "herd of mares" drifted to her ears. He quelled any backhanded chattering with one steely glance. As the sunlight waned, the twinkling lights of a town in the distance locked a grip of ice on her heart.

"How close are we?"

"It's Hawk's Bend. About ten miles from Cheshire." Her voice was tight and raw. Fear was a tangible entity in the air. Nicky could see Rebecca and Belinda were teetering on the edge of out-and-out terror.

"We'll stop there for the night."

Tyler's proclamation seemed to ease the tension that was madly escalating. He must have been feeling the effect of the unknown, too. Just what would happen?

Nicky pulled her hat lower over her eyes when they rode into town. It had been over three years, but someone could still easily recognize her. She had spent plenty of time in Hawk's Bend, and certainly people must know of Owen's unrelenting hunt for her.

Rebecca and Belinda climbed down from the wagon with Tyler's assistance. The two went inside the hotel to secure rooms. Tyler paused at the wagon. She felt him staring at her. Finally, her head slowly swiveled to him.

"Will you stay with me tonight?" he asked softly, so softly she wasn't sure she had heard him. For the past two nights, she had stayed with the two cousins, not daring to risk her heart further with Tyler. His quiet question knocked her completely off balance and made her heart thump so loudly she was sure he could hear it.

"Why?"

Tyler closed his eyes and took a deep breath. When he opened them again, the need for her shone brightly in their blue depths. "Because after tomorrow you'll be gone from me. Free to leave me, to go back to your family, the life you had. Tonight, I want you to be mine." He paused. "Please, magpie."

Nicky had to swallow hard to push back the lump that had risen in her throat at Tyler's honesty. He had not said she might be dead tomorrow, but voiced his fear over her loss by other means. She struggled to come to a decision in the face of her desires for her husband. She was spared when Rebecca and Belinda returned to gather their belongings for the night.

"I'll set up the wagon at the livery." Tyler held his arms up to assist Nicky down. She hesitated for a brief second before she stood and leaned into his big hands. She swallowed the groan that rose to her throat. She wanted to be in his arms forever.

When her feet hit the dusty ground, his hands lingered a little bit longer than necessary on her slender waist. The achingly familiar moment nearly tore Nicky's heart from her chest. She wrenched away from him, leaving him standing alone, scowling at her, with more than a hint of despair in his eyes. Turning her back, she walked away.

⁂ ⁂ ⁂

Nicky paced the empty hotel room. Her boots sounded hollow in the deafening silence. She cursed her men's garb as she silently wished for Tyler to stay out all night. The desk clerk, assuming she was a man, had put her and Tyler in a room together. She couldn't exactly explain to him that she was a woman, dressed as a man, on the run from the law. As Rebecca and Belinda went to their room, Nicky could only helplessly enter hers. She knew Tyler would think she had given in to his plea to spend the night with him. When he got back, she'd set him straight. It was the floor for him tonight. There was no way in hell she was sharing a bed with him. It's not that she didn't trust him, but that she didn't trust herself. She swore softly as she lay back on the bed.

It's just for a moment or two. I'm so damn tired.

Nicky rubbed her gritty eyes with the heels of both hands. Within a few moments, the exhaustion claimed her and she slept.

⁂ ⁂ ⁂

Tyler cautiously stepped inside the hotel room, and stopped short when he saw Nicky on the bed. After he closed the door, he broke out into a wide grin, then crossed the room to the bed. After stripping down to nothing, he gently removed her boots and gun belt, laying them on the floor next to his own. He eased his weight onto the small bed, trying not to wake her. He gathered her sleeping form into his arms and held her close, reveling in the small pleasure of her even breathing caressing his chest.

She was so important to him now, he didn't think he could even remember his life a month ago, much less resume it. But he knew the time would come when he'd have to let her go. He had coerced her into marrying him, bullied her actually. He hadn't known why at the time, or maybe he did, but he refused to acknowledge that even then, he had loved her. Tonight was the last night he'd hold her, and he was going to grasp that time with both hands and hold on tight.

Long into the night, Tyler kept his wife close, content to sleep with her, and not expecting more. This, for now, was enough.

⁂ ⁂ ⁂

Nicky woke first. She burrowed into the warmth of Tyler before full consciousness snapped her to reality. She was lying in his arms again. And it felt incredibly, deliciously wonderful. She dared not move too quickly since she didn't want to wake him. When she stole a glance at his face, those blue eyes were already open and alert. What she saw swirling in their depths stole her breath away. She saw peace, acceptance, and unconditional love. She could only gape at the feelings Tyler was expressing with his eyes.

"I don't know how you ended up in my bed, magpie, but for the rest of my life, I'll thank whatever forces brought you here."

"I was tired, and the desk clerk thought I was a man, and...and I guess I fell asleep."

"It doesn't matter. I have something to say so I'm going to get it out before I lose my nerve."

She stared at him, willing him to continue, wanting him to stop.

"Until I met you, I never let myself get close to anybody. You pestered, badgered, annoyed, and excited me like nobody else I'd ever met. You took my heart, woman. Lock, stock, and barrel." He smiled sadly as he ran his fingers slowly through her sleep-tousled hair. "When we say goodbye later, know that I will never, ever forget you... I love you, Nicky."

Four words rang in Nicky's ears louder than Tyler's declaration of love. "*When we say goodbye*?" Nicky sat up and her eyes felt like they were on fire with anger. "Goodbye?"

"What's wrong? I thought—"

"I know what you thought. You thought that's what I wanted to hear. You're wrong." Tears began to pool in her eyes and she swiped at them angrily. "You tell me you love me, then so long?"

"Nicky, you deserve a stable home and husband, which isn't as the wife of a bounty hunter. Do you know there are men out there that would kill just to *get* to my wife? I don't even want to think about what they'd do to you."

"I don't give a shit for what anybody else would do. I'm a big girl, Tyler." Her breath hitched audibly. "How could you?

How could you think of just leaving me? I love you too, dammit."

"I can't give you forever, Nicky."

She glared at him. "No one expects forever. I can hope for it, but you're not even giving us a chance. Our marriage so far has been a goddamned dime novel. I can't believe you are throwing this away."

He closed his eyes and took a deep breath. "I can't do it."

"No, you won't do it. You're a goddamned coward, that's what you are."

"You're the second woman to call me a coward in the last month." His eyes narrowed dangerously. "I don't think you should do that again."

"Coward! Yellow-bellied toad! Coward!" she yelled at him and she jumped from the bed.

He caught her wrist and pulled her back. She gasped when she realized he was not only naked, but aroused as well.

"Stop, Tyler, let me go," she said.

"I'm trying, but you won't let me."

She hit his chest with her fist, cursing the fact that she couldn't punch him with both hands, and ignoring the pain of the healing sprain. He captured her flailing wrist and brought her face to his. He kissed her salty tears and then kissed her lips.

"Tyler," she moaned into his mouth. "Don't leave me. Please. I need you."

"Shhh. No more words."

He gently removed her clothes, kissing the exposed skin as it was revealed. It was as if he was worshipping her. Her nipples were aching with need by the time her shirt was off completely. Her pussy damp and throbbing when her trousers were off.

"Please, Tyler…" she whispered, needing him, wanting him.

His hands touched her from the top of her head to her feet. His lips blazed a trail behind them as he kissed, licked, and nibbled her all over.

She was shaking with desire as she watched him rise above her. Her legs spread in welcome and he slid into her, deep, deep into her core. Tyler stopped, resting his forehead against hers, breathing each other's breath. Nicky's heart thumped and she felt whole again for the first time in a long time.

Tyler had healed her, had brought her to a place where she could be whole again. Oh, Lord Jesus, she loved this man.

After a moment, he started to move. The delicious friction caused tingles to scatter throughout her body. She rocked with him as he moved faster. Tyler's mouth found hers and his tongue thrust with the same abandon as his cock.

Faster and faster they reached for their peak together. She raised her legs and clutched him tightly as the passion of a thousand suns burned through her. Hot, scorching pleasure so intense she cried out his name, hearing her own echo back to her. Their bodies fused into one being.

Nicky knew there would be no one else for her but Tyler Calhoun. She would fight for him.

* * *

While Tyler went to retrieve the wagon, Nicky tapped on Belinda and Rebecca's door. She was surprised to see her hand shaking, and clenched her fist, chastising her weakness in the face of danger. It had been her constant companion for so long, it should not affect her so. Three years on the run with nothing but vermin—human *or* animal—for company should have honed her nerves to finely chiseled rods. But it hadn't. She felt as if there was already a noose around her neck and Owen Hoffman was about to drain her life out, along with her very soul. She hadn't settled anything with Tyler either. Her marriage, her future, and her life were dark unknowns. Today was the day the rest of her life, or lack of, was decided.

As Rebecca opened the door with frightened eyes, Nicky forced herself to be calm. "It's time."

⁂ ⁂ ⁂

After gathering their belongings, the three women marched somberly downstairs and directly outside, not even discussing breakfast. No one had an appetite anyway.

Tyler was waiting for them and helped the cousins into the wagon. As Nicky watched, three riders approached their little group. Her stomach clenched in fear as she thought of Nate. She tried to hurriedly finish checking the cinch on Ophelia's saddle before the strangers got too close. It was Tyler's turn to drive the wagon, so Nicky was riding her mare this morning. Her palms became wet with fear and her hands were slippery. Far too slippery to finish quickly.

One of them was on a gray gelding, which looked remarkably like Logan's horse Shadow, and he stopped at the hitching post next to her. As he dismounted, he landed directly in front of Nicky. She looked up, terrified, from under the brim of her hat, and realized that it was her brother Raymond. She stood up slowly and stared at him.

Ray looked as though he'd been poleaxed.

Tyler stepped up beside the speechless siblings.

"Move along, mister," he growled.

Raymond snapped out of his reverie and glanced at Tyler. His jaw visibly tightened.

"I said *move along*."

Ignoring Tyler, Raymond turned his attention back to Nicky.

"Ray."

"Do you need help?" He glared in Tyler's direction.

She shook her head no. She bit her lip to hold back the tears that threatened. Jesus, she felt like a watering pot lately. She felt Tyler's hand on her arm and looked up at him. Concern was etched on his handsome face.

"He's my brother."

"I figured that out. Do you want him to stay?"

She glanced at Ray and nodded. Ray hugged her quickly, then held her at arm's length to look at her. "I can't believe you're here. What are you doing with him? Isn't he...well, a bounty hunter?"

"Yes, but it's too complicated to explain right now, Ray. Don't worry, Tyler is my husband."

Ray's eyes widened in astonishment. That was probably the last thing he ever expected her to say. Her eyes beseeched him for understanding.

"I don't understand any of this, Nicky," he hissed.

"Please, we're going to try to clear my name, but I need you to keep silent about seeing me...for now. Is that Shadow?"

Ray nodded. "Jed Parker bought him out at the stagecoach station. I found him when I was looking for you and Logan, so I bought him back."

She smiled sadly. "I'm glad. Logan would have wanted you to keep him. He loved that horse."

"Ray, what's going on over there?" came a voice from the sidewalk.

Coming up behind Ray, another man leaned in to look at the trio. Tyler tried to block his line of vision, but he caught a glimpse of Nicky anyway.

"Sissie?" Jack gasped.

"Hello, Jackaroo.

"Holy shit!" He skirted around Tyler and grabbed her in a bear hug. "Jesus, we thought we'd never see you again. I thought you were dead." A mist of tears could be seen in his blue eyes as he stared at her in patent disbelief.

Tyler's jaw clenched. "We can have the family reunion later," he ground out. "Let's go, Nicky."

Jack finally looked at Tyler, and recognition flooded his eyes. "Ray, is that..."

"Yeah, but Nicky says he's her husband."

"*What?*"

He glared at his little brother. "Can you just shut your mouth for a minute, Jack?" Turning to Nicky, he said, "Is Logan with you?"

Nicky closed her eyes and shook her head. "He's been dead since the day I left, Ray. I made him, forced him to go with me, and oh God, he... I can't explain it all right now." She opened her eyes and forced herself to look her brothers in the eye. "Owen killed him because of me."

Jack's face turned bright red. "That goddamn two-faced son of a bitch!"

Ray sucked in a breath of outrage. "We all wondered why he was convinced that you were the one to blame for Burt's death, and the missing money. Folks had a hard time believing him to begin with, much less that it was you who was the ring leader and not Logan. He came to us with Logan's things about six months after you two disappeared, claiming he had been killed someplace in Colorado. I knew it didn't smack of the truth."

"I can prove he's guilty of Logan's murder, and some other things, too. Trust me, Ray. I need today."

"Hang on. Let me talk to Skip. I need to let Regina know where I am." He turned to approach the third man who had ridden with them, and had a brief discussion.

"Regina?" Nicky looked at Jack.

"Regina Goodson, well, Malloy now. She and Ray got married about a month ago." His look was a little sour. "They've been staying at the ranch while their house is built. Pa gave them five hundred acres up at the northwest corner."

Nicky remembered Regina very well. She had been a spoiled, selfish girl with a mean streak a mile wide.

"He married Regina Goodson. She wasn't exactly Ray's type as far as I remember. How did it happen, Jack?"

Jack shook his head with a grimace. "Don't ask."

"Is she...well, that is...am I going to be an aunt?"

Jack snorted. "Yeah, looks that way. At least I think so. I have my doubts it's even Ray's." He looked so fierce for a moment that Nicky forgot this was Jack. Sweet, gentle, funny Jack. Obviously Regina hadn't endeared herself to the rest of the Malloys.

As Ray turned back to rejoin his sister, Tyler shielded her from the line of vision of anyone on the sidewalk.

"I'm coming with you," Ray declared when he returned.

"Me, too," Jack added.

Tyler cursed softly and glared down at Nicky. She needed him to understand. "Please, Tyler. They're my brothers."

He nodded tightly. "Let's go then."

Chapter Seventeen

Nicky could not quell the shaking in her legs any more than she could slow the pounding of her heart as they stopped at the sheriff's office in Cheshire. It was almost as though this was a bad dream. Almost. Having Ray and Jack there was more than she had hoped for, and having Tyler by her side was her only anchor in the sea of dread in which she found herself drowning.

Be strong. It's almost over.

After helping Rebecca and Belinda down from the wagon, Tyler stood next to Nicky and enfolded her cold hand into his big, callused one. Silently, the grim group walked into the small building.

⁂ ⁂ ⁂

Sheriff Jim Weissman looked up from the ledgers spread open on his desk to survey the group that had just entered the building. He recognized Ray and Jack Malloy immediately as he nodded in greeting, but his attention was focused on the other two men who seemed to be holding hands. His surprise turned to outright shock when he registered the identity of the smaller man—Nicky Malloy. He stood abruptly, knocking one of the ledgers off the desk in his haste.

"Good God, Nicky, never thought I'd see you again."

"Neither did I, Jim. It's good to see you."

"Well, goddamn, it's good to see you, too. I mean, darn, sorry ladies." He inclined his head to Rebecca and Belinda. "So what are you doing here? You know I gotta arrest you, darlin'. Owen's been wanting your head for a long time."

Tyler spoke before Nicky could. "Nobody's arresting her, *darlin'*."

Jim looked Tyler over with a frown. "Who in the blazes are you?"

"Nicole is my wife, and *nobody* is putting her behind bars." Tyler's voice was as cold and deadly as the guns strapped to his waist. "Got that?"

Jim's jaw dropped. "Will someone please fill me in on what's going on here?"

Rebecca stepped forward and offered her hand to him. "Rebecca Connor, Sheriff. Perhaps we ought to begin with my cousin Belinda and me. I want to tell you the whole story, and to share it with Nicky's family, so that they can understand what happened." Her pretty gray eyes locked with Jim's as he shook her hand slowly.

"Yes, ma'am."

After the Connors were seated comfortably, the telling commenced. It began with Rebecca and Belinda.

⁂ ⁂ ⁂

As Jack listened in disbelief to the almost surreal story, he could barely contain his fury at Owen Hoffman for what he'd done to these two sweet innocent young women, and that poor boy, Jacob, who'd never had a chance to live. He admired them all for their grit and courage. When he listened to Nicky relay her portion of the tale, his fury turned to red-hot rage. What was done to them, to his brother, was unforgivable, unthinkable, and it made Jack want to howl at the moon and weep like a child at the same time. A memory buried deeply inside him began to shift, like a great slumbering giant awakening. He ignored the memory in favor of his rage.

"I'll kill him myself." He hadn't realized he'd spoken until Rebecca turned her gaze to him.

"Whatever punishment is due to that poor excuse for a human being will be meted out by the law and the Almighty Father, Mr. Malloy. I would be disappointed if I knew you exacted revenge on him."

He felt like a little kid being scolded by a schoolteacher. But hell, she was about the same age as he was. What was she doing preaching to him?

"Get used to disappointment, Miss Connor. I don't cotton to being told what to do by uppity women."

Rebecca's left eyebrow rose. "Uppity? Well, I can honestly say I've been called worse."

"I don't doubt that."

"Jack," Nicky scolded.

"It's all right, Nicky. Men do or say things in anger that they don't really mean." Rebecca's gray eyes dared Jack to deny it.

Jack muttered under his breath that he *had* really meant it. All of it. Every goddamned word. Miss Connor could take that to the bank. He wanted to kill Owen Hoffman. He'd half a mind to resurrect Burt Hoffman just so he could kill him, too.

⁂ ⁂ ⁂

Ray sat with his hands together, looking down at the floor between his knees, listening to his little brother exchange words with one of the Connor women. He understood Jack's rage, for he felt it himself, but he wasn't as quick to fly off the handle. Jack was a man of great passion, and he freely expressed it whenever he felt it. Ray let his simmer until it boiled over, which it was about to do, so he forcibly locked it away by focusing somewhere else. Later, when he saw Owen Hoffman again, he could release it fully.

Ray was positively overflowing with questions for his sister, but the look on her face stopped him. He'd rarely seen his little rough-and-tumble sister scared before now, except when she'd been locked in the root cellar by that bastard Owen. Then to have faced what she did in another root cellar made him nearly bloodthirsty for revenge.

He glanced at his new brother-in-law. He was holding Nicky against his chest with such a look of tenderness that Ray nearly wished them away. He'd never felt that with Regina, nor would he expect to. She had trapped him into this sham of a marriage, and now he was so caught in her web, he couldn't escape even if he thought it possible. In the end, he hoped Nicky would come out of all this mess intact. It would be a shame to lose what she so obviously shared with her husband. He was puzzled to see her pull away from him and Tyler's face become implacable. Perhaps their relationship wasn't as stable as it seemed. Then again, the world seemed to have turned topsy-turvy in the past hour, and nothing was as it seemed anymore.

Nicky approached Ray and took his hand, gripping tightly. "I need to know, can you ever forgive me for what I did?" Her voice was a hoarse whisper.

Ray frowned. "Forgive you for what, Nicky?"

Biting her lip, she continued with her eyes downcast. "You heard what I said. I had a chance to save him, but I hid like a coward and let him give his life for mine. That was unforgivable."

"There's nothing to forgive." Ray squeezed her hand gently. "You did nothing wrong, Sissie. You're not to blame for the things a monster like Owen Hoffman does."

She took a deep breath and swallowed.

"But if hadn't been for me..."

"There's nothing to forgive." Ray tilted her chin up to gaze into his eyes, so like his own. "Nothing." He enfolded Nicky in a tight embrace, trying to will away the guilt and fear he knew were wreaking havoc on her. She shuddered slightly in his arms.

"Thank you," she whispered into his neck. After a minute, she released him and walked to the window overlooking the street.

⁂ ⁂ ⁂

Jim Weissman was a shaken man. All the pieces to the puzzle fit now—why Logan Malloy disappeared and then mysteriously died, why Owen chased Nicky like a relentless bloodhound, why a girl like Nicky would suddenly be an outlaw on the run. The question was, what would he do about it?

"By law, I should arrest you, Nicky."

She had started alternately pacing and wringing the heck out of her hands. Her spine stiffened at Jim's softly spoken words. Her proclaimed husband widened his stance with his hands dangling at his sides, looking very ready to do battle for his woman.

"The truth is, I believe your story. But I'm not the one to decide innocent or guilty. I say we round up Judge Elms and ride out to Owen's. He's a fair man, maybe he can help us sort this out."

⁂ ⁂ ⁂

"Ride out to Owen's?"

Tyler felt the embers of his rage flare to life as he heard the fear in his wife's voice. Damn that monster for making her so afraid. He felt a kinship with Jack—he wanted to kill Owen Hoffman, too. The bastard deserved to be roasted in hell.

The sheriff crossed the room to stand in front of the young woman he apparently treated like a kid sister. “It’s the best I can do...legally, anyway. Otherwise, if you were to ride away, I never saw you.”

All eyes in the room locked on Nicky. Without a quaver in her voice, she said, “No, I’ve spent too long running from this trouble. I want to have it done. Today.”

She raised her eyes to Tyler. He nodded slightly at her unspoken question. It would end today, one way or another.

⁂ ⁂ ⁂

After Judge Elms listened to Nicky’s story, along with Belinda and Rebecca’s, he assured them that he would get to the bottom of Owen’s claims. He released Nicky to Tyler’s custody. Although the judge must be at least seventy, he insisted on riding out to the ranch with them. Rebecca and Belinda decided to stay at the hotel in town, rather than come within five miles of Owen again.

As they were getting ready to mount up, Nicky apologized to Jack for taking his pistols when she ran. She was glad to see he’d replaced them; she didn’t relish the thought of another one of her brothers being killed because of her. He hugged her tightly as he whispered in her ear.

“I’m glad you took them, Sissie. I’m glad they kept you safe. I would have given anything to protect you myself. I’m sorry I wasn’t there.”

“I’m not. I would have lost both of you.”

“If my death would’ve saved you the last three years, I would have gladly given it up.”

“I caused Logan’s death, Jack. Nothing can ever change that. And...and I thought none of you would ever forgive me.”

"Forgive you? There's nothing to forgive," he replied, holding her even tighter.

Nicky was nearly overcome by the identical proclamation from Jack that Ray had already given her. She needed their forgiveness as much as she needed air. There was so much love to be had, she wished she'd live the day to savor it.

The ride out to the ranch was like a funeral procession. The mood was as dark as a thundercloud, and tension was high. Nicky wouldn't even look at Tyler. On the other hand, Ray and Jack seemed to be boring holes into Tyler's back with their eyes.

⁂ ⁂ ⁂

Ray watched his baby sister as she deftly loaded bullets into her pistols—which looked remarkably like the ones Jack had lost a few years ago. She was as fast as a greased hog with those weapons even with one arm bandaged. He wondered what she had had to do to survive three years on her own. He himself had lain awake many nights wondering why she and Logan hadn't looked to their family to protect them. Now he knew Nicky had run away alone in guilt and fear, believing her family would condemn her for her role in Logan's death. It was the farthest thing from the truth.

It was as if that bounty hunter could read his mind. "She feels guilty. Blames herself for Logan's death," Tyler said quietly as he watched his wife's stiff back with a worried frown.

"How the hell would you know?"

"She told me. And she cries about it in her sleep."

"She *cries* in her sleep?"

Ray was once again shocked. He hadn't seen Nicky cry since she was eight years old and had fallen off a horse. After her brothers had laughed at her, she swore she'd never cry again, no matter what happened. It took a minute for the full impact of the bounty hunter's words to register on Ray's brain. He knew what Nicky did in her sleep.

"So she's your wife now? In the true sense?"

"What's between us is only between us, but know this." Tyler's lips thinned into a tight line of anger as he turned his gaze on his new brother-in-law. "Nicole is my wife. *Mine.* No one will hurt her. I'll stake my life on it."

Ray didn't know if he could trust this man yet, but there was a fierce protectiveness that appeared when he talked about Nicky. And they sure as hell would need it. After all, they were riding into the lion's den.

* * *

Owen Hoffman was enjoying his morning coffee in the dining room when his stable boy came rushing into the room. He was panting and gesturing, looking about ready to burst.

"Mister Hoffman," he practically shouted. "Riders—"

"Boy!" Owen barked as he slammed his coffee cup down on the table, shattering the handle. "Do not dare come into this room like a wild mustang and disturb me."

The boy quaked on his feet, but he stayed his ground. "I'm sorry, sir, dreadful sorry. But Red sent me in to tell ya riders are coming in. That big bounty hunter is with 'em."

Owen's eyes widened. So, perhaps the bird that had flown the coop had returned with clipped wings. He rose from the table and strode purposely toward the door, shoving the stable boy aside.

"It's going to be a beautiful day."

Chapter Eighteen

The time was now. Here. Nicky's heart was beating so hard it felt like a herd of horses had taken up residence in her chest. Outwardly, she retained her calm—a perfect match to her husband's demeanor. Cool as his ice blue eyes. That slight twitch in his cheek was the only sign of tension.

As they rode up to Owen's ranch house, the pain of remembering Logan's death right on this very spot began to squeeze her heart painfully. With physical effort, she pushed it away. *Not now.*

Then Owen came out of his house, strutting like a peacock.

"Calhoun, good to see you. Did you find her?" He surveyed the group, pointedly ignoring Ray and Jack. "Jim. Judge Elms. Are we gonna have a hanging today? I'll have the boys butcher a steer and we can have a celebration."

Nicky dismounted along with everyone else. *Courage.* She forced her chin up and walked toward Owen. With her hands resting on the Colts, she walked steadily. When she took off her hat, she saw the recognition in Owen's evil eyes.

"You did find her. Damn, but you are good. Did you at least sample the goods before they're permanently unavailable?" He chuckled.

⁂ ⁂ ⁂

Tyler's fists clenched into hammers, and he started toward Hoffman to kill the man with his bare hands. Ray placed his hand on Tyler's chest to stop him. It was like slamming into a tree branch. His chest stung from the contact.

"We don't need another excuse for a hanging."

As Tyler watched helplessly, Nicky approached Hoffman with determination in her step, fortitude in her eyes, and steel in her spine. He felt a sudden surge of pride for her. *That's my wife.*

⁂ ⁂ ⁂

"Why is she armed?" Owen's eyes narrowed.

"Because they're here to arrest you, you murdering bastard," she spat.

To her horror, he almost laughed.

"Me? *Me*? Hah! Being on the run must've jostled your brain, Nicole. Why would they be arresting me when you killed Burt and stole $10,000 of my money?"

"I didn't steal a penny, and Burt was killed when he tried to rape me. It was self-defense, nothing more. Your crimes are more accountable." Nicole held up one finger. "Murder." Two fingers. "Kidnapping." Three fingers. "White slavery."

Owen's good humor vanished. "Surely you don't believe the ramblings of an outlaw, Jim?"

"Well, I'm not sure, but I am likely to believe two lovely ladies by the name of Rebecca and Belinda Connor. They claim they were kidnapped in San Francisco, brought here to your ranch with a young boy, and they were ah...taken advantage of by you and your men," the sheriff said, and then paused. "I'd like to take a look in your root cellar, Owen."

"Preposterous drivel," Owen thundered. "Judge Elms, you know I'm an upstanding citizen. Surely you can see this is drivel concocted by this...this outlaw to escape from justice."

Judge Elms had stood quietly, observing each speaker in turn. His white hair waved silently in the cool breeze of the open range. "There will be a full investigation, Owen. Someone may remember the Connors from three years ago if indeed they were here. We will also look into your brother's death, and Nicole's role in it. As far as the $10,000 goes, we're just taking your word on it being stolen. Do you have proof?"

"What the hell is going on here?" Owen's eyes were livid with fury. "What lies have you been spouting, you bitch?"

He raised his hand to strike Nicky, but she had a pistol aimed and cocked in the blink of an eye.

"Don't you move, you bastard. I know everything about you," she hissed. "Including where you buried my brother's body."

The hammer on the gun clicked back slowly in her hand. Sweat was trickling down the center of her back.

"Nicole," Tyler's voice came to her on the wind. "Don't."

⁂ ⁂ ⁂

As she turned ever so slightly to look at her husband, Owen made his move. He grabbed her by the hair, and pulled the gun out of her hand in a flash. Tyler's body cried out in alarm as his heart clenched. Owen tossed the pistol to the ground and yanked the other one out of its holster before she could reach it.

"Let her go," Tyler growled.

Any doubt of Owen's guilt vanished as he slowly backed toward the barn, dragging Nicky by the hair. He pressed the nose of the pistol to her temple.

By God, Tyler realized, *she's not even afraid. She's furious.* Then he saw her slide a Bowie from her boot.

Seeing the knife in her hand, Owen kicked out, and the knife landed out of reach on the dusty ground. Tyler flinched at the viciousness of Owen's boot and hoped he didn't do any damage to her good hand.

"Come on boys, let's have us a necktie party."

A dozen of the seediest-looking ranch hands came into the clearing. Every one of them was armed, and looked ready to go a dance or two with Nicky's would-be rescuers.

"Shit!" Tyler glanced at Ray. "Who the hell are they?"

"Most are criminals, or wanted men. They're pretending to be ranch hands."

"How many can you take?"

"Two, maybe three."

"Same here. What's your plan?" asked Jack.

Tyler frantically tried to formulate a plan. His fear for his wife was making him slow. "He's got her as his leverage. What we've got to do is separate them, and then make a move."

"And how do you plan to do that?" Ray's voice was full of impatience.

"I don't know yet, Malloy. Give me a minute," Tyler snapped.

"She's only got a minute," Jack snapped back.

Tyler's mind was almost numb with fear for his wife. He watched helplessly as her hands were bound tightly behind her back. Nicky flinched as the knots were tightened on her healing arm. She was roughly tossed upon a waiting horse. God, she hated to be bound, and now to face the nightmare of Owen with her hands tied must be nearly making her insane. He knew it was having the same effect on him.

"Let her go, Hoffman!" Tyler bellowed as he rushed toward her. Two men grabbed hold of him in a punishing grip. A third held a gun to his head. Behind him, four more circled Ray, Jack, the sheriff, and the judge, with pistols and rifles trained on the group lest they interfere.

Nicky was kicking and twisting with all her might, but she was no match for four grown men. Tyler tried to break the grip of the two fools holding him back, but he couldn't reach her.

"You son of a bitch," cursed Jack. "Let her go and come after me."

"I don't want you, you snapping puppy," Owen snarled.

"Don't do it, Hoffman." Tyler's voice was hoarse with frustration and fear.

"Oh, yes, the reward." Owen slapped his forehead with his free hand. "You want the six thousand for bringing her back alive, right? How could I forget?"

Tyler's gaze locked with Nicky's. This was the moment when his love for her was tested. Hoffman pulled some money out of his pocket and shoved the greenbacks into Tyler's jacket pocket with an evil smile.

"Here's some of it. I'll get the rest after our hanging. Much obliged, Calhoun." With a small smile, Owen turned and walked back toward Nicky.

Tyler planted his elbow in the nose of the man holding his right arm, and threw the money at the back of Owen's head. His freedom didn't last long though. The two men had him constrained again in seconds.

"Keep it. I don't work for you any more, Hoffman."

The older man swiveled to stare at Tyler in disbelief. The breeze picked up the money and it whirled around Owen like green leaves around a rotting tree.

"She worked her wiles on you?" His gaze narrowed as he observed Tyler's struggle to be free. "You know, she wasn't all that sweet when I had her, but maybe your standards aren't as high as mine."

Lying piece of shit. He'd never "had" Nicky and it infuriated Tyler that Owen would dare suggest that he'd touched her.

"If you do this, I will make sure you suffer before you die. I have kept company with Comanches. I know ways to torture a man until he's ready to swallow his own tongue rather than face any more."

Owen seemed to feel a moment of apprehension, but then it passed. "Yes, yes, I'm sure you know many nasty ways to rid yourself of unwanted baggage. Are you sure you won't take the money?"

"She's my wife."

Owen's expression turned to astonishment. "Did you say wife? She's your fucking *wife*?" He turned to the woman sitting on the horse. "Make sure the noose is tight. That goddamn bounty hunter took what was supposed to be mine."

A muscular-looking Mexican finished making the noose and tested its strength. Tying one end to the tree trunk in front of the barn, he threw the rope over the highest branch. The noose dangled in front of Nicky's horrified eyes. Owen watched as the noose was fitted around her slender neck.

"Owen, you can't just hang her," the sheriff finally intervened.

Owen ignored the lawman as he circled the horse on which Nicky was held.

"Mr. Hoffman, really. Nicole is entitled to a fair trial," Judge Elms said.

"Well now, there's twelve of us here. Who says she's guilty?" Owen shouted to his men.

"Guilty," they all chimed in together.

"Guilty it is. Gentlemen, let's carry out the sentence." Owen rubbed his hands together with maniacal glee.

Nicky lashed out with one boot and kicked Owen as he passed by her. A trickle of blood oozed from a cut above his eye.

"You'll pay for that, you bitch. I hope your neck doesn't crack right away, so I can watch you suffocate." He punched her injured arm in retaliation. Nicky swayed, but maintained her posture.

Tyler felt like howling to the sky in frustration. He couldn't reach her. She was going to die right in front of his eyes, and he couldn't reach her. Just as his pa had died in his arms. He felt a soul-rending pain rip through his body at the thought of Nicky's death.

Jesus, please, no!

⁂ ⁂ ⁂

Nicky's gaze sought Tyler's. She silently mouthed, "I love you" to him, saying goodbye. His blue eyes were overflowing with anguish and frustration.

As Owen's hand was raised to slap the horse on the rump, Ray, Jack, and Jim all tried in vain to reach her. A sense of peace took over Nicky's spirit and everything seemed to slow down as she lived the last moments of her life. She looked at her husband as a single tear escaped and skidded madly down her dusty cheek.

In a blur of movement, Tyler wrenched his right arm free from the burly man holding him. He dragged his pistol from its holster faster than she'd ever seen him move. As the horse bolted, and the noose tightened on her neck, the sound of a shot split the air. The rope around Nicky's neck went slack, and she landed on the hard, dusty ground with a painful thud. Tyler's bullet had saved her life.

"Stop right there, Hoffman," came a voice from behind them.

"Papa?" Nicky croaked.

"*Si*, Señor Hoffman. I suggest you let my *Roja* go," came another voice.

"Hermano?" Nicky gasped.

Suddenly, there were more than two dozen men surrounding the lynching party.

Owen's ranch hands dropped their weapons as they realized the futility of giving their lives for someone else's vengeance. Tyler reached Nicky and picked her up, then nearly crushed her in a bear hug.

⁂ ⁂ ⁂

"Oh, my sweet little magpie," he whispered hoarsely. "You took ten years off my life. I thought I'd lost you."

Tears stood in his eyes as he silently thanked God over and over for sparing his precious wife.

"Can you untie me, Tyler? My arm is hurting like it's afire, and I think that bastard dislocated one of my fingers."

"Jesus, I'm sorry." He hurriedly cut her bonds. She closed her eyes and popped her finger back into place with a well-rounded curse. Tyler gritted his teeth for her, then helped her to stand. "Looks like Hoffman lost the war after all."

The Malloys arrived like a swarm of locusts. An older man, looking remarkably like Jack, came forward with his arms outstretched. Nicky rushed at him with a shout of joy and tears streaming down her cheeks, her pain forgotten.

"Papa."

As they embraced, Tyler stepped back to witness the reunion. All sorts of Malloys came to Nicky's side for a kiss or a hug. It was almost too much for a jealous husband to take.

"I don't know what to say," Jack said to Tyler. "Without you, she probably would have come home in a pine box."

"She almost did." Tyler wasn't willing to accept her family's gratitude. He had almost gotten Nicky killed. He couldn't subject her to a life like this. He loved her too much.

"*Roja.*" That damned Hermano strolled up with half a dozen of his men. They were an even sorrier looking group than the men that Owen had hired.

"Hermano," she cried and hugged him. Jesus, was she going to hug *everyone*? "You didn't have to follow me, you know."

He smiled. "I had nothing better to do. Besides, you and your bounty hunter have had some interesting adventures, no?"

She gasped. "You saw us?"

His smile got wider. "Not everything, but enough."

Tyler frowned at the bandito. "I don't think I like that."

Hermano shrugged. "I care? No, I don't think so. Now we are even, *Roja.* You save my life, I save yours."

She smiled at her erstwhile friend. "Yes, I guess we are even. Thank you."

"No thanks are necessary. You will always be *mi hermana roja.* My little red sister."

Nicky's father frowned at the bandito just as hard as Tyler was frowning. He would love to hear her explain this relationship to her papa.

Suddenly the hackles on the back of his neck rose. Tyler whirled to see Owen pull a derringer from his sleeve and aim it at Nicky's head. In an instant, it was over. Two shots split the air. One was Tyler's, the other Jack's. Hoffman lay on the ground with two bullets through the center of his chest. The two men glanced at each other and would have grinned if the situation had not been so grim.

"Well, don't that beat all, Nicky," said the sheriff. "Danged if you weren't telling the truth about Owen. What a low-down conniving bastard."

As Jim walked up to speak to Nicky and her family, Tyler strode away and mounted his horse. Breaking free from her family's embrace, Nicky grabbed hold of Sable's bit before Tyler could ride away. She gripped the leather tightly.

"And where do you think you're going, Calhoun?" she said testily.

"You're free, Nicky. Time to get on with your life. Get a real husband, have a couple of young'uns, grow old."

Let go, magpie. Please just let me go.

"I already have a real husband. For better or worse," she snapped. "And if you don't want this Malloy posse to hunt *you* down, I suggest you come on back to Papa's ranch with us. I won't even mention what Hermano would do for me."

Tyler tightened his lips to a thin white line, but he didn't ride away.

As Nicky's father approached, Tyler sighed, dismounted and met him head on.

"Tyler, this is my father, John Malloy." She linked her arm with Tyler's as he shook hands with her father. "Papa, this is my husband, Tyler Calhoun."

"Husband?" His graying brows nearly met with his hairline.

"Yes, Papa, I'll explain everything."

⁂ ⁂ ⁂

It was on the way to the Malloy ranch that Tyler saw the stable boy again. He had a bedroll tucked under one arm and was walking in the opposite direction. His head was tilted downward, and his posture drooped, as if in defeat. Tyler was transported back in time eighteen years and saw himself. It was a long, lonely road for a poor boy with no family, no luck, and no hope.

"Be right back," he said to Nicky before he turned and headed toward the boy.

Tyler knew the moment the boy saw him coming. He looked determined not to run from the thundering black horse and its equally dark rider. If nothing else, the boy apparently still had pride.

Tyler brought his horse to a stop a foot from the boy. He hadn't flinched or tried to run, which raised Tyler's opinion of the boy considerably.

"What's your name, boy?"

He cleared his throat when his first attempt to answer didn't work. "Noah Harper."

"Tyler Calhoun. Where you headed, Noah?" Tyler tilted his hat back and leaned his arm on the saddle horn with a leathery creak.

Noah shrugged. "Don't know for sure. I just knew I didn't want to work for Mr. Hoffman anymore." He paused a moment. "He sent you, didn't he?"

Tyler shook his head. "No, he's dead, son. Not coming after anybody anymore."

Noah's smile transformed his face. He was a truly handsome lad with a thick head of light brown hair, brown eyes, and a strong chin. Tyler could see the hint of the man he would become.

"You have any family, Noah?"

"No, sir."

Tyler rubbed his chin for a moment. "Neither do I."

Noah's eyes widened. "What about all those folks waiting for you over yonder?"

Tyler glanced over at the Malloys, and he thought sourly about Hermano and his group, who indeed were waiting for him on the next rise. "That's my wife's family and friends. My family is dead and buried nearly twenty years now."

"I never knew my pa, but my ma died about two years ago. She used to cook for Mr. Hoffman, so I already was working in the stable. He let me stay, but..." Noah trailed off, his cheeks coloring. Tyler surmised he didn't want to admit to anyone that he'd lived the life of a beggar, existing on scraps from a man like Owen. He had lived that life himself.

"Been there myself, Noah. More times than I'd like to remember. There's no shame in doing what you have to." Tyler held out his hand to the boy. "If you have no destination in mind, I've got need for a ranch hand like yourself."

"Me?" Noah's voice was incredulous.

"Sure, young and strong. Eager to learn and help. It's not much of a ranch yet, Noah, but I'd be happy if you could join me."

Noah looked at Tyler's hand with more than a little trepidation, as if he expected to reach for his hand only to have it snatched away.

"Don't be afraid. I won't hurt you, son."

Noah took a deep breath and placed his hand in Tyler's. He swung the boy up behind him on Sable.

"Hang on."

Noah wrapped his skinny arms around Tyler and held on as they raced back across the field toward the future.

Chapter Nineteen

As it turned out, the Malloys had been alerted through Ray's quick thinking. He'd sent a message to his father after he'd met up with Tyler and Nicky in Hawk's Bend. How Hermano knew what was going on was anybody's guess. The man seemed to be a living shadow. The rescue parties arrived in time to stop Owen's mad revenge.

The celebration at the Malloy ranch was in full swing. Brothers came out of the woodwork to glare at Tyler like a fly at the dinner table. Ray's blonde, pretty wife, Regina, was there as well. He didn't like the way she looked at him either, but it sure as shooting wasn't with hostility.

Noah was welcomed like a younger brother. He was given a bed in the bunkhouse and swaggered around like he was near to bursting with happiness. Tyler made it clear to the other hands that Noah worked for him, putting an extra measure of pride in the boy's step.

They were gathered in the great room at the Malloy house. It was a huge room encompassing the kitchen, eating area, and a living room, of sorts. Nicky's brothers hugged her so many times, he thought she was going to be sporting bruises from all of it.

Her mother, Francesca, wept copiously as she clenched her daughter's hand tightly. "Cherié, at long last," she kept murmuring.

Nicky told her story to the rest of her family. Jack and Ray had heard it earlier at the sheriff's office. It still twisted him up in knots to listen again. Francesca gasped in pain when she discovered how Logan had truly died. Vengeance was jumping up and down in the eyes of the Malloy brothers, but Owen was dead, and there was no one to visit their wrath upon, so it was swallowed down, and maybe eventually digested.

Nicky was pale and shaken when she had finished, waiting for the recriminations for what she had done that caused Logan's death, but none came. What he saw on their faces was more like regret mixed with respect. She had survived on her own for years, proving to them what her parents had known all along. The lone Malloy sister was stronger than they had ever suspected.

"Okay, I've kept my tongue long enough," Ray's voice boomed. "How in God's name did you *marry* this bounty hunter, Nicky?"

Tyler stiffened. Hermano's chuckle could be heard through the open window. Tyler knew he should have ridden away. Too many pairs of eyes turned to glare at him. He felt distinctly uncomfortable, a feeling that was completely foreign, and definitely unwelcome.

"None of your business, Raymond John Malloy. Tyler loves me, and I love him." She narrowed her eyes as she surveyed her five brothers. "And that's the end of it. I catch any of you giving my husband a hard time I'll beat your asses black and blue."

She turned to march upstairs. "Mama, can you help me?"

Francesca smiled as she followed her daughter.

After the two women left the room, Tyler's discomfort increased tenfold as Nicky's father regarded him steadily. "Is this a true marriage?"

"Yes, sir, it is." Tyler thought honesty was best at this point, but he readied himself for a fight.

"Good. Boys, make yourselves useful. This is a ranch," he barked. The Malloy brothers shuffled out of the room with more than a few hostile glances at Tyler, which he pointedly ignored. Regina paused to give him another saucy wink before she disappeared into the kitchen. He reminded himself to steer clear of that woman. Trouble with a capital T.

John turned to Tyler. "Welcome to the family, son. You can call me John."

As John reached out to shake his new son-in-law's hand, Tyler felt a strange tightening in his chest. He hadn't been called son in nearly twenty years.

"We're fixing to have a party tonight to celebrate Nicky's homecoming. Folks are bound to be curious about you, Tyler. Do you think you can handle it?"

"Being married to your daughter makes me ready to handle just about anything." Tyler grinned wryly.

John slapped his knee as he chuckled at Tyler's comment. Obviously, he knew Nicky pretty well.

"You can't imagine how glad we are to have our little girl back." He shook his head slowly. "I knew in my heart that Logan was dead, but somehow I knew she wasn't. She's a survivor, a fighter, and I'm damn proud of her. You'll do right by her, won't you, son?"

Tyler hesitated. He didn't want to promise forever to Nicky's father before things were settled with her.

"I love her, John. I love her more than I ever thought I could. If it's in my power, she'll never want for anything. I will always be there when she needs me."

"I'm glad to hear it. She's my only little girl, after all, and I don't want to see her suffer any more than she already has." His eyes were haunted. "She's been through hell and back, and I take a good part of the blame. I didn't see Owen Hoffman for what he really was. I pushed Nicky into getting engaged to him, and it cost me my youngest son. I'm hoping she'll get her own piece of heaven with you."

Tyler's heart felt almost too full. He had a wife whom he loved to distraction, and a new family. How could he turn his back on something so precious? He'd never be able to find it again in a thousand years. It was time to make his peace with Nicky so they could start living the rest of their lives, together.

⁂ ⁂ ⁂

Tyler didn't see Nicky again for hours. He went outside and helped his new brothers-in-law set up for the party. As they worked to hammer together picnic tables and make space for dancing, he felt their eyes full of mistrust skimming over him constantly. Only Jack seemed to be friendly to him. Jack, of course, was still a kid at twenty-three, but Tyler took an immediate liking to Nicky's favorite sibling, anyway.

That goddamned Hermano was still hanging around like a bad penny. His group of merry men seemed to have disappeared, but unfortunately, he promised Nicky he'd stay for the party. And then hopefully he'd ride off for good.

Noah was running back and forth delivering needed supplies of nails and lending a hand when needed.

"You're kidding." His brothers echoed Jack's look of astonishment. Noah stopped in his tracks to gape.

"No. It's the absolute truth."

"She started a saloon brawl?" Jack laughed heartily. "I can't believe it. Nicky sure did learn a thing or two from her brothers, didn't she?"

"I noticed a yellowed bruise or two," said Ray grimly. "I was hoping to find out how she got them."

"She saved my ass, and her own," Tyler said. "Nicky's a helluva woman."

His proclamation was met by silence.

"Yeah, she is a woman now, isn't she?" Ray's voice was contemplative. "I guess we've always thought of her as our baby sister."

"She has a spine of, how you say, iron," Hermano interjected from his lounging position under a tree. "Strong and tough."

"I knew she was tough," said Brett as he bracketed his hips with gloved hands. He had the look of Jack with dark brown hair and blue eyes. "But I didn't know how tough. Are you sure you can handle her, Calhoun?"

"Well, I might need some help now and then." Tyler's mouth quirked up in a smile. "Have you seen her when she's mad?"

All five brothers, and Hermano, burst into raucous laughter at Tyler's question. Tyler had found their baby sister, and had come away with respect, a family, and a wife to love for the rest of his life.

"I think you'll do fine," said Brett as he clapped his new brother-in-law on the back.

"*Si*, you will be fine," Hermano said.

⁂ ⁂ ⁂

As twilight settled in at the Malloy ranch, the crowd of partygoers was growing larger by the minute. Although three of the Malloy brothers, Jack, Trevor, and Brett, weren't married, the unmarried females at the party seemed to flock to Tyler like he was a shepherd and they were the sheep. Their bleating, flirting, and tittering were driving him mad. He kept trying to get away from them, but they followed him like a herd.

"Jack, Trevor, come over here."

Jack and Trevor were smiling as they approached him.

"Have you seen Nicky?"

"I heard Mama say she was coming down soon."

Tyler leaned over and whispered to Jack. “Help me out here, Jack. Get rid of this pack of hyenas.”

Jack’s smiled broadened. “I guess they like a hero, Tyler.”

Jack and Trevor sauntered away, leaving Tyler with five tiny females surrounding him. And that’s how Nicky found him.

Nicole. He blinked twice at her image and promptly forgot to breathe. In a man’s clothing she was beautiful. In a light blue dress with her curls sporting a matching blue ribbon, she was exquisite. The fabric hugged her curves like a loving hand, accentuating her delicious figure.

Nicky frowned at Tyler’s flock of women, and promptly disappeared amidst the throng of people.

As soon as the breath whooshed back into his lungs, Tyler tried to push his way through the crowd of women surrounding him.

“Nicky,” Tyler called as he fought to disentangle himself from the flock.

“Mr. Calhoun, where are you going?” twittered one of the sheep.

“Away from here,” he growled. “To my wife.”

Searching for Nicky in the party crowd, Tyler bit back a groan of frustration as her mother waylaid him on his quest.

“Mrs. Malloy.” He looked down into his mother-in-law’s face. He saw Nicky, as she would be in twenty-five years. She was a beautiful, older version of his wife, making him wish all the more that he could find her.

“Please, you must call me Francesca.”

“Francesca, do you know where Nicole is heading?”

“Probably to the stable with the horses. It is her favorite place.” Francesca paused. “She does not know she is beautiful, monsieur. She thought you’d see her in a dress and go running.”

He grimaced at her words. "She is the most annoying, frustrating, gorgeous woman on this side of heaven. And I'll be damned if I let her get away from me."

Francesca smiled. "Go."

He groaned aloud when Hermano stopped him a minute later.

"I am leaving."

"Glad to hear it. Not soon enough."

Hermano smiled slowly, his black eyes laughing. "I love your wife, too, you know. She is, and always will be, in my heart as my *hermana*. I keep my ears open. If she needs me, I will hear."

Tyler couldn't accept his words as anything more than a threat. "Are you threatening me, *amigo*?"

"No, no, not at all. I have said goodbye with *Roja*. She knows she can find me if she needs help. And you, *señor*, since she loves you, for why I don't know, you can count on me, too."

With that, Hermano disappeared into the inky black of the night beyond the house. Tyler shook his head. What a strange bandito Hermano was. Perhaps one day they may need his help, for example, when the igloos got crowded in hell.

He found her in the stable, talking quietly to his horse. Sable was nudging her playfully with his nose. Stupid horse was as lovesick as his master was.

"Nicky," he bellowed.

She jumped a foot at the sound of his voice. He grinned from ear to ear.

"Just remembering," he said as he grasped her and pulled her close. "When you walked out wearing that dress." He nibbled on her earlobe. "I had all I could do not to drag you into the nearest bedroom, tear it off you, and show you how much you mean to me."

"What about all those women out there, Calhoun? Obviously, you could have your pick of them."

"They're sheep."

"Sheep?"

"Mmm. Like a herd of sheep I couldn't get away from fast enough to catch my Nicole, my wife, my love." He nuzzled her neck and breathed in her fresh scent. She smelled of flowers again.

"I love you, Nicole. We've spent our time hurting and punishing each other, and I've had more than my share of that. I want you to be with me, always. I was so afraid of what we might have, of what we could lose that I almost lost you. I almost spent my life without you."

She pulled back to look into his eyes. He knew she found only love, more than she would ever need for a lifetime.

"I love you."

"Oh, Tyler, I love you too." She kissed him fiercely.

Dragging his lips from hers, he buried his nose into the crook of her neck. "Mmm, you smell so good. I want to make love to you, magpie."

"Please."

He backed her into an empty stall and laid her down in the sweet hay. They became a tangle of arms and legs. He briefly wondered what would happen if one of her damn brothers walked in, but decided he didn't care.

After a bone-melting kiss, he took a much needed breath. The wonder of being with her was filling his heart near to bursting. Tyler stared down into her gorgeous green eyes and swam in the love he saw shining up at him. She waggled her eyebrows and he smiled.

"Mr. Calhoun, I think you're trying to take advantage of me."

"I sure as hell hope so."

Nicky wrapped her arms around his neck and before he knew it, he was flat on his back and she was straddling him. Her warmth enveloped his erection, making it strain that much harder against his trousers. Her dress was partially unbuttoned allowing a tantalizing glimpse of freckled skin. Freckles he'd love to taste.

"I don't think you're wearing your lace underthings, are you?"

"You're about to find out." She stuck out her tongue and reached for the remaining buttons on her dress with one good hand. Tyler took pity on her fumblings and finished unbuttoning them for her.

When he pulled her dress off over her head, Tyler found that his wife was only wearing a pair of stockings and garters. It seemed she'd been nearly naked under that dress the whole time. His cock screamed to be let loose. She laughed after she caught a glimpse of his face.

"You have too many clothes on."

After Tyler was nude, she straddled him again, rubbing her wetness up and down his hardness. He closed his eyes and reveled in the hot slide of skin on skin. When she bit his nipple, his eyes popped open and her mischievous grin made him grin back.

He captured one perfect breast with his mouth. As he suckled the hardening bud, she slid backward until he was poised at her entrance.

"Put it in, magpie."

Nicky did as she was bid and he groaned at the perfection of being held so tightly by her body. It was pure bliss, plain and simple.

"God, you feel good."

He chuckled against her nipple. "I was thinking the same thing."

She rocked slightly, pushing him that much deeper. "You're going to have to let that go."

"Don't want to." He nibbled on the pink peak.

She clenched hard around his cock and he shuddered at the pulse of pleasure that rocketed all the way to his toes. He lost his mind for a moment. Before he knew what had happened, she was sitting up and had her hand braced on his chest. Little minx.

"Now I'm ready to ride."

Tyler had never been one to let the reins go easily, but for Nicky, he simply handed them over. She already owned his heart.

Nicky surely knew how to ride. She rode him like he'd never been ridden before, sliding up and down to her own slow rhythm, carrying him along. He held onto her hips, pushing himself deeper toward her center. She met his thrusts with her own, but she didn't increase her pace. She was torturing him.

"Lord have mercy, woman."

"Mmmm, no mercy for you." She leaned forward and licked his lips until he opened his mouth. Tyler wrapped his arms around her back and with a quick flip, she was under him.

"Cheater."

He suckled her neck. "All's fair in love."

Tyler pulled her legs wide, then laced his fingers with her good hand and gently cupped her sore one as he slid in and out of her core. The golden hay surrounded her head like a halo, her cheeks were flushed, and her mouth open.

"Love," Nicky repeated, then she whispered his name fiercely as she contracted around him, quivering and pulsing.

Her pleasure proved to be his. When he came, it roared through him so hard, stars sparkled in his vision. He gripped her hand tightly, as tightly as she gripped his. Their hands were as entwined as their hearts, their bodies, and their souls.

After he caught his breath, he withdrew and lay down, and tucked her under his arm.

"You are so beautiful." He picked up a lock of her sunset-colored hair between his fingers and marveled again at the silky texture. "You take my breath away."

Her brows drew together in a frown.

"You still don't believe me?"

"No one has ever told me I was beautiful, or even pretty. I'm just so tall, with gangly arms and legs. And this hair. Ugh, and the freckles across my nose."

Tyler proceeded to kiss each freckle. "I love your freckles. They taste like cinnamon. And I love the fact that you don't have to break your neck to kiss me. You fit right into my arms like you were made for me, darling. You're perfect, and the most beautiful thing I've ever seen."

She sighed contentedly as Tyler continued his ministrations. "Mmmm. I like that."

"I can't believe these Wyoming boys are that blind. No more old boyfriends for me to pummel, like Nate?"

"No," she laughed. "Not a one, but..."

"But what?"

"There might be a new flame soon."

"What new flame?"

"Why, the next member of the Calhoun gang, of course." She smiled as she pulled his hand to her flat stomach.

Understanding dawned. "A baby? Are you telling me we're going to have a *baby*?"

"I think so, but I'm not certain. I missed my monthly last week. Mama says it's possible. It must have been the first time we, well, you know, the morning after our wedding."

He blanched at the thought of her in Hoffman's grasp when she was pregnant. He could have lost more than he ever thought possible. He gripped her shoulders.

"Don't ever take a chance with your life like that again. You didn't need to confront Hoffman like that."

"Yes, I did."

After a few moments pause, he let loose a large sigh as he tucked her under his arm. "I hope you like Texas."

"Why?"

"That's where we'll live. Of course, we'll take Noah with us. It's not much, but my house is there and—"

"There you go again. Making up my mind for me." She sat up and starting rearranging her clothes.

"Don't yell at me, woman," he bellowed right back.

"Don't take me for granted, oaf."

"Never," he whispered as his mouth met hers in a fierce heat.

"First thing we're going to do is visit with my family for a while," she said when she finally pulled away from him. "Then we'll decide where to live. And, yes, Noah can come with us."

"Pushy witch."

"Sorry you married me?" she whispered.

"Never. I love you, Nicole."

"And I love you, Tyler."

As he thoroughly kissed his wife, Tyler heard the sound of boot heels in the stable. He froze in place. Nicky stared into his blue eyes with apprehension.

"I tell you, I saw him come in here." It was Ray's voice.

"Are you sure?" That was Jack. "I don't see them anywhere."

"Maybe they went for a walk," said Brett.

"Maybe they rode away," said Trevor.

"No, his horse is still here, and so is Nicky's mare. They wouldn't go anywhere without their horses," Ethan observed.

Nicky stifled a giggle as she heard her brothers' conversation. Tyler's brows grew together in a frown at his wife's obvious enjoyment of the situation. Even if they were married, he was naked, rolling in the hay with their nearly naked baby sister. Five against one weren't the best odds.

Why were they looking for them?

"Shit. Mama said we couldn't eat until we found them. Nicky's done it again. And I'm hungry," complained Jack.

"Me, too."

"So am I."

Tyler had to assist Nicky to hold back her giggles.

"What should we do?"

"Split up and start looking for them."

"I'll go to the house. Come on Trevor."

"I'll take the barn."

"I'll check the bunkhouse. Why don't you come with me, Brett?"

As the footsteps faded, Tyler released his grip on Nicky's mouth.

"What was all that about?"

"When I was little I used to hide at dinner time because Mama wouldn't start eating without me. As the baby sister, it was one way I could get back at them for all their teasing. Sometimes it would take them an hour to find me." She grinned impishly.

"Somehow I'm not surprised." He frowned. "We should get dressed and get out there if everybody is waiting for us."

She shrugged and let loose a little giggle that went straight to his nether regions.

"Keep doing that and they won't eat until Christmas."

After they quickly pulled on their clothes, he stood and helped her to her feet, kissing her thoroughly as he buttoned up her dress.

"You might want to get the hay out of your hair."

Tyler froze at the sound of Ray's voice. They both turned to find all five brothers leaning against the stall door.

"And button up your pants before you give Pa apoplexy," said Brett.

"H-how did you..." Nicky stammered.

"We know all your hiding places, Sissie." Jack grinned.

Tyler surveyed his brothers-in-law for hostile intent as he buttoned his pants, and Nicky pulled the hay from her curls. There was a moment of silence when he thought for sure it was going to end with fists.

"We wanted to tell you that we missed you, Nicky," said Ethan.

They each echoed the sentiment. Tyler was nearly taken aback. How lucky his wife was to have a family that loved her so unconditionally.

"Ray and Jack told us about how you thought we wouldn't forgive you. Please, next time, come to us for help," Brett continued.

"We'd never turn our backs on you, little sister," Trevor said softly.

"We love you, sprite, believe us when we tell you, there's *nothing* to forgive," said Ray.

Her eyes misting with tears, Nicky looked at each of her brothers in turn. "I don't know what to say."

"I do. Let's eat," Jack quipped.

Laughing, four of them turned and walked back toward the party. Only Jack remained.

"I'm glad we found you, Sissie," said Jack softly. His words carried more meaning than their simple message.

"Me, too," she said thickly as she embraced him quickly. He turned and strode out of the barn but not before they noticed the suspicious sheen in his eyes.

"Me, too," said Tyler.

As he gathered his wife into his arms, he realized how glad he was that he'd taken on Nicky Malloy's bounty. It had brought him to a place in his life that he'd never thought he'd be. And more bounty than he would need for the rest of his life.

Beth Williamson

To learn more about Beth Williamson, please visit www.bethwilliamson.com. Send an email to Beth at beth@bethwilliamson.com or join her Yahoo! group to join in the fun with other readers as well as Beth http://groups.yahoo.com/group/cowboylovers.

The Prize

Can't get enough of The Malloys? Here's an excerpt from THE PRIZE, *book two in the Malloy Family series by Beth Williamson, available in ebook May 2006 from www.samhainpublishing.com.*

The ground was too frozen to bury the foal, so Jack took stones from the pile behind the barn and brought them about twenty yards away. Rebecca didn't want to think the pile had been gathered for that express purpose. He shoveled a makeshift path to the burial site, and then brought the blanket-wrapped bundle. She walked behind him saying a prayer under her breath for the foal and its mother. Losing a baby, for any reason, was the worst kind of heartache a female, human or horse, could endure. This reminded her of her own pain, her own shame, and her soul-damaging decision three years ago. It still hurt so much it could snatch her breath away. She couldn't let Jack know how distressed she was, though. He must *never* know what she did. The shame would be too great.

Lying the bundle down on the snow, Jack went back to the barn for a moment.

"I'm sorry, baby," she whispered, hastily wiping frozen tears as Jack returned with a rifle.

"Can't be too careful," he said.

Setting the rifle down, he used the shovel to clear a larger patch in the snow, then picked up the foal and gently laid it down again.

He looked up at her as he started to pile the rocks in a circle around the blanket-wrapped bundle. “Did you want to say anything?”

She shook her head. “I said a prayer for it already.”

That seemed to satisfy him, as he nodded and continued to pile the stones around it, making an oval-shaped pyramid of sorts. Leave it to a man to know how to pile stones together as a grave.

In a split second, she found herself violently shoved from behind, face first into the snow. An inhuman scream split the cold night air followed by a rifle shot. Rebecca cautiously moved her head and tried to regain the breath that had been knocked from her.

“Becky?” came Jack’s horrified voice. “Oh my God! Becky?”

His hands were turning her over in the snow. She blinked up at him as he wiped the snow from her cheeks. She was finally able to suck in gulps of the frigid air.

“Are you okay? Did she hurt you? Say something, dammit!”

“Please don’t curse,” she whispered.

He tried to smile, but failed. “Goddamn cougar. I’m sorry. I should’ve been more on my guard. Those big cats are hungry this time of year. She was after the foal and squashed you like a flapjack.” He cradled her face in his hands. “Sweet Jesus, are you hurt?”

She mentally surveyed her body. “No, just winded I think.” She sat up with Jack’s assistance. He started to brush the snow off her back and stopped suddenly. He uttered a curse she had only heard once in her life, and it made the hairs on the back of her neck stand up.

“What is it?” she asked with no small alarm in her voice.

He pulled her to him and hugged her tightly. The feeling of being in Jack’s arms again was incredible. She could feel the frantic thumping of his heart beating against hers. And he was so warm!

"Thank God you're okay," he whispered. He pulled back slowly and his eyes reflected many emotions, not the least of which was worry. Then he lowered his mouth to hers in a bruising kiss that managed to steal the breath that she'd just regained. But oh, for such a different reason. His lips were strong, not insistent. His tongue roughly invaded her mouth and she was lost. Utterly lost. Twining her arms around his neck, she moaned and pushed herself closer to him. His grip tightened as the kiss grew deeper, hungrier. She felt as if she were caught in a whirlpool, spinning faster and faster. Her breasts were tight, her nipples hard nubs that she ground into his chest. Wanting to be even closer, wanting much more.

"House, let's go. House," he ground out.

Rebecca was about to agree heartily when Jack was ripped from her arms. The scream of another cougar singed her ears. A huge, tawny cat was biting and clawing Jack as he struggled for his life. Becky screamed and shouted his name. She scrambled backwards, searching frantically for the rifle. It was lying on the ground beside the grappling man and beast. The slurping, growling noises the cougar was making were quite possibly the worst sounds she'd ever heard. Jack was cursing and grunting and the snow was turning red with blood. His blood.

"Leave him alone, you bastard!" she bit out as she aimed and squeezed the trigger. The shot went wild, but the cat let go of Jack, screamed again and lunged for her with Jack's blood dripping from its mouth along with a puff of warm breath in the cold night.

This time, somehow God was guiding her hand, and her aim was true. The big cat was felled by the second shot, sliding the last two feet to land at her feet. She was breathing hard, gulping air like a small child drinking cold milk on a hot day.

She was also shaking so badly the rifle dropped from her hands into the snow.

"Jack!" Rebecca cried, running to his side. Kneeling down she willed herself to not be sick at the sight of so much blood. So much blood. "Can you hear me?"

She ignored the tears streaming down her cheeks as she looked into his glazed eyes. "Please, Jack. Say something."

Noah came running toward them from the barn.

"Noah, help me get him into the house. He's bleeding so badly."

Jack smiled at her. "You are so beautiful, Becky. Like an angel."

"Don't speak of angels, Jack. It scares me and I really don't need to be any more frightened that I am at this moment," she said, grabbing his hand and pressing the palm to her lips.

His eyes began to close. "My angel."

"Jack, dammit, don't you die on me!"

Learning Charity

© 2006 Summer Devon

Want more hot historicals? Read this excerpt from a Red Hot read—LEARNING CHARITY by Summer Devon, *available now in ebook from www.samhainpublishing.com.*

His large dark eyes sparked with a light of something. Curiosity? Humor? For the first time on meeting a customer, she felt a stirring within her.

No wonder. What a glorious man. On closer inspection, she understood that some of his features—a large mouth, slightly crooked nose, circles under the dark eyes—might be considered flaws. The whole effect of his appearance caused her body to prickle with the same joyful attraction she'd felt long ago for the curate in her village.

Pure pleasant excitement.

Only now she knew too well what men and women did and she knew he'd pay to do just that with her. Yet instead of feeling that strange distant sensation or revulsion, her two most common responses, she grew dizzy with something new. It took a minute for her to realize the heavy sensation and her quickening breath was anticipation. She imagined him undressed and her stomach gave a tiny flip and an aching heaviness began to throb within her.

He hadn't even touched her.

A hint of panic cut through her. Charity must keep apart once his hands reached for her. Cherry would take charge, though at the moment she felt too rattled to take on that confident persona.

She dragged her attention back to Madame, who had adopted her ‘customer manners’. The older woman gave a high-pitched imitation of a governess with the faintest trace of a false French accent. “My dear, the gentleman only wants to ask you a few questions about your interests.”

“No,” she whispered to Madame. “I do beg your pardon, but I-I—”

Madame’s dark brows knit. “I don’t think we have asked for too much from you.” A veiled threat. And no wonder. Cherry balked at standard house requests such as threesomes. She remained too shy, even after several weeks of employment.

“I understand.” She made a last attempt. “Madame, you have been very generous. I can’t explain.” She risked a glance across the room at the customer. He watched her, amused. Charity stumbled back into speech. “That is, I don’t wish to offend, but I am not at all sure I have anything of interest to say—”

The customer interrupted. “Thank you, Madame Suzette. I’ll take it from here. That’ll be all.” His drawl marked him as a foreigner. American, perhaps?

Madame winked at Cherry and blew the man a kiss. She closed the door quietly behind her.

He grinned at Cherry. “Did I do that right? Or should I have been more groveling, you suppose?”

She smiled, choosing not to play to his bantering manner. Lord, she hoped to get this one done fast. With a shrug and wiggle, she allowed her wrapper to fall to the ground. She wore only an elaborate lacy corset over short, gauzy pantaloons.

He gave her nearly exposed body an appreciative inspection, but as she walked to him, he held up a hand, palm out. “I hope you don’t mind, but might we talk first?”

Her smile remained plastered to her face, even as her mind raced. *Damn him,* Charity, behind the tattered curtain of

Cherry, cursed silently. *Blast him to the devil!* She wished she could think of stronger obscenities but could not, another consequence of her genteel upbringing.

She felt jarred, and as violated as if she'd never done this before.

Printed in the United States
149812LV00004B/2/A